P9-DGS-964

THE
GOD
GAME

OTHER DAN SHARP MYSTERIES

Lake on the Mountain
Pumpkin Eater
The Jade Butterfly
After the Horses

JEFFREY ROUND

THE GOD GAME

A DAN SHARP MYSTERY

DUNDURN
TORONTO

East Baton Rouge Parish Library
Baton Rouge, Louisiana

Copyright © Jeffrey Round, 2018

All rights reserved. No part of this publication may be reproduced, stored in a retrieval system, or transmitted in any form or by any means, electronic, mechanical, photocopying, recording, or otherwise (except for brief passages for purpose of review) without the prior permission of Dundurn Press. Permission to photocopy should be requested from Access Copyright.

All characters in this work are fictitious. Any resemblance to real persons, living or dead, is purely coincidental.

Cover image: ©shutterstock.com/BsWei
Printer: Webcom

Library and Archives Canada Cataloguing in Publication

Round, Jeffrey, author
    The God game / Jeffrey Round.

(A Dan Sharp mystery)
Issued in print and electronic formats.
ISBN 978-1-4597-4010-5 (softcover).--ISBN 978-1-4597-4011-2
(PDF).--ISBN 978-1-4597-4012-9 (EPUB)

    I. Title. II. Series: Round, Jeffrey . Dan Sharp mystery.

PS8585.O84929G63 2018   C813'.54   C2017-903400-6
                                                 C2017-903401-4

1 2 3 4 5   22 21 20 19 18

We acknowledge the support of the Canada Council for the Arts, which last year invested $153 million to bring the arts to Canadians throughout the country, and the Ontario Arts Council for our publishing program. We also acknowledge the financial support of the Government of Ontario, through the Ontario Book Publishing Tax Credit and the Ontario Media Development Corporation, and the Government of Canada.

Nous remercions le Conseil des arts du Canada de son soutien. L'an dernier, le Conseil a investi 153 millions de dollars pour mettre de l'art dans la vie des Canadiennes et des Canadiens de tout le pays.

Care has been taken to trace the ownership of copyright material used in this book. The author and the publisher welcome any information enabling them to rectify any references or credits in subsequent editions.

— *J. Kirk Howard, President*

The publisher is not responsible for websites or their content unless they are owned by the publisher.

Printed and bound in Canada.

VISIT US AT

dundurn.com | @dundurnpress | dundurnpress | dundurnpress

Dundurn
3 Church Street, Suite 500
Toronto, Ontario, Canada
M5E 1M2

This book is for

Stanley Almodovar III, age 23; Amanda Alvear, 25; Oscar A. Aracena-Montero, 26; Rodolfo Ayala-Ayala, 33; Alejandro Barrios Martinez, 21; Martin Benitez Torres, 33; Antonio D. Brown, 30; Darryl R. Burt II, 29; Jonathan A. Camuy Vega, 24; Angel L. Candelario-Padro, 28; Simon A. Carrillo Fernandez, 31; Juan Chevez-Martinez, 25; Luis D. Conde, 39; Cory J. Connell, 21; Tevin E. Crosby, 25; Franky J. Dejesus Velazquez, 50; Deonka D. Drayton, 32; Mercedez M. Flores, 26; Peter O. Gonzalez-Cruz, 22; Juan R. Guerrero, 22; Paul T. Henry, 41; Frank Hernandez, 27; Miguel A. Honorato, 30; Javier Jorge-Reyes, 40; Jason B. Josaphat, 19; Eddie J. Justice, 30; Anthony L. Laureano Disla, 25; Christopher A. Leinonen, 32; Brenda L. Marquez McCool, 49; Jean C. Mendez Perez, 35; Akyra Monet Murray, 18; Kimberly Morris, 37; Jean C. Nieves Rodriguez, 27; Luis O. Ocasio-Capo, 20; Geraldo A. Ortiz-Jimenez, 25; Eric I. Ortiz-Rivera, 36; Joel Rayon Paniagua, 32; Enrique L. Rios Jr., 25; Juan P. Rivera Velazquez, 37; Yilmary Rodriguez Solivan, 24; Christopher J. Sanfeliz, 24; Xavier E. Serrano Rosado, 35; Gilberto R. Silva Menendez, 25; Edward Sotomayor Jr., 34; Shane E. Tomlinson, 33; Leroy Valentin Fernandez, 25; Luis S. Vielma, 22; Luis D. Wilson-Leon, 37; Jerald A. Wright, 31 … we are all one pulse.

Pulse Nightclub
Orlando, Florida
June 12, 2016

The flower of politics is war.

— Mother Teresa

AUTHOR'S NOTE

ALTHOUGH CANADA IS SEEN BY many as a country where integrity and fairness are the rule rather than the exception, politics is still a messy business. In my depiction of the political landscape, I have dealt with a real-life scandal. Apart from the barest facts and characters already known to the public, however, all characters and events herein are entirely fictional and should not be construed as having any existence or validity outside the pages of this book or my own dark imagination.

PROLOGUE:
TORONTO, 2013

Disgrace

NEVER IN HIS LIFE HAD ANYTHING like this happened to him before. He was not the sort of man to be given the sack. And that was precisely why he'd been drinking for the past two weeks. *I am not the sort of man to be given the sack*, he told himself as he grabbed at his bootlace and pulled. *I am John Badger Wilkens III and I was not* — here the bootlace snapped — *born to be subjected to public ridicule and disgrace.*

He frowned and threw the lace down in disgust, glaring at the ragged ends as if they were to blame for his shameful dismissal. *John Wilkens, you are hereby suspended from your official duties for suspected inappropriate conduct until further notice.* He remembered every word. That was exactly what they had said when they came to remove him from his office.

He sat there, one boot on and one boot off, staring at the empty bourbon bottle sitting beside the empty tumbler on the otherwise empty table. What a dismal thing to be turned out for suggesting that all was not well behind the scenes at Queen's Park. A pack of lying thugs had taken over, besmirching his name in the process. And at Christmas, of all times!

He stared at the rebellious boot. If he simply bypassed the top eyeholes and tied the laces shorter — if he could just reach them — he leaned down and grasped. There! That would make sure it stayed on long enough for a tramp in the night air.

He needed to clear his head and think. What was to be done? Yes, what *was* to be done? Never had anything like this befallen him. Clearly, he was in a pickle. What could he do to fight the forces marshalled against him? He'd raised his voice above the crowd and dared to suggest that things were not all they seemed. And no sooner had he spoken those foul words than he'd found himself dismissed, facing allegations of personal misconduct and improper use of public funds. Absurd! To make things worse, they'd locked him out of his office, separating him from his files and suspending his computer password. How could he prove his innocence now? It was absolutely reprehensible for someone with his record to be treated so meanly. So rottenly!

He tugged at the other boot. It seemed to take ages to get them both on, one lace shorter than the other but secure at last. He tramped to the hallway. The closet swung open with surprising ease, clipping his nose in the process. He didn't know his own strength!

I don't know my own strength, he told himself. With a tug, he pulled his trench coat from its hanger and slung it over his shoulders, inserting his arms into the sleeves with difficulty. The garment resisted his efforts. When had he last worn it? The belt barely made it around his waist.

The vestibule opened onto an unseasonably mild December evening. A warm front had come in, creating a dense fog. Streetlamps gleamed like distant fireflies before vanishing around the corner. The whole world was murky. John stepped onto the porch, feeling the coolness surround him. The air felt good against his burning cheeks.

He patted his pockets for keys. Both sets were there, house and car, but he wasn't about to get into the driver's seat. All he needed on top of everything was to be stopped for driving while intoxicated. No, they weren't going to pin something like that on him. A taxi was also out of the question. *Leave no trail.* He'd been warned to come alone.

He was halfway down the street before he realized that the insistent tugging at his waist was because he'd mistakenly taken his wife's overcoat instead of his own. It crossed his mind how ridiculous he must look, but it didn't matter. Then he saw he'd also left with two mismatched gloves: one leather and the other Thinsulate. One pair for good and the other for shovelling. *For pity's sake!* he thought. *Whom the gods would humiliate ...*

If he'd taken a proper look before leaving, he might have noticed another small incongruity: the garage door left slightly ajar where earlier it had been closed, a coil of yellow nylon rope missing from the interior. He might have, but his thoughts were elsewhere.

At that moment, John was thinking about how that worm of a ministerial assistant had come to him late in the afternoon, ordering him to pack his personal belongings and leave. A distasteful man in so many ways. Clarence, the security officer, had stood behind him. They had said good morning to each other every day for the last five years. Now, the expression on the man's face made John sick. It was hard to conceive that he, too, believed the reports of John's dishonesty.

Staggering along the empty street, it came to him with a flash of drunken clarity: they were going to gang up and pin this on him. With the election coming, that egregious minister and his mob of supporters were cooking things up to besmirch his party. And they thought there was nothing he could do to stop them.

They were wrong! He had a secret weapon. He'd peeked behind the curtain and discovered a thing or two in the process. Knowledge. It was man's downfall before it became his redemption. He shouldn't have looked, but what choice had he had? Something was out of line and it had nagged him till he'd verified the facts. And, oh, what he'd discovered!

But he wasn't the only one who knew. He thought of the mysterious emails he'd recently received. *We both know what's going on here. I can help you*, their sender had offered, but whether they came from friend or foe, he couldn't tell. He'd left the first unanswered. The second was more straightforward: *You're running out of time. Talk to me.*

He'd tried fishing around to see how much the emailer knew: *Who is this? What do you think I know?* The reply was almost immediate: *What they're doing to you, they've done to others. We can discuss this.* And they *had* done it to others, John now clearly saw, while making a mockery of truth and public trust.

Whatever the sender knew, it meant John wasn't the only one sitting on such explosive information. Someone besides him realized what was going on. Someone outside the inner circle of ministers and flunkies in the government, maybe even someone with a vested interest in bringing the government down. With the election, everybody was skating on thin ice. What better time to clear his name? That's what his mysterious contact was hinting at. And he, John Badger Wilkens III, would gladly lend a helping hand.

From the start he'd tried to stay out of the rabble-rousing, to steer clear of the dirt and keep his hands clean. But the dirt had come to him. He'd thought it enough to act from pure motivations, but he'd been tainted by these shadowy intrigues. They were impossible to avoid. And, once he began to dig, it was inevitable that he would find something.

Nothing could have stopped him from looking once he had the idea. Because he had to know! How could he not? Nine hundred and fifty million! All that public funding down the drain! It still seemed impossible to believe, even when he'd seen the proof.

The final message came the afternoon he was suspended. *It's you or them. Deal with me or I go public,* his secret sharer had warned.

None of the notes had been signed, but he had his suspicions. They had all heard rumours of a mysterious, behind-the-scenes manipulator who could make or break you. A Magus. He hadn't believed in the Magus, but that had been naïve of him. It was just that much easier to do the dirty work if the world refused to believe in you.

When the problems surfaced, he'd thought of resigning to save face for the party, but now it was too late. They wanted a scapegoat. A martyr. He wasn't going to let them off the hook without a fight. He'd just received the final email when the security guard entered with the assistant. That snivelling worm, that ankle-biting cur. John had typed in his private phone number and sent off the reply to his mysterious would-be saviour, then looked up into the faces of his executioners.

Twenty minutes later he was out of the office, his reputation in ruins.

But now it was his turn. He was going to tell his mysterious contact everything he knew in return for clearing his reputation. One thing was sure, he wasn't going to have this pinned on him like some apparatchik run afoul of the Kremlin.

"Information for information," he said aloud to the fog as he stumbled along. "You tell me what you know and I'll fill in the blanks for you." A deal was a deal. Whoever he was about to meet would surely agree that was only fair. "You want to know what I know, then you tell me what you know and how you know it."

His breath swirled in the air, joining the wisps and curlicues of a diaphanous curtain. *Lost in fog.* That was the expression. He stopped and looked back. His home had disappeared in the whiteness. Thank goodness he'd sent Anne away. His cheeks burned with the memory of having to tell her that although he'd done nothing wrong, it might look otherwise until he could reveal a few simple truths. *I will clear my name if it's the last thing I do*, he'd told her. Because the whole fucking mess would come out in the wash sooner or later. And then he would be vindicated.

He stumbled along, wondering who he was about to meet. He had his suspicions: it was likely to be one of those beastly reporters hanging around the assembly, sifting the dirt, looking for a juicy story. Whoever it was had found a good one and locked onto the likeliest target: *John Badger Wilkens III*. To his everlasting shame.

Why do you want to go into politics, Badger? his father had asked years ago. *It's a dirty business. Don't you know that?* John had simply shaken his head, thinking of ambition. Thinking of righting a few wrongs in the world. But to do that, you had to stay clean yourself. *You're too good for the rabble, Badger. Don't besmirch yourself.*

In his father's day, politics meant that the big boys came in and assessed the scene, then hired the companies to mine for ore and, once that ore was found, they let the corporations bid on the right to extract it. Corporations owned by friends. Next they set hiring standards and got other friends to implement those standards into law and pay the workers, men too desperate for work and too ignorant of what safety meant to ever refuse a job. They came from all over the country, with their wives and children trailing behind. There were always accidents as they stripped the earth and polluted the environment till the vegetation died and the rivers ran rusty and someone cried foul, then safety standards were enacted and environmental laws set up to counteract the destruction until the day the ore itself ran out and the workers went elsewhere to start all over again, leaving behind ravaged landscapes and empty pockets for most, but swollen bank accounts for a privileged few, the company executives, who simply waited for the next big strike-it-rich opportunity.

And always there were secrets to be kept, names to be protected. Then more laws were enacted to shield those same men from legal repercussions as the whole thing went round and round again. It was not the men you saw, but the men you didn't see who made the wheels turn in their tortured, squeaking revolutions.

That was what his father had warned him about: those men you didn't see coming. The ones John had vowed never to become like or be outsmarted by. Ruthless and rapacious, they were adept at making up reasons to justify their selfishness. They were the ones who gave politics the bad name he now clearly saw it so richly deserved. And here it was happening all over again. To him.

It was a relief to know his father had died before finding out how true his words had been.

John stopped and peered into the fog, where everything seemed to disappear in a void. Houses, trees, cars. As if there was nothing left of the living world. His bootlace had come undone. He bent to retie it. At least his head felt clearer. Perhaps alcohol hadn't been the best idea, but it had given him courage. Purpose.

He looked around. Nothing was familiar. He might have been at the ragtag end of the universe, some point of land far from the known regions. He staggered to a corner to read the sign: *Heath Street*. How on earth …? In the fog and in his drunken state he'd ended up on one of those little cul-de-sacs backing onto the ravine. The signs had been warning him: *No Exit*.

Three cars were parked along the curb, their outlines hulking like camels bedding down for the night. The first, a black Honda, butt-ended a grey Audi. You didn't leave expensive cars on the road, even in this neighbourhood. The final car was white, a big utility vehicle of the sort that painters and repairmen drove. He thought he'd seen it once or twice in the lot at Queen's Park. Maybe it would turn out to be someone from the security division wanting a private word. A moment of optimism came to him: they were conducting an internal investigation and needed his co-operation, having known all along he was innocent. Well, by god! He'd be glad to give it to them after the way he'd been treated.

A private place, the voice on the phone had said. *Somewhere close to your home.* And then the promise of discretion: *Come alone. It's just a talk. We won't record anything. There'll be no witnesses.* At first John had hesitated. How did he know he could trust the other party? But then reason intervened. He'd done nothing wrong and had nothing to hide. What would it matter if they recorded every last word? It would only be to his benefit.

A fence loomed up out of nowhere. On his right, a pile of refuse threatened to topple over onto him. His life was a garbage heap! How fitting. His father had been right: politics was dirt, filth. And there was no one he could turn to except a mysterious emailer intent on discovering what he knew. Well, then. *Let me tell you what I know*, he would say.

The fog was thicker now, enveloping him with its ephemeral arms. He wanted to get on his knees and curl up in a ball beside the garbage. The refuse of his life. He felt the rage welling inside. He'd only done what was right!

He had stood up in the face of evil. But it had been smarter than him. Smarter and stronger. There was too much to fight against. Too much corruption and injustice.

Just shut up about it, John! It comes with the territory, he reproached himself. *You knew that before you began, so don't whine about it now.*

He reached the end of the alleyway. There was no way forward. The moon suddenly snapped into view, a bone-luminous light coming through the fog. Beyond lay the immensity of the galaxy, the universe spreading on forever. In that moment of illumination, he saw stairs off to his left leading down to the ravine. He was saved!

Then, just as suddenly, the light was gone again. Eclipsed. It dawned on him that it was nothing more than a streetlamp with a rickety connection. So much for the grandeur of it all. He stopped and laughed at the absurdity. They had him exactly where they wanted him.

It might have been the only moment of true perspective he'd had all week. *We are nothing,* he thought, peering into the swirling fog. *All this is for nothing! We live and die in the blink of an eye. A brief space between two eternities.* All the while, he wondered if it was the alcohol talking. Babble, babble, babble. Just like those fools in the legislature.

Then without warning he convulsed with shame at the memory of his dismissal. The tears came quickly, clouding his vision. In his grief he sat heavily on the pavement, groping with blind hands to feel the earth beneath him.

From a distance, footsteps headed his way. He jerked his head around, wiping his eyes and stumbling to stand, not wanting to be caught in this forlorn posture. Someone was coming toward him, silhouetted by the light, monstrous and grotesque, like a giant alien enlarged and projected against a screen of fog.

Suddenly he felt stone-cold sober from fear.

It was a little past seven when the fog began to lift. An early-morning jogger looked up to see the figure suspended from the bridge, an outline coming in and out of the mist that clung on in the ravine. It was a man in dishevelled garb — a woman's overcoat, mismatched gloves, and boots tied with broken laces — suspended by a yellow nylon cord.

At first the police thought it was a tramp, a vagabond living in the gully, until they emptied his pockets and took a look at the ID he carried. This was no ordinary man who'd hanged himself. This was a man who'd recently been publicly disgraced. And soon the awakening city would know why.

ONE:
TORONTO, 2014

You or No One

THINGS WEREN'T GOING WELL FOR private investigator Dan Sharp. He had just spilled coffee on his new suit, and he sat dabbing ineffectually at the stain with a damp cloth. Just five minutes ago, he'd learned the warehouse that housed his investigations office would close permanently come summer, to be gutted for condominiums. This was prime real estate overlooking the Don River; it was bound to happen sooner or later. Like it or not, he had three months to find a reasonable substitute for the place he'd thought of as a second home for the past five years.

On top of that, the food for the wedding had come in priced at nearly twice what he was expecting. They'd already tossed out the idea of flowers as an unnecessary expense, but this was a gay wedding and food was a *must*. It went without saying that theirs had to be a spectacular menu.

Weddings were not Dan's idea of fun. Not because he was afraid of commitment; he just didn't like circuses, whether three-ring or of the domestic variety. For Dan, a vow meant giving your word and sealing it in your heart. Ceremonies were for the crowning of monarchs, the consecration of altars, and the opening of shopping malls and theme parks.

Getting married was Nick's idea. At first, Dan had laughed. He thought his partner was joking. They'd barely known each other a year then. He shook his head and said, "Thanks, but I'm not the marrying kind." Nick had stared him down. "Well, I am." Then he got up and left the room, leaving Dan sitting there dumfounded.

That wasn't the end of the subject. Not by a long shot. Dan wasn't sure whether they were having an argument or just a difference of opinion. Nick could be garrulous one moment and silent as the grave the next. Something about him demanded attention. Put it down to all the police training. Even off duty, cops commanded authority; they didn't confer it on others. Any time they disagreed, Dan felt as if he were being given the third degree by an officer of the law investigating with probable cause.

For Dan, it boiled down to whether he wanted to buy into an institution that had long denied the validity of non-traditional relationships. But he hedged, couching it in material terms when they next discussed it: "It's a racket, Nick. Thousands of dollars for what? To say 'I love you' in a church?"

"How much is my love worth to you?" Nick asked.

"Low blow," Dan countered. Still, he knew better: to give Nick an inch was dangerous. He went in for the kill. "As an institution, marriage is conservative and backward thinking. I've given you my word. Do you need to own me on paper like some sort of real estate transaction?"

"It's a statement, Dan. A very radical statement. It says we're willing to stand up and be counted in a world that denies our legitimacy. They hate us. They outlaw and kill us in many places around the globe. Why not say we're proud of who we are in one of the few countries where we can do that? And in case you're wondering, I wouldn't marry just anyone. It's you or no one."

In the end, they had compromised: a small ceremony, but legal. Not much pomp and lots of standing up to be counted among those who mattered to them. Which still didn't mean Nick was willing to settle for cheap, Dan reminded himself. And that was why he found himself staring at a quote from a very chic catering company offering a menu created by a three-Michelin-starred chef for twenty-five people at four hundred bucks a plate. Maple-glazed bison on black truffle pasta, grilled Mission figs stuffed with Stilton and wrapped in prosciutto, wild boar meatballs in almond sauce, an arugula-walnut-cranberry salad, and lemon tiramisu with white chocolate lace pastry to finish. All this with hand-selected cheeses and wines. Nothing but the best. Yes, it was more than impressive, but was it worth it? Dan struggled with that. Ten thousand dollars would go a long way toward paying for his son Kedrick's education, for instance. Or feeding a homeless person or getting LGBT youth off the street and into safe living conditions.

Being conscientious had its price.

Dan pushed the quote aside and picked up the phone to tell Nick they needed to find another caterer. He was interrupted by a knock. A shape hovered over the frosted glass like a milky alien outline. Cold calls were rare in Dan's world. Most first-time clients were either fearful of consulting a private investigator or else so obsessed with their privacy that they contacted him by phone or email.

This one apparently wasn't put off by such concerns. The door opened on a big man with a bulky torso, bristling with energy. On seeing Dan, he entered without waiting to be asked and offered a large, furry hand. "Peter Hansen."

The name sounded vaguely familiar.

"Dan Sharp."

Hansen's gaze went around the office, gauging and appraising: old furniture, raw brick, original art, classic texts on the bookshelf. A man in a hurry. Better to make your assessment first and then decide what you want.

"You come recommended," he said, seemingly satisfied. "Yeah, you're the one I want."

It wasn't much of a compliment, but Dan could tell a man like Peter Hansen wouldn't have come had the recommendation been half-hearted.

He named a client Dan had worked for several years previously. The case hadn't been unusual or noteworthy, but Dan's results were both quick and decisive. That, more often than not, was why people kept coming to him.

Hansen placed a valise on Dan's desk, snapped it open, and slid a black-and-white photograph under Dan's gaze.

"My husband," he said in a tone that suggested a deep ambivalence.

Dan looked down at a thin, handsome face whose expression hovered somewhere between uncertain and fearful. A man trying to escape notice.

"Name?"

"Tony Moran."

"How long has he been missing?"

Peter regarded him warily. "How did you know he was missing?"

Dan looked him up and down. "You don't look like the kind of man who would pay someone to sort out his domestic affairs if you thought you could do it yourself."

"Fair enough. Tony's been missing since the weekend. Friday, probably. I was away for the evening. He wasn't home when I got back in the early hours on Saturday."

"I'm sorry to hear that."

"I don't want sympathy. I want you to find him."

Dan overlooked Peter's abruptness. "Do you suspect foul play? Kidnapping? Anything dire?"

Peter shook his head. "Not at this point."

"Where do you think he might be?"

"He's got a fear of flying and he doesn't drive, so chances are he's right here in the city. I've cut off his credit cards."

"Any obvious reasons for disappearing? An affair, perhaps?"

"No." Peter paused. "Maybe. We had an argument. Over money."

"Did you hit him?"

Hansen made a face. "No."

Dan pushed the photo back and looked at Peter. "Well, then that pretty much covers it. My guess is he'll come home when he cools off and runs out of places to stay."

"I'm not so sure," Peter added. "He's a gambler. He lost a lot of my money and doesn't want to have to confront me over it."

Nor would I, Dan thought. "How long have you been married?"

"Three years."

"I still say he'll be back when he's ready."

Peter stabbed Dan's desktop with an angry finger. "I came here to hire you."

"And do you want your husband back or just the money?"

Peter bristled. "Just find him. Please. Before he causes me any more embarrassment."

"Have you been on my website? Do you know my terms?"

Peter nodded. "I have. I do."

"Okay. I'll take a look around. If I agree to take on the case, I'll draw up a contract and we can set up a time to go over it together in the next couple of days."

Peter shook his head. "No contract. I don't want anything on paper."

Before Dan could protest, Hansen put up his hand. "I'm in politics, Dan. My boss is a high-profile minister at Queen's Park and there's an election coming up. I can't have a whiff of this hitting the street. I want no paper trails. I need your absolute discretion."

He reached into his case, drew out an envelope and placed it on the desk.

"Here's your retainer. I don't want a receipt. All I care about is results. Everything you need to know about Tony is in here." He glanced down at the caterer's quote on Dan's desk. His eyebrows went up. "Thinking of getting married?"

Dan nodded.

"My advice? Don't do it. They're always more trouble than they're worth."

He turned and strode to the door. Then, with one hand on the knob, he looked back at Dan. "If you need more money, let me know."

The door opened and closed. The whirlwind subsided.

Dan waited till Hansen's footsteps receded, then slit open the envelope. He thumbed through a pile of thousand-dollar bills, ten in total, wrapped in a sheet containing Tony Moran's particulars. His eyes ran down the page. Tony was a high school graduate, with a further couple years at a business college. A few of his past jobs were noted, including a stint as assistant manager of a Wendy's franchise. Not a big achiever, then.

Dan glanced at the picture again. Despite Tony's good looks, there was something skin-deep about them suggesting he might attract a certain type of partner quickly, but not stay the term. His polo-shirt-and-sweater combo smacked of conservative taste, but with a narcis-sistic undertone. Then again, he had a low-rent sort of sex appeal. The sort of man a Peter Hansen might look on as material for moulding, someone to impress with a helping hand out of the gutter. Pygmalions were a dime a dozen.

Three local addresses were listed at the bottom of the sheet. Dan suspected they would turn out to be gambling dens. He picked up the bills again. It was a lot of money, far more than what he normally asked for as a retainer. It seemed Peter Hansen was serious about wanting his hus-band returned. Maybe Nick would have his chi-chi caterer after all.

Dan turned to his laptop and did a search on Hansen. A series of links appeared, including an article about his marriage to Tony Moran on a downtown Toronto rooftop three years earlier. It looked to have been an impressive affair. The premier and several prominent ministers had attended, which might explain why a major paper had covered a gay wedding. They weren't a bad-looking couple, Dan thought. Not mismatched the way a wealthy older man might seem with a cute but brainless younger man. But where Peter's face showed force and determination, a tenacious grit, Tony's showed something softer, more malleable. Dan knew which one of them he'd rather be friends with, if it came to that.

Dan realized why Hansen's name had sounded familiar. He'd worked hard campaigning for civil rights, proving a standard-bearer for LGBT issues, though one article suggested he'd lost an election four years earlier by being openly gay. Thus he'd ended up as special assistant to the educational reforms minister instead.

Dan was about to close his laptop when a headline caught his eye. It was dated just before Christmas: *Disgraced Queen's Park MPP found dead in ravine.* He clicked on the link. A cheerful-looking man in his mid-thirties met his gaze. Dan recalled the story: John Wilkens had been the opposition critic for a man named Alec Henderson. Peter Hansen's boss. Despite his relative youth, Wilkens was once regarded as a contender for House Speaker, and possibly prime minister material, until he'd been dismissed for improper use of government funds. An investigation had been pending at the time of his death. The coroner's ruling was suicide.

Dan scanned a follow-up piece. There were the usual official condolences from party leaders for their deceased colleague: *John Wilkens was a good man who believed that public service was the most honourable way to serve others*, etc. No mention of his indiscretions with public funds. Never speak ill of the dead. Wasn't that what they taught?

The dead minister's lineage was impressive. He'd come from one of the most established families in Ontario, scion of a proud race of industry leaders and charity funders. It was the usual muck, a political whitewash. The dead had no enemies. Dan smelled a story larger than what was written here, but the formal speak of politics had closed ranks around the dead minister, leaving the truth gagged once again.

He picked up his cell and dialed the number on the paper. Hansen answered.

"Dan Sharp here, Peter."

"Yes, what? Anything wrong?"

"You left an awful lot of money on my desk."

"It's yours. Keep it."

"It's far more than a retainer."

"Consider it a bonus if you find him."

"I won't keep it unless I earn it. I'll put it in my safe for now."

There was a pause. "You may need it to find Tony."

"Meaning?"

"Spend it if you have to." He hung up.

Dan sighed quietly. He hadn't even begun to work on the case and Peter Hansen was already turning into a pain in the ass. It worried him. Something smelled wrong — he just wasn't sure what. He glanced over the paper with the scant facts of Tony Moran's life. Maybe the answer lay there, but it wasn't much to go on.

He picked up his Day-Timer and wrote Hansen's name along with the time of his visit. Beside it he wrote *$10,000 CASH*, underlining the entry.

In the space below he wrote: *Find another caterer.*

TWO

Sweet Domesticity

DAN WAS COMFORTED BY THE smell of roast chicken on arriving home. Apart from being a great companion, Nick was also an excellent chef. It was just one more thing that made him an outstanding partner.

There was no dog at the front door, but that wasn't unusual these days. Ralph the Geriatric had given up his duties as official greeter to anyone he knew returning home. Only strangers still merited that calling.

Ralph had been many things in his long life, including a rabble-rouser and back-porch broadcaster of neighbourhood news, but he was now enjoying his retirement. Dan had named him after the unmarried uncle of one of his exes, whom he'd met one Thanksgiving. Uncle Ralph had had bloodshot eyes and been wracked with a terrible croup. It turned out he'd also briefly been the secret lover of actor Rock Hudson back in the 1950s when the term "confirmed bachelor" covered a multitude of sins. After dinner, Dan jokingly declared to his ex that he wanted a dog like the uncle. Stopping by the pound on a whim a month later, he found a ginger retriever pup with blood-shot eyes, just recovering from kennel cough. He brought the dog home for Kedrick. While the boyfriend soon deserted and the namesake uncle died not long afterward, taking Rock's secret to the grave, Ralph was still around fifteen years later. Of late, however, he spent much of his time lounging on a cushion, thumping his tail when called, and surveying his kingdom from this private throne.

In the kitchen, Ralph looked up with an approving glance before settling back down again. Dan gave him a pat on the head, then reached for a mug in the cupboard. He turned on the tap and heard a yelp from upstairs. Nick was in the shower. The touchy thermostat had no doubt given him a sharp reminder of its finicky nature.

When they met, Dan had been single so long he wasn't sure he could let another man into his life while retaining his emotional balance, the outer signs of self control so important to him. Still, Nick had given him reason to try. Surprisingly, gratefully, Dan had concluded that domestic life agreed with him so long as the man at his side brought more happiness than grief. In the meantime, to his pleasant surprise, a recurring stress disorder retreated to the far shores of consciousness till it was a mere echo of the turmoil and anxiety he'd once lived with daily.

So far, with Nick, there'd been little to regret. Dan had worried about dating a cop for all the usual reasons, but for the most part they turned out to be unfounded. True, Nick had a peppery temper, but it was as sudden as it was brief. Here and gone, like a summer squall. He had emotional depth and he was patient. He was also refreshingly direct.

Dan liked that Nick could be funny and serious in equal measure but never hid his true feelings. He was his own man. "You'll never have to guess with me," he'd told Dan at the relationship's outset. Not entirely true, Dan discovered, as Nick's emotions and moods changed like quicksilver. But he was reliable, loyal, and loving.

Dan was still not entirely sure how Kedrick felt about Nick, however. Ked had been happiest when Dan was with a man named Trevor. But Trevor had been unnerved by Dan's choice of profession, living in constant fear for Dan's safety. The split had been amicable, but since then Dan was never entirely certain of Ked's approval of any man in his life. The problem had been temporarily resolved when Ked moved to B.C. to pursue a degree in oceanographic and environmental studies and could only vet his father's boyfriends at a distance. Still, Dan would have preferred to know that Ked approved of his choice of mate.

Officially, Nick and Dan did not live together, though that was set to change with the marriage. Till then they were owners of two residences, one a spacious condo on Toronto's coveted waterfront and the other a modest-size home in newly chic Leslieville. When Dan bought the house, it had been advertised as "two bedrooms plus den with basic backyard," though in reality the latter turned out to be a veritable wilderness. At the time, Leslieville had been anything but fashionable, scorned by both hipsters and yuppies alike as an unremarkable lower-class pocket sandwiched between the Beach and genteel

Riverdale. The yard reflected the city's neglect. It consisted of a tottering wire fence enclosing a plot of weeds nearly four feet high. Dan cut the grass, built a deck, and erected a winding rock wall to shore up the flower beds before adding a pond in the far corner. High hopes. The pond's goldfish supply was repeatedly plundered by marauding raccoons. An exploratory pair of turtles suffered the same fate, as did the half-dozen piranha Dan bought to nip some sense into the pesky thieves. While rats and cockroaches ruled the rest of the world, Toronto was lorded over by its well-fed Procyons.

A few indigenous plants made a strong showing the first season: rhubarb and wild roses, even garlic sprang seemingly out of nowhere. Later, Dan introduced cultivated roses and miniature lilacs. Tulips, daffodils, crocuses, and trillium soon reared their heads alongside everything else. Before long, he'd established a backyard sanctuary that was frequented by a variety of birds and insects, as well as the occasional skunk and fox.

The house, too, had been in a questionable state when he moved in, but it soon sported new doors and windows and a new roof. Dilapidated hardwood floors walked on by the house's original inhabitants a hundred years earlier were soon refinished, while the fireplace, sealed for decades but now newly refurbished, took pride of place in the living room where he now stood.

Dan stroked the lid of a decorative box perched on the mantel, sliding it open to a trove of snapshots. His cousin Leyla at ten, tomboy bangs and a grin, lay on top. She'd been like a sister to him. Next came Aunt Marge, his substitute mother, jolly and robust like the good wife from a fairy tale. From her he'd learned love and compassion. Dan's real mother, Christine, had died when he was four. Her image lay further down. He knew where to find it if he wanted to. Those were the older photos. There were newer additions, many recent: shots of Dan and Nick together, of Ked right before he left for university, and of Ked's mother, Kendra, a Syrian-born immigrant who had crossed Dan's romantic horizon briefly, though neither had been contemplating parenthood at the time.

Some of the pictures were pleasant reminders, others bittersweet. His long-time friend Domingo, who'd died of a recurring cancer, smiled up alongside Dan's best friend, Donny, and Donny's own bit of domestic bliss, the charming Prabin. They were his Found Family, though sometimes they felt more like a Lost and Found, these disparate bits and pieces of his life. Dan wasn't given to sentiment, but all of them held meaning. His wedding photos would one day find a place alongside the others.

There were no photographs of his father. Stuart Sharp had been a brutal man given to harsh words, black moods, and, when his son displeased him, a quick swing of the hand. The latter hadn't happened often, if only because Dan learned early to stay out of his way, but on at least one occasion the drunken Stuart had slammed his son into a doorframe, giving Dan a lasting scar on his temple, a lightning bolt that was a permanent reminder of his father. Dan didn't need photos for that.

In truth, he felt he'd long since made peace with his father's memory, coming to understand him as a frustrated and bitter man constrained by a lifetime of crushing labour in the mines, with few joys outside. He'd had little to give to others once his wife died and left him to raise a son who felt more fear for his father than any other emotion he could readily name.

It had been a hard life in a city of rock. Sudbury: the nickel capital of the world. A rough place for rough people. Dan remembered a classmate, Pelka, whose father had drunk battery acid in a failed attempt to kill himself, and a shy, fatherless boy named Rex whom Dan had claimed hopefully as his best friend for a single semester before Rex and his itinerant mother moved on again for parts unknown. Another girl, Shirley, always had a boy's haircut and wore blue jeans. She came to school looking alternately frightened and angry. No one spoke about these things. Dan had made the best of things while he lived there, knowing nothing else, then put it behind him when he moved away and somehow, inexplicably, wound up a father in the largest city in the country at age twenty-four. Over time, parenthood had proved the dividing line between the largely deserted shores of his past and the well-populated shores of his present.

An additional marker was reached when Kedrick left for university, a day Dan had long known was coming but still felt strangely unprepared for when it arrived. Ked's upcoming graduation would be the first time they'd seen each other in more than six months. And soon Dan himself would be facing yet another landmark: marriage to Nick. He hoped it suited them both.

From upstairs came the sound of heartily shouted song lyrics under the shower's stream. It was like having a teenager in the house again, Dan thought. After nearly two years, the ups had well outnumbered the downs of their relationship. Even their sex life had turned numerous corners, and it was still alive and well. A good sign for two men verging on middle age.

They slept together when Nick wasn't on the late shift and ate meals together when he was. Now all Dan had to do was make sure he didn't get fat and lazy. Nights spent in front of the fire with Nick seemed filled with all the bliss in the world. All that he needed, anyway.

Weekends, Dan felt no desire to stray from the idylls of his backyard, lounging beside the moss-covered wall beneath the locust tree and imagining the long-vanished snapping of goldfish foraging for food in the empty pond. Was there anything better?

The thump-thump-thump of footsteps announced Nick's arrival as he came downstairs wrapped in a towel, sleek and glistening from the shower and suitably hirsute. Without a regular trim, his chest would sport a full-frontal rug. He kissed Dan on the top of his head, then disappeared into the kitchen, humming to himself before returning with a tray of drinks like an exceptionally polished waiter, minus the tux.

"Lounging again, your majesty? May I offer you a cranberry cordial?"

Dan took up a glass, admiring Nick's torso. It made life easy when your partner had a certain physical appeal, but Dan was sure he'd still be in love with this man when he was eighty, should they both live so long.

"I could do with an appetizer," he said with a wink. "Something hot and spicy."

"All in good time, sire," Nick said. "Supper's in ten minutes. Let's not ruin your appetite."

With a quick bow he ran back upstairs to dress, leaving Dan to ponder his luck at having snagged the perfect partner. Nick had come to Canada from Macedonia as a teenager. In his twenties he'd picked up a wife briefly before deciding it wasn't a life he was suited to. Before they could fight over the much-loved son their union had produced, the child died, precipitating a decade of alcoholic abuse on Nick's part.

By then Nick had grown accustomed to Canada's rights and freedoms, including the right to determine one's own sexual behaviour, and came out. As if to make up for the ease of choice, however, the following year he entered a rock-solid bastion of homophobia — the police department. It had been hard at times, and it meant keeping his private life private, but he'd survived. Then came Dan.

Nick returned now, fully dressed. Dan let him in on the day's news. Crisis one: he was being evicted from his office space. Crisis two: they needed to find another caterer for the wedding. Nick shrugged off both of these.

"If we start looking now, we can find you something suitable at a good rate in the next couple of months."

Dan was inclined to be gloomy. "Have you looked at rental rates lately? I could end up in some godforsaken neighbourhood on the far end of town trying to match the price I pay now."

"Then I'll provide you with a police escort every morning. As for the other ..." He glanced over Dan's shoulder toward the kitchen. "Maybe I can put the menu together myself."

"I suspect you'll be too busy on the day in question to be producing a gourmet meal. In the meantime, I've come into a bit of unexpected revenue, so perhaps we can afford a little more than I thought."

"Lucky day at the races?"

"In a manner of speaking. I got a new case. That's assuming I want it."

Nick cocked his head. "Why wouldn't you?"

"Because it came with a very heavy cash retainer in a brown envelope. Ten thousand dollars heavy, to be precise."

Nick whistled. "You think it's gangster money?"

"Close. It's political money. Ever hear of a guy called Peter Hansen?"

"Sounds familiar. Didn't he run for a seat at Queen's Park a while back?"

"He did, but he didn't make it. Now he's special assistant to the educational reforms minister. He's gay and his husband has disappeared. Gambling debts, from the sounds of it. But he wants it kept out of the media. Apparently the legislature has had its share of scandal lately. An opposition critic committed suicide at Christmas."

Nick's eyebrows rose. "Yes, I remember. He hung himself in the ravine."

"Not quite. You're hung. He was hanged. There's a difference."

Nick tried to suppress his smile. "Okay, Mr. Pedant. But it's a given — where there are politics, there are scandals." He paused. "Any connection between the suicide and the missing husband?"

"Nothing I can see. Tony Moran isn't *in* politics, just married to it. The suicide was cooking some books, by the sounds of it."

Nick shrugged. "It's always the Conservatives who get greedy when they're in power. The Liberals are egotists who make a mess of things because they think they know better, and the New Democrats are a bunch of flakey do-gooders."

Dan laughed. "Well, that pretty much covers the board. Between the crooks and the flakey do-gooders, I guess there's no hope for the rest of us."

"Don't underestimate the Green Party. The future is green, I always say."

Dan shook his head. "You're a very funny policeman, Officer Trposki."

"The way I figure it, as long as I can make you laugh you'll stick around for the wedding. After that, it'll be too late to change your mind." Nick glanced toward the kitchen. "Supper's ready. Let's eat."

They had just sat down when the hall phone rang. Dan stood to answer it.

Nick gave him a warning look. "Don't be long."

"I promise." Dan picked up the receiver. "Hello?"

There was a brief silence, then a man's voice said, "Is this Dan Sharp?"

"Yes."

"Mr. Sharp, I understand you're working for Peter Hansen to find his husband, Tony."

Dan's mind went on the alert. "Who's calling?"

The man's name meant nothing to him. The caller continued. "Peter Hansen gave me your number. He said I could talk to you about the case. Do you mind answering a few questions?"

"I do mind. If you want to know anything then ask Peter Hansen."

He hung up, fuming. First Hansen had showed up unannounced at his office, tossing money around while demanding discretion, and now he felt free to give out Dan's private number to someone Dan had never heard of. Peter Hansen had all the makings of a nightmare client.

THREE

Humpty Dumpty

DINNER OVER, DAN CLEARED THE plates and brought them to the kitchen. To the consternation of nearly everyone he knew, he did not own an automatic dishwasher. And because he had no dishwasher, the person who ended up washing dishes was usually him. That was the accepted arrangement when he and Nick ate together: chef gets to relax after the meal. Donny and numerous other well-meaning friends had tried over the years to convince him that modern technology had its merits, but Dan merely scoffed.

"For one thing," he'd say, "I don't trust a machine to do as good a job as I can. For another, I like washing dishes. It relaxes me to submerge my hands in the soapy water and get scrubbing. It's my happy space."

These statements usually elicited a few gasps, especially among a sophisticated downtown crowd. Sometimes there were murmurings of sympathetic understanding, but usually not.

"You're more than welcome to it," Nick told him, after offering to buy a dishwasher and being turned down flat.

More often than not, Nick sat at the table and nursed a coffee while Dan washed up, rather than rushing off to read or lounge in front of the television. Completely comfortable in each other's presence, they were seldom apart during their off hours. Anyone seeing them might suspect there was an invisible force constantly pulling them together.

Dan finished the dishes, then followed Nick into the living room. He plunked himself down on the sofa and grabbed the TV remote.

"News?" he asked.

Nick grumped. "Why? It's always bad. I get enough of that at work. In fact, I can tell you the news without even turning on the TV: somewhere there will be wars, somewhere else a natural disaster, while closer to home we'll have a suspicious fire and a car accident that tied up rush-hour traffic."

"You forgot politics," Dan added.

"Yes, I did. On purpose."

"You are one of the few people I can truly say is more curmudgeonly than me."

"Glad to hear it."

Dan aimed the remote. "Let's brave it anyway."

They sat through the commercials with the sound muted until the news began. As Nick predicted, there was coverage of fighting in Africa and the Middle East, with an earnest detailing of the collapse of last-minute peace talks. The World Health Organization reported an outbreak of Ebola in West Africa. Disaster was the through-line, distressing despite its seeming remoteness. Only the local news featured a bright spot, with mention of a donation to SickKids hospital.

Dan was about to turn it off when a shot of Peter Hansen and Tony Moran appeared onscreen as the anchor's disembodied voice stated that the husband of the special assistant to the educational reforms minister had been declared missing. A former candidate for the legislature, Hansen had hired a private investigator. Dan felt a jolt when he heard his name cited. The anchor closed by saying that both Peter and Dan had declined to comment on the case.

Nick's hand stole over and gripped Dan's thigh.

"Did you know about this?"

"No," Dan said grimly. "So much for my client's request for discretion."

Just then his cellphone rang.

Dan looked at Nick. "What are the chances?"

He picked up and heard Peter Hansen's gruff tone.

"Why did I just hear my name and yours on the evening news?" Hansen demanded. "What is this? Some kind of publicity grab? I told you I didn't want this getting out."

"Wait a minute. I didn't contact the press," Dan said. "Someone called me to ask about the case. He said you gave him my number. I didn't tell him anything."

"Who was it?"

Dan repeated the name he'd been given.

"Never heard of him," Hansen growled. "Those fucking barracudas!"

"Who?"

"The political reporters. They must have followed me to your office, or else they're hacking my email."

"We haven't had an email exchange."

Peter snorted. "My phone, then. Who knows how they get this stuff!"

"I would advise caution from now on. Let's talk directly in person when we speak about it."

"A little late for that!" Hansen rounded off his conversation with a few well-placed expletives. "Sorry. Not professional of me."

"I understand."

"Please just find Tony."

"I will," Dan assured him.

He'd just put the phone down when it rang again.

"Sharp."

There was a short pause followed by a tenor voice asking, "Could I get a comment on the Peter Hansen situation?"

"Who is this?"

"Simon Bradley. I'm a journalist. I cover local politics."

The name rang a bell, Dan thought, but from long ago. This voice sounded too young.

Bradley continued. "I'd like to ask a few questions about Tony Moran. I might be able to tell you something in return."

"Such as?"

Dan heard cars whizzing past on the other end, a busy highway.

"John Badger Wilkens. The Queen's Park minister who committed suicide at Christmas."

"Why would I want information on him?"

"I'll explain, if you meet me."

Dan looked over at Nick, who had busied himself with a magazine.

"When?"

"I'm just heading back into town. Say half an hour?"

Vesta Lunch had been open on the corner of Bathurst and Dupont, night and day, for as long as Dan had lived in Toronto. It never closed and never seemed to change. Not the servers, not the clientele, not the menu. As greasy spoons went, it was one of the best. Late-night comfort food for the lonesome and early-morning remedies for the hungover. Even an emergency shelter in a snowstorm, if need be. No matter how far your fall from grace, it was a place to hang your hat and call home.

Simon Bradley stood upon Dan's arrival. He was young and easily six-foot-four, with a slim build under an Armani jacket, a confident smile, and a haircut that must have cost two hundred dollars. Dan recognized him as an occasional on-air broadcaster, the type who showed up in the midst of swirling snowstorms to report on traffic jams, house fires, derailed trains, and the other detritus that made up the bread and butter of the all-news stations. Apparently he'd been transferred to doing pieces of a political bent. Someone must have thought his mug worthy of the cause.

"Was it your father or your grandfather?" Dan asked.

The question caught Simon by surprise, but he quickly got back on track.

"Grandfather," he said as they shook hands. "You remember him?"

"As a kid, yes. The name mostly, but I think I recall a resemblance."

Simon Bradley Sr. had been one of the names reverberating through the Sharp household, spoken with
reverence, when Dan was a boy. The names, including
old-school politicians such as Lester Pearson, hockey
players like Jean Béliveau, and broadcasters like Simon's
grandfather, were laid out as evidence of the glory days
now past. They'd been legends back in the day when
television ruled and you couldn't get through the bleak
northern Ontario winters without one.

"You're right. I got his name and his looks," Simon
said. "But my dad got all the literary rights to his books."

There would have been dozens of them, Dan recalled.
Bradley had been one of Canada's mainstays as an on-air
journalist, and before that as a historian famous for his
coverage of the Cold War. Now here was his grandson
trying to make a name for himself in the same field.
Sometimes the pressure to live up to a forebear was more
trouble than it was worth.

Their server heard them talking and stole a look at Simon
as though he was considering asking for an autograph.

"You somebody I should know, man?" he asked, setting down a plate of fries alongside a chicken-and-gravy
sandwich.

Simon shrugged. "Only if you watch television."

The waiter shook his head. "Nah. Waste of time," he
said, glancing over at Dan.

"Just coffee," Dan told him.

Simon grinned as their waiter walked away. "That
puts me in my place."

The server returned with a cup of coffee, managing to
slop it into the saucer as he set it on the table. He looked at

it as though it might merit a second pour, then shrugged the gaffe aside as not worth his bother.

Dan tipped a single cream into his cup and sipped. It was always great coffee. He watched as Simon picked up a gravy-covered fry and slipped it into his mouth with a satisfied grin.

"So good! Love this place."

"Just to remind you, Mr. Bradley, the meter is ticking."

Simon gave him a reproachful look, as if he'd just insulted their new friendship. Suddenly he looked like a kid straight out of journalism school. "Sure, sorry, Dan. What do you know about John Badger Wilkens III?"

Dan shrugged. "The minister who committed suicide? Not much, really."

"Well, let me tell you a few things. At twenty-five, John was the youngest elected minister in the legislature. He was a five-time debating champion in university, as well as a crackerjack lawyer and chartered accountant. Word is he was being groomed to be party leader in a few years. Which is to say he was considered by many to be a likely fit for future prime minister. Conservative, of course."

"Naturally."

"He was voted most popular member of the legislature before he turned thirty," Simon continued. "Then last year something happened. From being leader of the pack, John's star dimmed suddenly, and he was shunted to the backrooms. His party advisers stopped pushing him in front of TV cameras. Then came the revelations: missing money from a public portfolio. His fall was unthinkable after such a quick rise."

Dan recalled Nick's depiction of Conservatives as being prone to financial scandals. "What happened?"

"I don't know for sure, but similar things have happened to others. Before him there was Sharon Timmons. Remember her?"

Dan nodded. "Another up-and-coming star. The New Democrats. Wasn't she implicated in some scandal or other?"

"Drugs. Though she and her husband both proclaimed her innocence. For a while it looked like it might have been the teenage son, but they vigorously denied that as well, saying it was a plant. But it tarnished her reputation. The party eventually dropped her, too."

"Curious, but how is this supposed to help me find Tony Moran?"

Simon leaned forward, as though to emphasize their intimacy. "What if I told you John Wilkens was murdered?"

Dan gave him a skeptical look. "It would make an interesting aside, but I thought we were here to talk about Tony."

"This is related."

"How?"

"I was in touch with John right before he was given the sack. I think he knew something he wasn't supposed to know. It had to do with the cancellation of the power plants contracts. It was a last-minute campaign promise that got the Liberals re-elected. When it was first announced, the estimated cost was something like two hundred million and change. Then came news of the cover-up. The Auditor General recently quoted the cost to the province as more than nine hundred and fifty million dollars. John and I had planned to meet so he could tell me what he knew. Only he got himself killed first, see?"

Dan shook his head. "I don't see anything. The power plant scandal is old news. Both the premier and the energy minister resigned. I understood Wilkens killed himself because he was disgraced for embezzling public funds. But it had nothing to do with the scandal. Why do you think he was murdered? And how does Tony Moran fit in?"

Simon stuffed a forkful of sandwich into his mouth, wiping his lips with the back of his hand.

"When the money disappeared, Wilkens's party dumped him. He'd become a liability and they didn't want to get their hands dirty. Wilkens claimed he'd been set up. I think he found something irregular. He offered to help unmask the corruption at Queen's Park. A few days later, he turned up dead. Pretty strange coincidence, no? As for how it relates to Tony Moran, ask yourself how Tony might have stumbled onto the same info as John Wilkens."

"I couldn't possibly begin to guess, Mr. Bradley. You work the political beat. You would have a much better idea than me."

Simon gave him a satisfied grin, the Cheshire Cat in person.

"We're talking about the cover-up of corruption on a grand scale. Whatever happened to John Wilkens, whatever he uncovered, somehow Tony Moran found out about it, too."

Dan nodded, feeling boredom creep in. There was something about Simon's hair that made it hard to take him seriously. "Does Peter Hansen know about it?"

"I don't know. I tried to contact him, but he won't return my calls."

"Have you gone to the police?"

"No."

Dan sipped his coffee. "Why not?"

"They probably wouldn't believe me, for one. For another, I want the story. Once I get the police involved, I'll be pushed aside."

"If it involves murder, the police have to be informed."

"There's no proof. At least, not yet. I intend to find it."

"You think you're going to unmask a murderer?" Dan shook his head. "Braver men than you have done stupider things and lived to regret it."

"Braver men maybe, but not smarter." Simon winked. "We all see what we want to see. Sometimes it's a matter of choice, other times it's in the presentation. Take me, for instance. I can say nearly anything and it will be believed. Why? Because I'm in front of a television camera when I say it. That makes it real to most people. If I were irresponsible, I could make up all kinds of allegations about people, really hurtful things. They might make me retract them later, but the damage would have been done to their reputations."

"What would be the point?"

"Exactly! What if there were a person designated to do such things? Someone who could make or break your career simply by having things appear one way or another?" Simon lowered his voice. "I think John Wilkens believed there was such an individual, or possibly a small group of people, who could get rid of up-and-coming political contenders. Some promising candidate suddenly bows out of the race and takes a very cushy job, for instance, leaving the field open for another candidate ..."

"Is that legal?"

"Not strictly, but so long as there's nothing connecting the job offer with leaving the race, you can't really point a finger, though some might question the timing. It could be a bribe or it could be a threat. In John's case, it was a matter of suspicious activity with departmental funds. In Sharon's it was drugs. You see what I'm getting at?"

"Maybe."

"It's really a matter of what you choose to see. Money changing hands in a questionable manner, expenses written off for unusual purposes. Suddenly a front runner getting all the prominence and attention he craves becomes a backbencher to keep him out of sight."

Simon looked over to see that the server was busy taking an order before he spoke again. He leaned closer till he was within inches of Dan's face.

"Someone is playing chess with people's careers and reputations. What does that tell you?"

"That politics is a dirty business."

"Very dirty! There's a rumour in the legislature that when something needs fixing, they call in the Magus to get results."

Dan frowned. "The Magus? You're kidding me."

"I'm not. That's what John called him, anyway. He believed it was one individual acting on the directions of a small group of people with vested interests in who rises and who falls. When something needs fixing, they call in this guy. The result? Rumours spread about misplaced funds, accusations of drugs or sexual harassment. In politics, there's nothing so fragile as a reputation. Once broken, it's impossible to repair. It's the Humpty Dumpty syndrome."

It was possible, Dan thought. A man falls from grace, joining a long list of political failures. Then again, all political leaders face their day of reckoning. And when it comes, the fall is never pretty.

"Can you prove it?"

Simon wiped his mouth with his napkin, folded it, and left it draped over the plate.

"I believe Tony Moran knows what I'm talking about. That's why he ran off and why I need to find him. I haven't been able to crack Peter Hansen yet, but I will." He eyed Dan. "In the meantime, I'm prepared to share with you anything I find out."

Dan shook his head. "Even if I find him, I can't make Tony talk to you. How could I?"

"I'll worry about that when the time comes." He pulled out his cell and checked the screen. "I've got your number. How about we just agree to stay in touch for now? I'll call you from time to time to let you know what I learn. If you hear something, you can call me."

It was late by the time Dan returned. He parked the car and glanced up at his house. The bedroom light was off. He sat in the backyard, the scene of many happy family gatherings. The singsong lullaby of crickets in summer and brief glimpses of stars through clouds all year long created an oasis of peace. To be able to see the night sky in the city's midst was a rare thing. It had kept him sane at the worst of times, and there'd been plenty of those before Nick came along. He thought again of Simon Bradley's allegations of the goings-on at Queen's Park.

From the depths of memory a name surfaced, someone who might give him some insight into the murky waters of politics.

FOUR

Queen's Park

QUEEN VICTORIA IS JUST ONE OF more than a dozen famous people residing in effigy at Queen's Park in the heart of Toronto. She shares the space with monarchs alive and dead, Canada's first prime minister, the Fathers of Confederation, the leader of the Upper Canada Rebellion, a token poet, and even Jesus Christ himself. But it's her park, nonetheless.

It's here that the Ontario legislature has resided and where the province's laws have been debated, refuted, enacted, and challenged since the country's inception. The legislature's ceremonial mace, an ornamented staff of wood and metal representing the ruling monarch's authority, was stolen by the Americans in the War of 1812, a series of cross-border skirmishes that gained them no ground but inflamed nationalist identity on either side of the Great Lakes. For their part, the British got a second go at the Colony That Got Away three decades earlier. As for the Americans, they acquired a national anthem and the above-mentioned mace, until Franklin Roosevelt ordered its return in 1934. Their only real victory, the much-lauded Battle of New Orleans, came some two weeks after the signing of the peace treaty between the two nations, news of which apparently had not reached them soon enough.

There are always winners and losers in times of conflict, as Dan was well aware, and while both the British and Americans claimed — incorrectly, as it turned out — to have won the war, the only clear losers were the aboriginal peoples, betrayed by their allies on both sides while sustaining heavy casualties and further loss of land before being shunted off to reservations. In the ensuing years, native land claims were just one of many contentious issues presided over at Queen's Park. It seemed to Dan that not much had changed in the intervening centuries.

While Canada's history was less bloody than most, of late Dan felt his fellow Canadians had developed a smug attitude toward politics. So it had come as a shock to them when the folks at Toronto's city hall were forced to deal with a crack-smoking mayor who befriended gang members and became the subject of police investigations, raging and rampaging at foes and allies alike, his infantile behaviour making headlines around the globe. Torontonians suddenly woke to the reality that even they could look like buffoons if their leaders were not cut from a finer cloth.

While politics at Queen's Park tended to be of a subtler nature, it was not without scandal. Making his way up the steps of the legislature, Dan thought of Simon Bradley's allegations about the opposition critic who may or may not have committed suicide, about Peter Hansen's missing husband who gambled away large amounts of money, and the rumours of a master manipulator who could make and unmake the reputations of political aspirants. Verifiable or not, it was juicy stuff.

Dan checked his watch. He was early.

Inside the doors was a modest collection of paintings by Robert Bateman, one of Canada's acclaimed nature artists. Fur and feathers. Nothing radical to shock the visitors. Farther along, behind glass, were collections of aboriginal art: tusk, bone, and soapstone looking pristine and sterile out of their natural environment, a testament to the acquisitive nature of power.

At the front desk, Dan leaned in to inquire when the next tour of chambers began. The receptionist beamed a glossy smile at him, apparently thrilled to be working in the hallowed halls of government.

"You're in luck! It starts in five minutes," she announced.

Beside her, a woman many years her senior who looked as though she'd had her fill of governmental regulations, frowned. "Council's already in session today, so you won't be going into the gallery," she snapped, more than happy to spoil his visit.

Dan joined a group of schoolgirls and tourists and they were soon on their way. The guide, an earnest young woman of budding theatrical leanings, indicated a series of stern portraits on the surrounding walls just beyond the lobby.

"Here we have the House Speakers. The Speaker is chosen by anonymous ballot," she announced with gravity, as though describing a Masonic initiation rite. "Generally, he comes from the ruling party, but there have been rare exceptions. Whoever becomes Speaker must agree to drop his party allegiances and act impartially at all times."

Dan smiled to himself, thinking it would be like putting an alcoholic in a bar and telling him not to drink while everyone else was knocking back their fill.

"Historically, the Speaker represented the throne," their guide continued. "This proved disadvantageous when at least seven Speakers were put to death for bringing news displeasing to the king. The Speaker no longer represents the ruling monarch, but instead represents the interests of the House."

A wise career choice, Dan thought as they trooped upward, gathering briefly before a large panel window on the second floor. Behind the glass, images flickered on playback monitors, spotlighting members of the legislature in another room. A garrulous blonde had the floor. She spoke animatedly, her face contorted with the urgency of her message, though her words remained unheard on this side of the wall.

"What you are seeing is the current debate in the assembly," their guide informed them. "We're not allowed to enter while council is in session, however ..." Here she stepped smartly up to a switch on the wall. What had been silent images, mimes in motion, suddenly came through first in English, then in French, as she flicked the switch up and down. "We're bilingual!" she exclaimed, as proudly as if she'd invented the switch herself.

The group broke into hesitant applause. Their guide led them on till they stood gazing up at another series of dour-faced portraits. Time-ravaged, colour-muted, the founding fathers of the legislature looked to a man as proper as an English parson, as though not one of them had so much as contemplated a dirty deed in his life. In the late nineteenth century, Dan knew, symbolist painters had begun eradicating human figures from their landscapes as they sought to depict a mystical vision of life. Humankind struck from paradise. *Portraitists should do the same with politicians*, he mused.

Among the subjects, a single woman stood out from the group, as though to belie the myth that Canada's founders had been only men and moose. This, the guide informed them, was Laura Secord. While Paul Revere had been warning of the impending approach of the British south of the border, a lowly Canadian cowherd had risked her life to warn of marauding Americans to the north as they spread their war of aggression.

"But I don't understand," spluttered a white-haired senior who had earlier declared himself a visitor from New York. "Why is the war considered an act of American aggression?"

The guide answered calmly. "Because the U.S. declared war on Canada."

"But that was because the British burned Washington!" the man huffed.

"It's true the British burned Washington, sir," the guide said. "But that was in retaliation after the Americans burned our parliament buildings." She smiled, gleeful at her small rebellion. In her mind, it was tit for tat. Aggression made easy.

"That's not what I was taught in school!" the man protested, stupefied by this seditious refutation of sacred truths.

And that, Dan thought, *is the nature of politics.*

Mindful of the pitfalls of history, the guide shepherded her flock down the hall. Dan lingered to admire the portrait of the daring Secord, waiting till the guide's voice passed out of hearing. Alone, he glanced over to the assembly chambers. The door was unguarded. He slipped into the gallery during a pause in the proceedings and took a seat.

Pillars reached up grandly, forming arches on all sides. From below they resembled oversized molars whose roots extended down to form a giant mouth. Which, in essence, was what the assembly was, Dan thought. A giant mouth that never stopped talking.

The gallery's partitions had been decorated by a gifted carver. Bats, wolves, and foxes gambolled about, a sly nod to the true nature of the political animal. While unwary visitors expecting an air of decorum might have been surprised by the gruff voices emanating from the floor, Dan was well aware that political discussions were not infrequently conducted like hockey games, one of the nation's favoured pastimes after drinking beer and complaining about the weather. Violence and vitriol were common, the participants treating each other like the bitterest of enemies until the need for compromise arose and something like détente occurred. It was as hypocritical and dishonourable an occupation as any to be found among human affairs, so who could resist?

Dan kept his eye on the House Speaker, the same one whose antecedents had been historically prone to execution. Forced to give up party interests, he came dressed for the part in a black-and-white harlequinesque veneer of neutrality. A fitting ensemble for the house dealer. *Look at me, ladies and gentlemen of the assembly: nothing in my hands, nothing up my sleeves. Nothing but impartiality here!* The symbolic mace was always at his side. No House business could occur without it. Perhaps the Americans had thought they'd successfully stalled the government for the hundred and twenty-two years it was absent. Fortunately, there was a spare.

The Speaker recognized Alec Henderson, minister of educational reforms, Peter Hansen's boss. The minister waited for the room to settle before introducing his bill: the new proposed sex-education curriculum, a subject cutting right to the heart of the bigoted and intolerant. In its initial stages, with the potential for controversy spread across its pages, the bill's contents were as likely to offend one group as another, while the minorities it was designed to protect — progressive folk, women, and that subversive LGBT crowd fomenting change and rocking the foundations of civilization in their pursuit of equality — had been cast as villains in the drama. Nothing new in the annals of politics.

Demurely attired, Henderson stepped up to give the galley a view of the Sensible Moderate Advocating Change. *Am I not a reasonable man?* he seemed to ask, clutching his vest at the arm pits, the very vision of normality despite the load of treason he carried in his folder.

He addressed the room in his real voice, his true voice, its inflections ringing with virtue and justice. Though perhaps it was just one of the many voices he was said to possess — who could tell? Meanwhile, he was still that same politician who never stopped ticking off the potential votes of everyone he met, like a real estate agent who can't help evaluating the worth of every house he enters. Naturally, there was always the next election to consider. Sell your soul for a good price, but always include a buy-back clause. You can screw the voters today, but never forget they still need to love you tomorrow.

A *basso-continuo* murmuring could be heard from the galleries, where a sour and unpleasant lot had gathered to hear him speak, pushing their own interests in the guise of public concern.

"What if we don't want this filth foisted on our children?" demanded a woman who looked as though she'd given up a round of afternoon cosmos to be there.

Henderson's smile was gracious, expressing his sincerest sympathy and understanding. It should have been — he'd practised it enough. "No one will be forced to take this course. Your child can simply opt out of the scheduled period."

"And then they'll be picked on and bullied by the other kids for not taking it!" someone else shouted.

The Speaker clacked his gavel, eyeing the insurrection. "The minister of educational reforms has the floor," he reminded them, though they were all well aware of the fact.

"Thank you, Mr. Speaker," Henderson said, managing to sound as though he had never at any time transgressed those very same rules of conduct himself.

Dan was impressed as the minister stared his critics down. His shrug could have been an apology or a dismissal. "Although I understand your concerns, the fact is you can't have it both ways. If you don't want your child to take the course, it shouldn't prevent someone else's child from having the option to attend."

Cries of assent came from his side of the scrum. While he had the room's attention, he would ride the wave of public opinion. He was the man with the silver tongue and the populist views. A man of the people. That night, his party would parade him through the streets, held aloft on their shoulders. In another age, dissenters might have carried him straight to the gallows. Views that made you a reformer a century ago might have been those of today's knee-jerk reactionary. Meanwhile the crowd railed, their voices pressing in from all quarters, replete with the echoes of history: *Free the slaves? Unheard of! Women's suffrage? Madness! Same-sex marriage? The end of civilization! What further lawlessness and insanity will be thrust upon us tomorrow by this reckless government?*

"Yes," Henderson assured a questioner, "the bill is intended to be fair and unbiased. It's based on an in-depth survey of more than four thousand parents whose children are in the current school system."

"And just who," someone demanded, "were these four thousand parents and how were they chosen?"

Another shrug. "They were chosen at random with a lottery-style method of selection," came the minister's long-suffering reply.

It was a reply evincing fairness enough to satisfy the harshest critic. But the voices of dissent were everywhere. A funereal-looking man with a cravat spoke up. "My constituents expect me to stand up against this sort of immorality. I need to give them the representation they asked for with their vote. Why else do we elect officials but to speak in our name?"

Henderson turned to the robed harlequin. "Exactly my point, Mr. Speaker. The people have elected us to speak for them and that is precisely what we are doing!"

The crowd was in an uproar: *This is against our religious teachings! … We don't want these things discussed in our schools … Yeah, well, my taxes pay for your kid to go to school and I don't want them learning hatred and prejudice … Then why don't you start your own school?* It was a textbook lesson on intolerance brought over lock, stock, and barrel from the Old Country. Never mind that they'd all been killing each other for centuries in the Old Country. If they had their way, that tradition would continue, too.

"I will have order in the House!" the Speaker cried at last, glaring out over the room even if deep down he didn't give a damn if they tore each other's eyes out, bored as he was with this farce of decorum and manners flouted by contrary schoolchildren.

Dan checked his watch. It was time for his meeting with an old friend.

FIVE

House of Rumours

To Dan, Will Parker had been an almost mythic personality, revered by many for his social activism but known by very few. Their paths had crossed often during Dan's early years in the city, both of them drifting in and out of various LGBT organizations, the first being the Suicide Prevention Hotline for which he and Will went through training together. When it came time for the real thing, Dan had been in awe of how Will instinctively filtered out the noise to get to the root of a caller's issues: coming out to family, suicidal urges, AIDS scares. Will seemed to have it all down pat, carrying a suitcase full of advice in his mind. The ease with which he discussed these and other topics was inspirational.

If Dan had to sum up what set Will apart, he would have said Will made you feel as though he knew you intimately after only a few minutes of chatting. Having compassion at his fingertips and an ability to share his convictions were Will's trademarks. He knew the stats on poverty, child abuse, sexual assault — social inequities of every variety — and he could quote them at will. Dan tried looking them up once and found them current and accurate. For a while, Dan had thought he might be falling in love with Will, but Will had taken that in stride as well.

"I don't have time for an affair, Daniel," Will told him flat out. "There are a lot of things I want to achieve. My personal life is secondary to those goals."

A man with his priorities in order.

Serious in outlook and committed in his actions, Will was a new-world cowboy with the unruffled calm of a priest. Although he claimed to be bisexual, Dan knew no one who had actually dated him. He was a mystery, aloof but kind. An icy exterior with a burning flame at its centre. Getting to know him was a challenge. Gentle reserve was his default mode, and helping the less fortunate was his only passion. Dan had expected him to go into medicine, but it was no surprise either that he'd ended up studying law and getting involved in politics, trying to make a difference.

These were Dan's memories as he left the assembly. He hadn't long to wait for the reality. Once outside, he turned and there was Will. The years had been more than good to him. He looked lean and extremely fit, with a touch of grey around the temples.

His smile caught Dan off guard. Not so serious now, it seemed. "Daniel, it's great to see you. Good of you to make yourself at home in our hallowed halls."

Will indicated the way. They fell into step, heading away from the assembly.

"I took the tour to see what it's all about before we met up," Dan said.

"And what did you learn?"

"That politics and high school are not far apart when it comes to the participants. The only difference is their relative ages."

Will laughed. "You're not wrong. Sometimes I think this place is a distillery for deviant behaviour." They reached the end of the corridor. Will stretched an arm in the direction of the next wing. "I'm just around the corner."

He opened a door and led Dan into a hushed interior that suggested arcane matters and state secrets were regularly discussed here. The furniture was old, intricate, and uniformly made of wood. An auctioneer might have a field day trying to scry the provenance of the pieces before laying them out on the auction block. Dan ran a hand over the grain of a writer's desk with a fold-up top that was stately and demure as someone's kindly grandmother. Shelves were crammed with volumes of legislative history and legal tracts, the makings of civilization great and small. From atop an imposing shelf, busts of Pierre Elliot Trudeau and Plato cast discerning gazes over the room. The father of modern Canada who had tossed the state out of the nation's bedrooms, and the man who had laid the foundations of western civilization after declaring love a mental illness were contentedly seated together. They would have good conversations, Dan thought.

"You've done well for yourself."

Will nodded. "If this is the sort of place you want to end up in, then yes."

"You didn't?"

"It's not what I envisioned back when I was a young student leftist trying to reform the world. I had more radical things in mind then, though they stopped short of the Baader-Meinhof Gang." He winked. "I'm sure you'd agree this is what we called 'selling out' back in our younger, more idealistic days."

"Then you've survived the transition nicely. Maybe we should have called it 'buying in' instead."

"A diplomatic answer," Will replied. "I'm surprised myself at how long I've stayed. Some days the level of duplicity is mind-boggling."

"You're the only lawyer I ever trusted, because you could still be shocked by bad behaviour. That and the fact you once refused a client you knew was guilty."

"Yes, well there's crime and then there's crime. Stealing pensions from old ladies and labourers deserves to be punished. I couldn't use my talents to free someone who clearly admitted his guilt but wanted a loophole to squeeze through."

"Is he still in jail?"

"Last I heard," Will said. "Probably why I'm still alive. If he'd broken a law I personally disapproved of then I'd have thrown myself body and soul into his defence. But nothing like that here, of course. I just advise and adjudicate a lot of musty, fusty old laws someone wants upheld or, with luck, dispensed with when their time has come. There's a lot of dead wood. Ministers wanting things on the books that will allow them to repeal gay marriage, for instance. It won't happen at this level. It's up to the feds, though it's not proving a popular fight. Times have changed, but I wouldn't put it past the prime minister to try to sneak it back into parliament. The last time he did, it got rumbled pretty quickly, but we have to be vigilant. That's the price of freedom. Isn't that what they say?"

"Truer words," Dan said with a nod.

Will leaned forward over his desk. "It's good to see you again, Dan. Life treating you well?"

"Very well, in fact. My son's in university in B.C. He's about to graduate."

"Terrific! Kedrick, wasn't it?"

"Yes. Good memory. On top of that, I'm about to get married. His name's Nick. He's a police officer."

"Well, congratulations, then." Will gave him an appraising look. "I assume he's stellar material like you."

"Thanks. He's a really decent guy, the sort I thought I would never meet. So far he hasn't been scared off by me. How about you?"

"Six years of marriage. A wife and two kids." Will looked at Dan. "I know what you're thinking: I went the safe route."

"I wasn't thinking that at all. I was remembering how I envied you for having the choice. I also remember thinking that dating you would mean there'd be twice the competition."

Will laughed. "True enough."

Dan's eyes roamed the desktop. "Any photos?"

"No. I keep my private life private. Just the nature of the business here."

"Understandably."

"So. To what exactly do I owe the pleasure?"

"Peter Hansen and Tony Moran."

Will gave him a quizzical look.

"Do you know them?" Dan asked.

"Yes, of course. Peter I know personally. I've met Tony at one or two social functions."

"Then you may have heard Tony has disappeared. I've been hired to find him."

Will's expression turned serious. "I'd heard he was missing. Is he in danger?"

Dan shook his head. "No immediate danger, at least according to Peter. It seems Tony has a gambling problem."

Will shrugged. "Rumours are rife. One can't help overhearing them in this place."

Dan half expected him to quote statistics on recovering gambling addicts, as he might have cited other demographics in the past. "I don't think it's a question of money borrowed from questionable sources or anything like that. At least not as far as I know."

"That's good, then. I had a client once who lost everything to some unscrupulous sorts who loaned him the cash. In the end, there was nothing he could do but sign over everything he owned. I wasn't able to save him. There was no question of violence against him, just compulsive behaviour that led to significant loss. I heard he made it back in two years and lost it all over again. It's a significant illness."

"I know a thing or two about addiction."

Will regarded him shrewdly. "You're quite the drinker, as I recall."

"Was. Past tense." Dan nodded thoughtfully. "Do you know a journalist named Simon Bradley?"

Will's mouth twisted into a hollow smile. "The muckraker. Of course. And not half the journalist his grandfather was, unless you count digging up scandal as journalism.

I've had to threaten him with legal action on behalf of the government more than once. He always skirts the edges of what's legally acceptable with his reporting and his dubious sources. What's he done now?"

"Nothing so far as I'm concerned. But he seems to think Tony's disappearance is connected to John Wilkens's death."

"The MPP who committed suicide? How?"

"Bradley thinks Wilkens was murdered."

Will's expression darkened for a second, then he shook his head and laughed. "That sounds like Bradley all around. Trying to make something of nothing."

"Is there any chance Wilkens could have been murdered for a cover-up?"

"Cover-up of what?"

"Bradley thinks it has to do with the power plant cancellations a couple years back."

"That issue is dead. What happened was disgusting, but as far as I know it's all come out in the wash."

"Bradley thinks otherwise. And he believes it got John Wilkens murdered."

Will glanced off, as though gathering scraps of thought in the dark corners of his mind. "It's politics," he said at last. "It's a nasty business. Many have killed for it and many more have died."

"So it's possible."

"Possible, yes. Likely, no. Wilkens was suspended for suspected misappropriation of funds. The allegations against him were pretty serious. Everyone seems to think he committed suicide to avoid the charges that no doubt would have been coming his way down the line. I've been looking into some of them, in fact. I can't discuss —"

Dan put up his hands. "I'm not asking you to do that. I was just wondering what you might have heard."

"I can't think of any connection between Tony Moran and John Wilkens, except that John was the opposition critic for Peter's boss, Alec Henderson, as you've probably discovered."

"I had."

"Other than that, I doubt there was much opportunity for their paths to cross. John was old money and a long-time Conservative with an attractive wife. Tony and Peter are working-class boys, openly gay, and pretty far left as Liberals go. I always wondered why Hansen wasn't with the NDP. In any case, the abyss between them and John would have been very wide." He paused. "Funny thing, though. John was said to be a likely candidate for House Speaker if the Conservatives ever got back in power. It shows a willingness to put aside his own views in the interests of impartiality. Maybe that indicates an ambivalence in his political views. Who can say how deep his convictions really were?"

"Have you heard of any behind-the-scenes shenanigans by people trying to fix elections?"

Will's expression was incredulous. "Fix elections? You meaning rigging ballot boxes and such? That's Third-World politics, Dan. It doesn't happen here."

"What about people hired to help swing votes by the manipulation of media buzz, and so on."

Will laughed gently. "That happens all the time. They're called opinion makers. Sure, there is always something afoot. 'Uneasy lies the head that wears the crown,' as they say. It's completely legal, so long as you don't say anything untrue about the candidates. If you do, you're going to be facing libel charges. Probably from me."

Dan shook his head. "What about someone hired to damage political careers? Making sure candidates are sidelined for one reason or another?"

"Hired by whom?"

"I don't know. This is the theory Bradley's working on. He tells me there's an individual who can make things happen to promising candidates, who then quietly or otherwise fade from prominence. He calls him or her the Magus."

"Like some sort of mysterious conjuror? C'mon! You're kidding me."

"I'm not."

"A fixer, in other words. Someone who can make or break a promising career." Will shook his head. "While it sounds good on paper, it doesn't work that way in reality. It's the popular vote that counts. Look how many people voted for Mayor Ford in the last election. Even after that crack-smoking video surfaced, the man is still popular. There's no accounting for stupidity, Daniel. You know what they say: people get the government they deserve. All we can do is put up a better candidate and hope good sense will prevail next time."

"One would hope."

Will glanced at his watch. "I'm sorry to cut things short. I've got a caucus meeting in five minutes. One of the parties is hiring a campaign strategist for the upcoming election. Apparently my opinion is important." He smiled. "My mundane life. You know how it goes."

Dan stood. "Thanks for your time, Will. I appreciate your candour. You were the first person who came to mind when I heard Bradley's allegations. I also thought it would be good to catch up."

"I wish you luck in finding Tony. For what it's worth, and totally off the record, I never believed Peter and Tony would last. I always felt Tony was too lightweight for a political spouse. Maybe he's just trying to get away."

Dan nodded knowingly. "And taking the bank accounts with him. It wouldn't be the first time."

"And for what it's worth …" He held Dan's gaze. "I don't think John Wilkens was murdered."

"I didn't take the allegations too seriously. I just wondered what you thought."

Will held out his hand. They shook.

"Watch out for Bradley. He's trouble. In the meantime, if I hear of anything, I'll let you know. You know what they say — the walls have ears. Doubly so in politics."

"Thanks. I'll do the same."

SIX

The Devil's Bible

Dan left Queen's Park and headed east, armed with the list of addresses Peter Hansen had said his husband frequented. He'd been right in thinking them gambling dens of various sorts. The first two looked as though they'd been visited by legal authorities not long before he got there. Heavy padlocks and wire grills pulled across the entrances warned would-be bet-makers that their luck had run out, at least for now.

If Tony Moran gambled for excitement, Dan knew, then chances were it wasn't simply the lure of the wager that attracted him, but also the need to be where he could share the roller-coaster highs and lows of winning and losing. In that case, the fixed-wage betting booths like Champions on the Danforth, where old men in short-sleeved shirts and linen trousers hung about on the sidewalks waiting for a favourite horse to come in, would not have held his interest long. No, it would have to be someplace grittier, someplace disreputable. Winning in public had its appeal, but for the type of gambler who likes the thrill of beating the odds, an audience of peers is required. Or maybe there were other factors sending Tony to dens in dismal basements. Loans, for one thing. If he'd had his funds cut off, as Peter declared, then he would need to find another source. There was always some shark willing to loan out what he knew he could get back fourfold by the end of the day. It didn't take higher math to calculate the odds on that one.

No one knows for sure who laid the first wager. It might have been old Satan in the Garden of Eden tempting Adam and Eve with his apple trick: *Go ahead, the odds are good today. Chances are no one will see you do it. C'mon. Whatcha wanna bet?* If it was that moment, then house bias was already in play long before anyone could outlaw it.

Many of the old games are still popular today: poker, craps, blackjack, and roulette have been around for centuries. Legend has it a form of keno was used to raise the funds that built the Great Wall of China. There are as many ways to gamble as things to gamble on. Whenever anything contains an element of chance, someone will lay odds on the outcome. Sports, political elections, the sex of a royal baby, the statistical probability of whether a single bullet loaded in the barrel of a gun will fire when it's your turn to pull the trigger, or the added frisson of betting whether the cobra in the wicker basket will bite you or the fool seated beside you when it's loosed. But there is always a bright side: if you lose, there's no need to worry about collecting.

Gamblers have pressed four-leaf clovers into their wallets, while others have turned to charms like allspice and horseshoes the way the devoted light candles to the saints. Animal body parts have long been prized as talismans, the most popular being lucky rabbit's feet (*not so lucky for the rabbit*, Dan thought), alligator teeth, and even a raccoon penis (a.k.a. the "coon dong"), the latter said to be especially potent when wrapped in a $20 bill. But then gamblers weren't always the smartest or luckiest people on earth. Sometimes they needed all the help they could muster while their wives sat at home cursing them and the kiddies wished daddy would just come back and eat a decent meal with them once in a while. Losing your husband to another woman was bad enough, but when that woman turned out to be Lady Luck herself, she was damn near impossible to beat.

As addictions went, Dan knew, gambling was one of the less physically harmful. It caused none of the vein depletions and skin lesions of heroin and crack. It wouldn't dry your liver or rot your brain. In fact, many gamblers lived to a ripe old age. But as psychological addictions went, it was one of the worst. For centuries, mothers had lamented it, lovers feared it. Families had been sacrificed for the roll of a die, kingdoms lost to the turn of a card.

And that was just for starters. Many were the men who ended up face-down in a freshly dug grave for want of a payback plan to satisfy their backers. Others spent their last few moments of conscious recollection on riverbeds or falling from bridges over ravines and gorges designed for more spectacular viewing pleasures.

In olden days, upper-class women were not supposed to gamble. But set up a prohibition and eventually someone will try to get around it. Thus the fashionable women of England in the late eighteenth century who came to be known as the Faro Ladies came about, hosting private parties and turning cards late into the night.

Most countries today allow gambling, but if you can't find something to suit your tastes you can always turn to the internet to squander your wages. It's said that the Fool, the tarot card designated with the number zero, is a man ruined by gambling. One of the most popular folk-rock songs of all time tells the fate of a card shark who goes down to infamy in New Orleans.

Dan Sharp's Aunt Marge called a pack of cards the Devil's Bible, adding gambling to the list of sins she asked young Danny never to engage in — swearing, drinking, and lying chief among them. At ten, he'd promised away any and all future indulgences just to put a smile on her face, never for a moment thinking he might wish it otherwise as he grew older. Later, he'd been amazed that sex hadn't been number one on that list. Perhaps she'd thought his only salvation there lay in total ignorance.

He thought of his Aunt Marge with a smile when he finally struck it lucky at an address in Little Vietnam. The street was tucked away on a rise behind the train tracks. The man leaning against the door twirled a toothpick between his lips as he scrutinized Dan, giving a hard look at the scar on the side of his face.

"Tony Moran said I might have a good game in here," Dan said.

A grin cracked the man's otherwise non-expressive face. He inclined his head and nodded Dan inside, shutting the door quickly behind them.

A Buddha sat amid an offering of oranges and incense sticks, winking a knowing eye like a jolly proprietor. It was Fat Buddha, the Buddha later in his career after he'd passed many trials and penetrated through to the core of reality and found nothingness there, as well as a whole lot to eat. Fat Buddha is the guy you want on your side when you're looking for luck. Fat Buddha is the key to happiness. Dan winked back as he passed the Buddha by.

From outside, the house had appeared to be a modest bungalow. Inside, however, it was deceptively long and labyrinthine, with a dark hallway twisting along to a partially concealed door. The man gestured for him to follow. One flight down revealed a concrete floor and bare walls, with storage space for an ancient washer-dryer. It was the smell of smoke seeping up from somewhere unseen that gave the next level away. Dan followed his keeper down a second flight of stairs in near darkness.

At the bottom, a door opened onto a low-ceilinged chamber hollowed out among the rocks and supported by beams of wood. It might once have been intended as a bomb shelter. Dan thought it unlikely the crypt-like space would show up on any city plans. Even the rats would give it a pass.

The room resembled a cliché of gambling dens circa the late eighteenth century: dimly lit, smoke-filled, and with consumptive-looking men seated around small tables. All it needed was for someone to be inhaling from an opium pipe and a few prostitutes lingering off to the side for local colour.

Dan sniffed. The air had a peculiar tang to it: the smell of loss and desperation. For all the brightness and warmth of the day outside, in here there was a chill that probably never left the room. Thirteen men crowded around two tables. A baker's dozen. None of them resembled the traditional card shark dressed in a natty suit and making smart quips between plays. This was not a Las Vegas–style operation. Most of them looked as though they'd spent far too long in that windowless dungeon two floors below street level.

The game was blackjack. In a place like this, Dan knew the stakes were on individual skill. Best player wins. A casino relied on luck and the odds that said you can't hold out forever in a game of chance where the Wheel of Fortune is the ultimate winner. But not here.

Dan approached one of the tables and took a seat. Five pairs of eyes flickered in his direction, as if noting a change in the air currents. No one looked at him directly. It was a coded match. To do or say anything overt might be dangerous. The trick lay in deciphering eye movements and hand gestures. This wasn't a place for casual greetings and social get-togethers. These men were serious about their game. And, for the moment at least, not much else. Air raid sirens might go off outside and none of them would stir until the last card was turned.

When it came his turn, Dan looked at the dealer and nodded. The man's eyes showed no glimmer of light. His teeth were long and wolf-like, jaundice yellow. He flashed what was meant to pass for a smile. It was like looking into the face of Lucifer himself.

A card shot in Dan's direction. He picked it up — a black deuce — and stole a look at the anchor on the dealer's right. The anchor's expression was less forbidding, but still inscrutable. His hair was coiffed and he'd come dressed a bit nattier than the rest of the chancers and gamesters surrounding him.

His eyes flickered in Dan's direction. Dan caught the glance. Was it just curiosity about a new player or was his gaydar ticking? No, there it was again. A kindred soul had sent him a glance, ferreting him out. Where a straight man might look at you once in curiosity, a second time in contempt, a gay man would keep coming back for more till he could be sure.

Nimble fingers turned the cards as hand followed hand. One of the men flexed his fingers, knuckles cracking like a gunshot in the tiny space. Four pairs of eyes glanced around nervously for a millisecond, then moved on.

They played for an hour. Not a word was spoken; nothing existed outside the game. Dan was down $480 when someone called for a break. These guys were good, way out of his league. He stood and went to the bathroom, splashing his face with water and smoothing his hair as he stared in the mirror. When he came out, the anchor stood in the hallway.

"Walter Temple," Dan said, holding out a hand.

"Good to meet you, Walter. I'm Jack Dawson."

They shook.

"I see you like to play anchor."

Jack shrugged. "I'm a bit of a lightweight here. The others know it, but that doesn't stop them taking my money." He laughed. "Still, it makes me feel secure to be the last bidder, so I play anchor when I can."

"Makes sense."

Jack gave him an appraising look. "Haven't seen you here before, have I?"

"No. Good eye. I'm a friend of Tony Moran's."

Jack held his gaze. Dan sensed his puzzlement before he remembered that Tony's name had been splashed all over the news yesterday.

"Is he … I mean, did they find him?" Jack asked.

"Sorry?"

"Tony. Isn't he missing?"

Dan gave him a blank look worthy of one of poker's best. "Really? I hadn't heard. I actually haven't seen him for a while."

Jack nodded eagerly. "I haven't either. Maybe he's back. Tell you the truth, I was worried about him. The last time I saw him he lost nearly twenty thousand dollars in one night."

Dan whistled. "I didn't know he had that kind of money. Way out of my league."

"Mine, too." Jack shook his head. "Not just that. He was betting erratically. It was almost like he wanted to lose it. I told him he might want to seek help. He shrugged it off."

"Was he angry that you said that?"

Jack shook his head. "Nah. You know Tony — he never loses his cool."

"Right. So there's no betting limit?"

"Not on Friday nights. It's *banque ouverte*."

Sky's the limit. Dan had seen the sickened looks on the faces of players when confronted with an astronomical bid from a cagey opponent. Good bluff or a confident hand? Who could tell? Open bids were a freefall waiting to happen. Not the paltry odds of the legit gaming tables, but the edge of an abyss that threatened to swallow a gambler whole. A pulse-quickening dare for high rollers, but not for the faint of heart or the empty pocketed.

"I know the stakes have to be high enough to keep the game interesting, but ..." Jack shook his head. "Tony made a lot of people nervous that night. They asked him not to come around for a while. It upsets the other players to see that sort of recklessness. You start to think it's mafia money being tossed around. Next thing you know, someone will be breaking down the door and scattering gunshot at the rest of us."

"I always limit my bets," Dan said.

A restless look came over Jack's face. "You were down four-eighty, wasn't it?" A man with numbers in his blood. He probably dreamed in hearts and spades.

"Something like that." Dan shrugged. "What about you?"

Jack's mouth stitched a nervous smile. "I was up about seven-fifty at nine this morning, but now I'm down nearly eight hundred."

"At nine? What time did you get here?"

"Oh, I've been here since last night."

"Maybe it's time to cash in," Dan suggested.

A bell tinkled somewhere behind them.

"Not yet." There was an electric gleam in Jack's eye. Chairs scraped in the other room as the players returned to their seats. Jack twitched like something skewered on a stick. "I've got to get back in there. Coming?"

Dan followed him. The others had resumed their positions like mannequins in a window display. Twenty minutes later, after two lucky plays, Jack was up nearly two hundred dollars. A smile returned to his face. The game was back on, winning in his grasp once again.

The dealer looked at Dan, waiting to deal him in for another round. They could go on all day and into the night.

Dan considered. He'd lost more than six hundred dollars. Even with Peter Hansen's advance, that was still a good dent in his wallet. If he stayed another hour and really concentrated, he might make some of it back. He felt the itch, the prickling that said *this* could be the hand that put him back on track. Just a few good cards, just a bit more daring with his bets … say, fifty a throw rather than twenty or thirty.

He felt the chill coming through the floor as he calculated the odds. Truth was he could lose his shirt. He could go on to lose all of Hansen's money, just like Tony Moran. If the bug really got him, he could eventually lose his home and then some.

The dealer was waiting. Dan felt all eyes on him as he checked his watch. It was later than he thought. Nick would be wondering where he was. Gravity seemed to have increased ten times since he'd first sat in the chair. It pulled at him, keeping him in his seat. A clear sign that it was time to go. At heart he hated to lose. That was a relief, of sorts. As long as he felt like that, he would never make a real gambler.

He shook his head and left.

SEVEN

Understanding the Third Reich

DAN OPENED HIS EYES. LAST night's dreams had been plagued by memories of his underground gambling episode. Visions of card suits twinkled and vanished as he rubbed his eyes. He got up, showered and dressed, then headed out.

Taped to his office door was yet another reminder that the building needed to be vacated by the end of July for a planned condominium development. Requests for extensions would not be considered. Signed, *The Management*.

And fuck you very much, Dan thought.

When he first arrived, the premises had been owned by a former client, a friendly man who'd given him a helping hand by offering the space at a reasonable rate. It enabled him to establish himself, working solo for the first time. That arrangement had ended with the new owners. From the start, they showed themselves to be more interested in establishing a bureaucracy than helping tenants cope with the change of management, announcing their ownership via form letter and implementing a series of rules restricting after-hours access for no reason Dan could see. Now, it seemed they were intent on turning over the premises and maximizing a cash grab.

Still, it was a good reminder that Dan needed to find a new place if he intended to stay in business. It had occurred to him to transfer his office to his home, but then he might not leave the house from morning till night, impinging on both his comfort and Nick's.

His cell pinged. It was Simon Bradley: *Thought you should see this.* The link took him to an online article covering the Queen's Park beat. Dan read the opening paragraph but the article stopped there. A second link at the bottom offered an app granting access to the entire website.

Praying he wasn't opening himself up to spam, he clicked. In less than a minute he had access to the entire paper. He read Simon's article from top to bottom. It hinted at scandal and made veiled allegations of government corruption — what would likely prove to be simple incompetence if properly investigated, Dan felt — but there seemed little of pressing interest. He had just started to type a note asking why Simon wanted him to see the piece when he realized he hadn't clicked on the photo.

It was a crowd shot, people in formal wear gathered in a ballroom, the event impossible to guess. He searched the faces and found John Wilkens standing next to Tony Moran. The placement might have been accidental, random atoms moving in space, but while everyone around them looked amused by the goings-on, both John and Tony appeared grim, as though they'd been discussing something perturbing. It was nothing most readers would notice. But then most people wouldn't be looking for a connection between two men at opposite ends of the political spectrum. It was like discovering two abstainers in a crowd of drinkers. There was no telling what they'd been discussing when the snap was taken, but it clearly linked the two.

Dan grabbed his jacket. He hadn't bothered with breakfast before leaving home. Perhaps a nosh in the city's west end and a good espresso to wash it down was what the morning needed to get going. That and a little Q&A with his newest client.

From the street, the house proclaimed: *We're nobody special*. Still, it had its charms. A well-tended garden surrounded the modest dwelling. The wraparound porch seemed designed for gatherings, with a mishmash of chairs and a cedar swing for conversing with the neighbours. Old-style politics. Hand-shaking and a personal touch. Dan wondered just how often people actually dropped in on Peter Hansen and how much was for show.

Though short on social status, Little Portugal was a neighbourhood with a big heart thanks to its friendly eateries and popular bar culture. It said a lot that Hansen chose to live there. Clearly, the message was that he saw himself as a man of the people. A glance through a lead-paned window revealed Peter on his cellphone. He waved Dan in. The door wasn't even locked. Welcoming, accessible. Another deft touch.

A grey corgi announced his intrusion with a series of sharp yips, twitchy and demanding like an officious little butler. Dan held out a hand. The dog took a sniff and backed off, no doubt smelling Ralph. With a warning growl, he promptly turned tail and ran back to wherever he'd come from.

The hall echoed with Dan's footsteps, giving a regal feel to the modest-size home. A designer's touch showed in the handpicked furniture and fashionable colours. Dan wouldn't have been surprised to learn the couple had regular consultations: "How Your Home Can Reflect the Latest Trends" or "A Politician's Guide to the Buzz on Today's Palette." He could almost see the decorator's anxious hand-wringing, hear the spiel on his personal vision for the pair.

Peter's voice carried in from the next room.

"I don't think it's a good idea for the minister to meet with the press before the conference," Peter said. "I'll be there in an hour. Tell him not to make any decisions without me."

Dan peered around the corner. Peter held up a peremptory finger. A man used to giving commands.

"Good. Works for me." He ended the call and turned. "Welcome. Have you found Tony?"

"Not in the flesh, but I've made progress. I went to an address you gave me and met someone who knew him at one of the gambling houses. Tony was asked not to return after losing twenty thousand dollars in a single evening."

Dan waited for a reaction. There was none.

"I'm not shocked, in case you're wondering," Peter told him.

"Why do you think he would be so reckless as to lose that much money?"

"If you know anything about addictions, Dan, then you'll know it's not something you can control easily. I've had to keep a keen eye on Tony at all times."

"It's a hard road, keeping your eye on someone else's addiction."

"Yes. It is."

"Did Tony resent that you made more money than him?"

"He did not. I understand human nature very well. I would know if Tony resented me. Is that what you came to ask me about?"

"Actually, I'm in the market for a new office and this area was suggested. I was just passing and thought I'd stop in to give you an update."

Peter gave a short, unexpected laugh. "Checking up on me, you mean. I can give you the name of the top real estate agent in the neighbourhood, if you're interested. But let me show you around, if it will reassure you."

He waved Dan into an ante room. Modern art dominated the walls — loud, brash, and pricey. Here was the showy side of the people's candidate.

"Let me introduce you," Peter said. He stepped in front of a grainy photo close-up of a man's biceps. A tattooed cross showed deep pores, the skin's flaws. Energy and sensuality fused. "This you may know. It's a Robert Mapplethorpe."

"Very nice."

To the left a large panel of near-naked skinheads loomed in aggressive postures. The collision of sexuality and virile machismo was disconcerting, suggesting that savage brutality and gay attraction were not that far apart.

"Attila Richard Lukacs," Peter said, as though introducing an august forebear. "Despite the subject matter, the formal qualities of his work are quite accomplished. I believe he may be the great gay artist of our time, as Francis Bacon was to an earlier generation." He was the art critic now, elucidating his time-honed opinions. "Lukacs is a fan of Jacques-Louis David, one of the most important artists of the French Revolution. David was the first truly modernist painter, presenting history without embellishment. He personally signed the edict sentencing Marie Antoinette and King Louis XVI to death by beheading."

"Not easy times."

"Politics is a messy business."

Dan was reminded of the Queen's Park tour guide extolling the benefits of bilingualism as Hansen flipped a switch and a paint-splattered garbage can lid appeared, glittering beneath a pin spot. On its surface, a crudely painted red devil's head squared off against a green cow's skull. Were it not for the light, the piece might have been mistaken for a cast-off from the street.

"This is an original David Wojnarowicz. One of my favourites. He isn't as well-known as others of his generation, mostly because he didn't live long enough for his name to proliferate, but he was an important figure nonetheless." He gently touched the metal rim. "Wojnarowicz painted his rage at the world. He was a street hustler and early AIDS victim. In his day, he was as famous for his activism as his art. Much of his work was destroyed, because he considered the world his canvas. Some of his best pieces were done on abandoned piers on New York's waterfront, even on street pavement. A true rebel."

Dan looked beyond the work to a tall window. It gave onto a garden where a cherry tree was struggling into bloom. Security was nil. "Not worried about thieves taking off with all this?" he asked.

"Canadians only know about fine art. Their precious Group of Seven and whatnot. And we all know fine art hangs on walls in museums." Peter laughed at his own joke. "This stuff is too decadent. Too weird. No one would steal it. They wouldn't have a clue what it might be worth."

Over in a corner, a framed pamphlet caught the light like a rare specimen trapped under glass. Someone had sketched a swastika on the lavender paper. Dan's eye dropped down the page: *die faggot cocksucker scum! AIDS carriers you are doomed we will kill you and that leftist minister of yours commie bastards!*

"Art?"

"Of a rather venal sort. All the usual pleasantries. It was my first death threat when I came out." Peter shrugged. "Some say it cost me the election, but I can't hide who I am. That's the trouble with politics. You have to pretend to be something other than what you are. That's the one thing I'll never do. I give Ford credit for that. He's an ass, but he doesn't pretend to be anything other than the colossal jerk he is. I don't condone his behaviour, but at least with him you always know which way the wind is blowing. It's the ones who hide their agendas I worry about. Our current prime minister, for one. He's managed to disguise his crypto-Nazi agenda well enough to make himself palatable to a sizable proportion of the population who would otherwise be loath to vote for an obvious fascist."

He nodded to the pamphlet.

"I could tell you tales that would raise the hairs on the back of your neck. There's an up-and-coming Liberal minister who's a classic homophobe. Well-disguised, of course. But he's much too popular for the party to expose him. If he gets into power, the clocks could go back about a hundred years on gay rights. Women's rights? Don't even think about it. As far as he's concerned, God created women to serve men, and all queers deserve to be castrated. End of discussion. You wouldn't think it in a country as socially advanced as Canada, but it's true. Rob Ford should be a lesson to us all. The fight is on."

"Ignorance, poverty, and someone else's dogma," Dan said. "That's where it all begins."

"Yes, true, but try changing things. That's why we have to keep our eyes on the board. The game can change overnight. People scoff when I say a man like Hitler could take power again, but the Weimar Republic had a very advanced gay community and liberal values. It was a golden era with many holding the same ideals we prize today. Gay nightclubs by the dozen, books and films dealing directly with queer issues. But Weimar led straight to Hitler and the Nazi takeover. Without realizing it, the entire country was just one step away from total insanity." He held up a finger: from art critic to social historian. "The lessons of history are hard, Dan. In case you didn't know."

"You think we could lose everything we've gained?"

"Sadly, I do. Weimar was an era of immense cultural expansion, a time of philosophical and scientific achievement often compared to the golden age of Athens. It was also a time of progressive social reforms. Workers' rights, public health insurance, child welfare, unemployment benefits. In short, all the things we value today. Germany had it all before the rise of the fascist clowns. Only they weren't very funny. What we have gained here could all be gone in the wink of an eye."

"If we don't learn the lessons of history …"

"Absolutely. Make no mistake. Exactly how did they go from Weimar to the Third Reich? That's what we all need to understand if we don't want it to repeat. There are many out there who hate the very mention of people like us. They'd rather we ended up in the ovens with the Jews. If another Hitler gets into power, we won't stand a chance." His eyes swept the room, as though seeing what would befall his beloved art collection if the Reich made its return tomorrow. He turned back to Dan. "Drink?"

"I don't drink as a rule."

"Problem?"

"Not if I watch myself."

"Very good. I understand."

A phone rang in another room.

"Please excuse me."

"Of course. Might I use your washroom?"

Dan followed Hansen's nod to a powder-blue room at the end of the hall. The carved vanity looked as if it had been designed for some preening southern belle anxious to reassure herself before entering a room full of beaux. *Fussy*, he thought, though whether it was Louis Quinze or Art Nouveau he had no idea. Donny would, of course.

He opened the medicine cabinet. Inside was a regular little pharmacy containing a dozen or more plastic vials. Perusing the labels was like reading a medical tract on mood management. Tony Moran's name was on every one. Was his anxiety due to a flawed genetic legacy or more recent problems of some sort?

Dan shut the cabinet and stepped into the hallway. Behind the next door was a small bedroom. A shelf held sports trophies — baseball, soccer, lacrosse — above a double bed. Here was the simpler personality. Tony's room, Dan knew without asking.

A mahogany dresser sat against the far wall. Old and well-preserved, like an aged ballerina. The photo on top showed Tony with an older woman, smiling timidly. His mother, Dan guessed. He twisted a thick black key and pulled open the top drawer. Inside were all the usual things: socks, underwear, T-shirts. Even a Moran family Bible. But also something not normally locked away in a dresser: a cellphone. Dan flicked the On switch. No password required. Perhaps that was why it was hidden.

His thumb scrolled down a list of texts. Some went back months. Tony apparently liked to keep records of his conversations. Sweet nothings between him and his husband. A birthday greeting from a friend. A single exchange stood out, dated just before Christmas:

NUMBER BLOCKED: What did you hear?

TMORAN: I'm afraid to talk about it.

NUMBER BLOCKED: Don't worry. I'll protect you.

TMORAN: Will I need protection?

NUMBER BLOCKED: Not if I talk to the Magus.

TMORAN: I'm worried about the money.

NUMBER BLOCKED: Don't worry. It will be there.

The conversation ended there.

Dan pocketed the phone and stepped back into the hallway. Peter's voice carried from the far end of the house.

One door further along led to a master bedroom. A small end table stood to one side of a king-size bed. Dan slid the drawer open. Inside lay a .32 Magnum revolver. Death threats, Peter had said. Perhaps he took them seriously. He pulled a tissue from a box and used it to pick up the gun, checking the magazine. It was empty. For show, then.

Dan closed the drawer and returned to the hall. The corgi put in a reappearance, giving Dan a worried look. He heard Peter's raised voice, followed by a brief laugh. Another governmental crisis averted. Footsteps approached. Peter appeared.

Dan looked over. "By the way, I meant to ask you: what was Tony's connection with John Wilkens?"

Peter looked genuinely surprised. "My late colleague?"

Dan nodded.

"None that I know of. They may have met at some function or other, but John was the enemy, if you'll pardon the expression. Tony wouldn't have had much to say to him. Why?"

Dan ignored the question. "Would you say there's been a marked change in Tony's behaviour recently?"

Peter scratched his head. "Tony's always been a bit high-strung, but maybe, yeah. The past few months or so he's been a lot jumpier."

"Since Christmas?"

"Possibly. It may have started before, but I've been quite busy with my job. Why do you ask?"

"Is there someone Tony's afraid of?"

Peter frowned and shook his head. "Afraid of in what sense? What are you getting at?"

"I'm just trying to get a better sense of who Tony is and why he might have wanted to lose twenty thousand dollars."

Peter gave him a sharp look. "Why do you say 'wanted to'?"

"According to the person I talked to, Tony's betting was very erratic that night. I thought he might have been trying to lose the money. Why do you think that might be?"

Peter stiffened. "I hired you to find my husband, not make judgments or accusations about him."

"What do you know about someone at Queen's Park known as the Magus?"

Peter stared for a moment. Dan expected him to deny any knowledge of a Magus or, like Will, to laugh it off. Instead, he nodded.

"All right. Since you brought it up, we've all heard of the Magus. Frankly, I don't believe such a person exists. And even if he did, I wouldn't waste one minute worrying whether or not he could harm me. Everything I do is totally above board." He shrugged. "How is this relevant to finding Tony?"

"I'm not sure yet."

"I made my bid to be a Queen's Park minister and I failed through my own efforts because I came out at what some would call an inappropriate time. There was no Magus involved. If I thought someone was trying to hurt Alec Henderson's career, I might think otherwise, but I don't intend to waste time worrying about the bogeyman."

Dan flipped Tony's phone toward him. Peter caught it and glanced down at the screen.

"Perhaps you'd better start," Dan said.

EIGHT

Going to the Chapel

THE MEETING HAD BEEN SET AND reset for weeks, but each time something had made them postpone it. Now, at last, it was about to happen. The topic: weddings. Getting married was no easy matter, as both Dan and Nick had discovered, and gay weddings were no exception. With so much to be sorted out — the menu, the venue, the guests, the attire, the décor, the DJ, the official photographer — there was seemingly no end to the choices awaiting the beleaguered couple, and no end to the mounting costs for their special day. Which presumably was why so many of them ended as nightmares rather than dreams come true.

Looking slim and cool, Kendra was first to arrive. Ralph came out to greet her, received his requisite pat on the head, then retired back to his cushion.

While waiting for the others, Dan brought out a bottle of Elderflower tonic and splashed some into two tumblers.

"Here's to twenty years of parenthood," he said, clinking glasses.

"Do you think he'll come home after the graduation or have we lost him forever?"

"You mean, have we lost him to the splendour of the ocean, the scenic backdrop of the Rockies, the clean air and easygoing lifestyle of B.C.? Why ever would you think that?"

Kendra smiled. "He insists he and Elizabeth are still an item. She's had the patience to keep going back and forth all this time. I give her full credit. I didn't want to suggest that he look around while he's out there. It would have been disloyal. And besides, we all love Elizabeth."

"Elizabeth is a lovely girl. Ked told me just last week that she's thinking of moving out there and joining him if he gets a job. I didn't want to say anything either. It's a big decision and I don't want to be *that* kind of parent, giving gloomy forecasts about the long term."

They smiled knowingly. Each had seen the other through numerous relationships, so many that the only constant seemed to be the platonic ideal of family they shared. No sex, no co-habitation, but total loyalty and commitment to one another's aspirations. It was the dream match, as far as they both were concerned.

Donny and Prabin arrived next. Their relationship, too, had started off as a casual arrangement, but Prabin had bolted at the first sign of seriousness on Donny's part. Too much pressure from the Indian community to marry a woman from his own culture and to have children had tipped the balance into an untenable overdraft. But somewhere along the way Donny wore all that down and convinced him they had something worth struggling for. That and an adopted son, Lester, introduced to Donny by Dan after he'd rescued the boy from the rough and tumble world of the sex trade. All together, they were their own little UN faction.

Last but not least, Nick arrived fresh from the gym.

"And here comes the lovely …" Donny began, then stopped. "What are you? The top or the bottom?"

A look passed between Dan and Nick.

"It doesn't matter," Prabin said. "I'm sure neither of them will be wearing white to this wedding."

"Speak for yourself," Nick said. "I'm a winter."

"And I'm wearing white for surrender," Dan added.

Donny shook his head. "Really! After all this time you still won't say? You guys are *too* discreet, and meanwhile gossip queens are dying in the streets for lack of scandal." He pulled out a checklist and sat poised with his pen. "All right, first things first. Where is the marriage licence?"

Dan turned to Nick and Nick to Dan. Each pointed a finger at the other.

"You did apply for one, didn't you?" Donny pressed.

"Didn't we?" Nick asked.

Dan shook his head. "Don't look at me. I thought you did!"

"All righty then," Donny said, scribbling a large *X* with a flourish. "No marriage licence. Fortunately you can apply online fairly quickly, but you would have to work together to make it happen."

"I think we can manage that much," Dan said.

"One would hope," Donny concluded. "Next question. What about the reception hall? Your guest list is pretty small, so you can rent a room from the city for a reasonable fee. What's your preference?"

Both Dan and Nick stared blankly at the faces waiting for an answer.

"Um ..." Nick sheepishly began. "Sorry, I guess we aren't really prepared for this."

Donny waved his protests away. "That's why we're here. I was thinking you might want to rent a boat. Very stylish. It's not as expensive as you might think. You can hire something affordable to tour around the Toronto Islands. A nice little sunset cruise."

"The last time I attended a wedding on a boat someone fell overboard and drowned," Dan offered.

"Maybe not, then." Donny made another large *X* then looked up. "If you don't mind something simple, Prabin and I would be happy to host it at our place."

"That would be a lot of work for you guys," Nick said.

"Not really," Prabin countered. "We'd love to do it for you."

"We discussed it last night," Donny continued. "It helps that we don't dislike any of your guests. And to tell the truth, we're just relieved you didn't want one of those awful destination weddings where you make people pay a lot of money to sit on a beach and watch you sweat in your tuxes while the waves roll in. If you had opted for that, I was going to un-friend you so I wouldn't have to come. Either that or try to break you up."

"You're so colourful," Dan offered, glancing at Nick. "And yes, we'd love to accept your offer to host."

Nick nodded his agreement.

"Good, so that makes one check mark," Donny said with another extravagant flourish. "Now comes the food."

"I looked into it," Dan said. "I'm not crazy about the prices I've been quoted."

"You've probably talked to all the chi-chi gay places ... Chez David, Antoine's, La-Ti-Da's."

"They're all a bit over the top."

"Of course, because they're gay. They always need to impress somebody. On the other hand, we could just do pizza and wings and time it for a baseball game."

Dan shrugged, glancing over at Nick. "One of us might be a bit too fussy for that."

Donny glanced back and forth between them. "Oh, really? Which one?"

"That's where I can help out," Kendra piped up. "You both love my cooking, so why don't I cater?"

"Excellent idea — check!" Donny said as he looked around at the gathering. "Now we're getting somewhere. Maybe we should just stop asking the happy-but-oblivious couple what they want and let the rest of us decide everything."

Nick nodded. "Sure, why not? Weddings made simple."

"We're happy to accept the help," Dan said, "but we don't want you paying for things."

"Agreed," Nick said as his cell rang. He looked around apologetically. "Sorry, I better ..."

"That would be the Batphone," Donny remarked. "Better answer it. Gotham City needs you."

Nick put the phone to his ear and headed for the doorway. "Officer Trposki."

Prabin grinned. "I love it when he says that!"

"I have a feeling Officer Trposki won't be with us for much longer," Dan said. "So if there's anything you need to ask him, let's do it now."

Donny ran a finger down his list. "Photographer, cutlery, napkins, music. Nothing you can't handle, I suspect."

"I'll do my best, but I guarantee Nick will want his say."

Nick returned, looking rueful as he placed both hands on Dan's shoulders. "Duty calls. My charming, long-suffering husband-to-be can update me. I give him permission to venture my opinion, though I reserve the right to change my mind later, if need be. Coercion optional, of course." He kissed Dan on the cheek and ducked out of the room.

"See what I mean?" Dan looked around and shrugged. "The lonely life of a policeman's other half, what can I say?"

"Now's your chance," Donny said conspiratorially. "Just between us girls in the powder room, is it all going the way you want?"

"Hey, I'm easy. Don't forget this whole thing is Nick's idea. I'm just going along for the ride."

Donny eyed Prabin. "Said in the true spirit of coupledom. We know what that's all about."

"Let's finish the list," Kendra volunteered. "I know how to convince Nick of what he wants."

As they went through the remainder of the items, suggestions were made and more check marks landed on Donny's list. At last, he sat back with a sigh.

"Time to wrap things up," he said. "I've got somewhere to be in half an hour and some of you might have actual jobs to attend. Danny will put on his superhero cape and save the city yet again, and I'm sure Prabin needs to go make sure the stock market doesn't crash."

"And I have a corporate customer to stop from looking distraught," Kendra said. She kissed each of the men coolly on the cheek and took her leave. "I'll let myself out."

"Well, this has been productive." Donny closed his notebook with a snap. "Let's all of us good capitalists go back to the grind, spreading greed and the epistle of luxury." He paused. "Oh. In other news, I want to remind you that Lester's concert is tomorrow. I've got tickets for all of us."

"Let us pay for them," Dan protested.

"No need, but donations are being gratefully accepted for the group's first video."

"Happy to contribute," Dan said, walking them to the door. "Thanks for coming. We want you guys to know how much we appreciate what you're doing for us."

"Not at all," Donny said. "It's time for you to leave the single life behind. Permanently."

"Speaking of which," Dan replied, "I saw my first big crush the other day. I met up with Will Parker."

Donny's eyebrows rose. "Handsome Will? How's he doing?"

"Very well. He's got himself set up at Queen's Park."

"Good place for him. That was one political hound, from what I remember."

"And still is, from what I can tell. He went over to the dark side and got himself married to a woman."

Donny's look stopped Dan from saying more.

"He what?"

"He got married to a woman. You didn't know Will was bisexual?"

"I had heard that and other things, but no matter. It's a big world. There's room for everyone." Donny shrugged. "I probably shouldn't say it, but Will is the sort of guy I always thought you would end up with — someone deep, serious, and dialectical. The no-nonsense, no-flirting, I've Got a World to Change type. Instead, you've got Mr. Fun and Sensuous."

"Do you think I took a wrong turn somewhere?"

"Not at all! Two lead balloons do not a flying machine make." Donny smiled. "You need to be with someone who blows up all your ponderousness. As you may recall, when you first told me you were dating a cop I had a moment of doubt — a moment as deep and wide as the Grand Canyon, no less — but once I got to know Nick I knew you'd snagged a winner. 'Don't screw this one up, buddy,' I thought to myself. And, hey! So far you haven't."

"Thanks for the vote of confidence," Dan said.

NINE

Dust

DAN HAD JUST SAID GOODBYE to Donny and Prabin and shut the door behind them, when his cell buzzed in his pocket. He pulled it out and saw Nick's name, then put the phone to his ear.

"Missing me already?"

"I'm at Mount Pleasant Cemetery. How fast can you get here?"

It was his official voice. Dan could always tell the difference between Nick the man and Nick the cop, even over the phone.

"We just wrapped things up. I'll head right over. Any clue as to why I would want to come, other than to see you in the flesh?"

There was no softening to Nick's tone. "There's been a break in the search for your missing client. I thought you'd want to be among the first to know."

Dan snapped to attention. "You found Tony Moran?"

"Not exactly. We have a lead. A vagrant brought in some clothes and ID belonging to Moran. I gather he was hoping there might be a reward. I'm about to join a team to see if there isn't a body to go along with it."

Dan grabbed his wallet and car keys.

"I'm on my way."

Ten minutes later, Dan turned in at the gates and passed the cheery, red-brick visitation centre. *All is well here*, it said. *Be at peace with us*. Then he swerved around the corner and the cemetery sprang into view.

Dan wondered at what point humans had decided they could outsmart Death by creating monuments to the deceased. Pyramids, mausoleums, catacombs, and ossuaries all served the same purpose: to deny the inevitable. *Cemetery*. A Greek word meaning *sleeping place*. But who is fooled into thinking the dead are only sleeping? Much better to shuffle off this mortal coil, give up your material remains, and let your eyes be pecked out by eagles on a high mountain crag than be shoved into some damp, worm-infested hole evermore. The aboriginals had it right when they swung grandpa into a tree and left him to rot. The Hindus were ahead of the game, building a funeral pyre and setting everything alight, followed by a feast for the mourners. What better send-off could there be? But to stick a body in a box and pay a small fortune for a plot of ground … who benefited from that?

In London, there's a cemetery for prostitutes known as Cross Bones, and there's another in Madrid for Jews, Protestants, and suicides. In Yekaterinburg, Russia, there's a mafia cemetery for murdered gangsters. Everyone has their own version of undesirables. It was the French, of course, who came up with the first pet cemetery: *Cimetière des Chiens*. Unless you count the Elephant Graveyard, that is. A pile of ivory tusks or a handful of dust — it all amounts to the same thing in the end.

Dan parked.

The investigations unit had cordoned off a section of grounds the size of a baseball diamond. It took in several family mausoleums and a row of tombs, marked by yards of yellow crime-scene tape flapping in the wind as though someone had been prospecting and set up a claim to the netherworld. Not far off, a dozen figures bent and swayed beneath a copse of trees, performing synchronized tai chi in slow motion. Dan thought of them as human windmills, arms rotating while the core remained at a standstill. Life's curious tick-tick-ticking away, even here under the sleepy elms of death.

A handler restrained a pair of hounds over by a wooden fence, the dogs clearly eager to give chase, the owner playing a reluctant bridegroom waiting for the right moment to pounce.

Nick saw Dan arrive and sauntered over. Dan hesitated, unsure how to greet him. Clearly a kiss wouldn't be appropriate, but his possessive gene had a momentary flare-up and he put a hand on his partner's arm. Two constables saw the gesture and exchanged glances. Nick caught their looks.

"They're trying to figure you out," he said.

"Let them. It's the twenty-first century." Dan saw Nick's concerned expression. "Don't worry, I won't give you away."

"Not worried. I can fight my own battles."

He turned and stretched an arm to the row of tombstones.

"Someone found a jacket and wallet with Tony Moran's ID tossed inside the Eaton mausoleum. Or at least he said that's where he found it. If he stole it looking for a reward, it could have come from anywhere. There are indications someone slept in the crypt overnight. It might have been Tony, but frankly it could have been anyone."

"What's with the hounds?"

Nick indicated the south end of the property where it dwindled into a grove of trees. "There's a large storm drain not far from here. The river isn't deep, but the water is high because of the storms. So far we haven't found a body."

Dan glanced over to the officers examining the ground in the distance.

"Anything that might indicate violence?"

Nick looked over at the canine handler. "The dogs don't seem overly excited, so I doubt it." He eyed Dan. "Here's the odd part, though. I looked in the wallet. Tony had a business card for John Wilkens, that politician who committed suicide at Christmas."

Dan stared. "Simon Bradley claimed Wilkens was connected with Tony Moran. He sent me a link showing a photo of the two of them standing side by side at a political event. Bradley says Wilkens was murdered. I didn't believe him, but I didn't entirely discount it, either."

Nick whistled. "Does he think Tony had something to do with Wilkens's death?"

Dan eyed him. "If it turns out that John Wilkens was murdered, then maybe he did."

They watched as a TV crew pulled up outside the perimeter outlined in tape. A cameraman jumped out and headed for the mausoleum.

Nick nodded in their direction. "You may find this case has been taken out of your hands, now that the media is onto it."

Dan heard his name called out. He turned and saw Simon Bradley heading toward him with a second cameraman in tow.

"Speak of the devil," Dan murmured.

"Good to see you again," Simon said, coming up to him.

"You got here awfully quick."

"So did you. One might think you had inside information."

He gave a knowing look in Nick's direction. Dan's internal danger sensor flickered into the red zone.

Simon smirked. "Word travels fast in my game."

"Very fast," Dan noted.

The operator mounted the camera on his shoulder, pulled the lens into focus and trained it on Simon.

"I'm at Mount Pleasant Cemetery, where police are looking into the disappearance of Tony Moran, husband of Queen's Park Special Assistant Peter Hansen. With me is Dan Sharp, private investigator." Bradley turned to Dan. "Has Tony Moran been found?"

"Not to my knowledge, no."

"What can you tell us about recent developments in the case?"

"Absolutely nothing."

Undaunted, Simon went on. "Are there indications of violence at the crime scene?"

Dan shrugged. "I haven't looked at any so-called crime scene. You'd have to ask the police."

Simon's inquisitive look stayed glued to his face. "Can you speculate on how Tony Moran's ID came to be found in a cemetery?"

Dan's incredulity turned to outrage at the mention of ID. "I haven't got a fucking clue, but I'm pretty curious how you found out about it so fast."

Simon turned to his cameraman. "Strike that." To Dan, he said, "I thought we were on the same side."

"Don't make assumptions about me."

Simon shook his head and turned to his camera operator. "Let's head over to the cops."

The pair turned and walked away. Nick had been watching the exchange. He smirked. "Good one."

"Old trick. If you don't want to be quoted on prime time TV, just swear."

A howling in the distance announced that the dogs had been let off the leash. Dan turned and watched them dash for the south end of the field, in the direction of the river and the storm drain.

TEN

Tea and Privilege

THE DOGS FAILED TO DISCOVER any further trace of Tony Moran. Either someone else had left Tony's wallet in the cemetery or, if he'd been there at all, he was exceptionally skilled at covering his tracks. Dan never knew whether to be relieved when a search turned up with negative results. It could be good news or simply a postponement of the inevitable. On the whole, no news was simply no news. In this case, however, it served to inflame his curiosity about one thing.

He took a final look at Simon Bradley and his cameraman scouring the cemetery for something newsworthy, then said goodbye to Nick, got in his car and headed east. By coincidence, John Wilkens's family home lay a mere three blocks away in one of the city's most established neighbourhoods. Despite a reputation for being "where the old money lives," Rosedale was no longer the white, Anglo-Saxon domain it had been when the city was first settled. It had since fallen to others who likewise believed that affluence conferred status, flocking there while the younger generation of WASPs moved out to seek its own values, leaving the diehards and the newcomers to battle it out over privileges they felt were their birthright.

Gays, too, had their status symbols, but following old wealth around generally wasn't one of them. Dan hated neighbourhoods like these on principle, but without any real vehemence. Rather, he found them curious anachronisms, like the English class system or American gun culture.

The home of John Badger Wilkens III, Dan learned, had been in his family for three generations, thus the *III* designation. It turned out to be a surprisingly modest two-storey house surrounded by birch trees on a quiet street corner. Up close, there was nothing particularly reprehensible about it, apart from the hundred-and-fifty-thousand-dollar vehicle in its drive. Dan admired its gardens, noting the enviable distance between the Wilkens property and the neighbours. Maybe that was all the race for money was about: misanthropy, plain and simple. A desire to live in the city, but with as much distance as possible from the nearest resident. He could sympathize on that count.

The young woman who answered the door was dressed in a pink blouse and grey tweed skirt. You might have thought she'd shipped over from Scotland circa the 1930s. Her eyes were blue and sharp, her face pleasing, though there was nothing suggesting warmth under the coolly efficient features. A rose, but one with thorns. Little got past her, Dan could see. She was the public school teacher everyone feared. She clearly didn't like his looks either, but held back from saying so. Had she been a hotel desk clerk, he would have ended up with a windowless room on the top floor of a creaky walk-up.

He held up his identification. "Mrs. Wilkens?"

"Do you have an appointment?"

Her expression said she knew very well he didn't.

"I'm a private investigator. I'd like a word, if I might."

"On what matter?"

"It's a private matter concerning Mrs. Wilkens."

The frown she gave him suggested she would speak to her mistress and do everything in her power to discourage a meeting, but at least she went. She was back in a minute, followed by another woman. Or rather, a shadow of a woman, noticeably thin and dressed entirely in black. She teetered as she stood there, the Duchess of Windsor on her fifth gin martini. If he hadn't known better, Dan would have thought her John Wilkens's mother rather than his widow.

"Mrs. Wilkens?"

"Yes. Who are you?"

Her eyes were large and solemn. Something said grief had taken up permanent lodging there.

Dan held up his identification again. "My name is Sharp. I'm a private investigator. I'm looking into the disappearance of a man named Tony Moran. I understand your husband knew him."

Her eyes darted over Dan's shoulder. Perhaps the presence on her doorstep of a private investigator required a close watch on the neighbours, lest they get too curious.

She turned to the woman at her side. "It's all right, Doris. I can handle this."

Doris went reluctantly away with a last look, as though memorizing Dan's face for a future police line-up. *That's the rich for you*, Dan thought, *hiring someone just to shoo away unwanted visitors.*

The woman in black turned to him. "Tony Moran? I don't recall the name. I doubt I can tell you anything."

But she made no effort to close the door. Perhaps she was just amusing herself by keeping him there with no intention of helping him out with his query.

"Mr. Moran is the husband of a ministerial assistant at Queen's Park. Your late husband's name and address were in Mr. Moran's wallet, which was found discarded earlier today."

She drew herself up. "Why wasn't I informed of this by the police?"

"I just learned it myself. The police may call to ask you about it in due time."

"I see." Her look was pure skepticism. "Still, I don't recognize the name."

"What about Simon Bradley? Does his name mean anything to you?"

Her eyes narrowed. "I believe Mr. Bradley is a reporter of some sort. Are you associated with him?"

Dan hesitated, more from fear of frightening her unnecessarily than from any sense of delicacy. "No, I'm not. But it was Mr. Bradley who first suggested there might be a connection between my missing client and your husband."

Her face was stone. To some women grief gave a dramatic expression, an overwhelming look of loss, while in others it took everything away. An emptying, a depletion. She was definitely of the latter type.

"What connection might that be?" she asked at last. "My husband was a man of considerable virtues and high personal standards. If this has anything to do with his dismissal, I can only say what I know to be true from the bottom of my heart: John was innocent."

Here was the missing link, Dan saw: a woman seeking to redress the wrongs her husband was accused of. This, if anything, was his way in. Whatever the truth of the matter, she believed in his innocence. It wouldn't be the first time a gullible spouse had stood by an absconding bastard.

"Did Mr. Wilkens feel he was in any way threatened or being framed by someone?"

She hesitated, then pushed the door open.

"Come in, Mr. Sharp. Let's not stand on the doorstep forever. There's obviously something you want to say to me."

He stepped inside a dimly lit hallway and waited as she closed the door before following her to a salon appointed with plush carpeting and antique furnishings. For a moment it seemed as if they had entered another century. The clavichord in a far corner might once have been played by Mozart. The entire room seemed to indicate a desire to eradicate the passage of time, a return to what some erroneously believed to be a gentler, kinder age.

They sat among various family portraits and the bric-a-brac of years gone by. Someone's grim grandparents glowered down from behind a clock encased in glass, its pendulum stopped dead. Vases with crackled patinas sat beside weighty-looking candlesticks on gilt side tables with marble inlay. A bronze eagle stretched its wings in imitation of flight, while behind it, a sword plunged into a scabbard hung on the wall. Below, two laughing, scantily-clad figurines curled flirtatiously toward one another, their amorous advances forever stilled by the chill hand of time.

Dan looked for signs of recent mourning, but saw little apart from the solemnity of the room with its air of a mausoleum, which he suspected was its normal state. Family history. It buried you long before you died. Some managed to get out from under its weight, but not many, by the sounds of it. Whatever state you were born into was usually yours for life, without a reprieve. It was the outcasts — the gays, the intellectuals, the radicals — who broke away from the pack, when they weren't driven off and forced to reinvent themselves. Even they sometimes returned, he knew. The undertow of family was strong.

Mrs. Wilkens stood by the fireplace, her frown turned up to full volume. No longer an agitated duchess, but a pensive lady-in-waiting.

"I was just about to have tea. Would you care for a cup?"

Given her state, he wondered if she meant it as a euphemism for something stronger.

"Or perhaps coffee," she added, seeing his confusion.

"Please, that would be nice."

"Which?"

"Either. Both. Would be fine."

She smiled at his awkwardness. "Tea, then."

She called out. The Scottish rose came in quickly, as though she'd been standing right outside the door waiting.

"Please serve the tea in here, Doris. With a cup for Mr. Sharp."

Doris nodded and vanished again.

Dan looked around at the photographs. One in particular caught his eye. A young man in ruffles. Little Lord Fauntleroy, a real mama's boy. It was a private-school photo, Dan suspected. You'd have to have a forceful personality to get away with that getup in a public school.

"That's John," she said in response to Dan's inquisitive glance before pointing out another photograph. "And that is me."

While she looked considerably younger in the photo than she did today, it was clear the Wilkenses had had a May-December marriage. *Mama's boy indeed*, Dan thought.

"You're thinking my husband was younger than me. You're correct," she confirmed. "We were fourteen years apart."

Dan had long held the belief that when people confessed their secrets without prompting it was a passive form of boasting: *Yes, I'm nearly old enough to be his mother, but I nabbed him for my loving husband and bedmate.*

"Actually, I was thinking what beautiful eyes you have," he said.

She smiled grimly. "You're a liar. But thank you for the compliment. He chased after me, in case you're wondering. In the beginning, anyway."

He was right again.

"I'm sure you were very happy together, Mrs. Wilkens. And if I didn't say it earlier, I'm sorry for your loss."

Somewhere in the distance a kettle came to a boil with a long, drawn-out sigh, followed by a sound like mice scurrying as tea leaves were scooped from a container and dropped into a pot.

"He should never have gone into politics," Mrs. Wilkens said abruptly.

"Because of what happened to him?"

Her look said he could never understand. "Because he was too good for it. From the start we knew he was special. John was not made for this world."

The rich seldom are, Dan thought.

"If you think this sounds like the beginning of a fairy tale, I can assure you I am not mistaken in my assessment of my husband. He had a long history of public service. That was what motivated him to go into politics."

Dan nodded politely.

"After what happened, even his party dropped him. Like a sacrificial lamb, as they say. What could he do? He tried to tell the party higher-ups, but they wanted nothing to do with it."

"Tried to tell them what?"

"That things were awry, things were amiss. But they couldn't afford to get their hands dirty. Well, now they've got blood on those same hands. They did this to him. When he's cleared of the charges, as he will be, I'll see that the blame is laid where it should be."

"What things did your husband believe were amiss?"

Her startled glance told him perhaps she had said too much. "I …"

Before she could answer, a tray arrived, carried in by the same conservatively dressed young woman.

"My sister, Doris," Mrs. Wilkens said, as though to dismiss any idea of privilege he might be forming. "Mr. Sharp is investigating the disappearance of a man whose wife works at Queen's Park."

Doris passed them each a cup and sat on the settee beside her sister.

"Husband, actually," Dan corrected. "Tony Moran is married to a man."

"My mistake," Mrs. Wilkens said. "One never knows these days."

Dan could detect no undertone of condescension in her statement. "My client's name is Peter Hansen."

He saw the change of expression on both women's faces.

"And it's Peter Hansen's husband you believe had some connection with John?"

It was the sister, Doris, who asked. Dan was right — she had been listening at the door.

"That's what I'm trying to find out. I'm sure the police will call and speak to you about it soon," Dan told them. "For now, all I've got is the assertion by Simon Bradley that John and Tony knew one another. This is partially substantiated by a photograph of them together at a public function, though that doesn't prove much."

He brought out his phone and showed them the photograph. They looked at it warily, as though anxious to restrain their curiosity.

"Do you recognize the occasion?" Dan asked.

Doris shook her head then turned to her sister.

"I'm afraid not," said Mrs. Wilkens. "It could be any official function."

Dan nodded. "I'm looking into the possibility that a third person had some connection with the two of them, possibly someone who in some way represented a threat to your husband. And now to Tony Moran."

"What sort of threat?"

"I don't know yet."

The older woman put both hands around her cup and looked down, lost in thought. Dan wondered what she saw there. Memories wavering in and out of the wisps of steam. Or maybe she saw her dead husband's ghost, his spirit vexed and wandering. She looked up again, pushing the visions aside, and returned to her current state of gloom.

"You asked if … if John felt threatened. I don't know whether this is exactly what you meant, but he did say he felt he was being pushed by various people within the government to perform distasteful tasks."

"Could you elaborate?"

"Mr. Sharp, if you knew my husband, you would know he was one of the most honest and honourable men who ever lived. John was suspended for suspected bribery. The idea that he paid someone to cover up illegal activities is simply unthinkable. The stress of those allegations obviously ruined his mind for him to … to do what he did to himself. It drove him to the edge of madness. He thought night and day of how to reinstate his good name, even before the press got hold of these unfounded allegations."

"So, your husband felt his reputation was under attack even before the allegations were made public?"

She placed her cup on the saucer. "John was being hounded well before the news came out. By politicians and media alike. They're all the same."

Her sister wrapped an arm around her shoulder.

Dan recalled the official statements regarding Wilkens's death, the eulogizing of a dead colleague. Guilt, perhaps. Or party pressure. He wasn't about to tell her what Simon Bradley believed, namely that her husband had been murdered, possibly by someone who had tried to threaten or coerce him.

"It's possible the people who were pressuring your husband may also be behind the disappearance of Tony Moran. That's why I wanted to see you, in hopes that you might remember a name or some instance when your husband felt he was being unduly influenced by others. Do you have any idea what things he might have felt were amiss?"

She shook her head. "He didn't confide much of his political life to me." She turned to her sister. "Do you know, Doris?"

"No. I'm sorry, I don't."

They sat quietly subdued, as though the room's inertia had robbed them of their movement.

Dan looked over at them. "Is there any reason you can think of that Tony Moran would have carried your husband's business card in his wallet?"

Mrs. Wilkens shook her head. "No, none at all. It truly surprises me."

"Was Mr. Wilkens a gambler? Even occasionally?"

The older woman laughed. It was as close as she'd come to showing a sense of humour. "Not a chance. If you knew John you would know how ridiculous the suggestion is."

"Had he many dealings with Simon Bradley?"

"As few as possible, I believe. There was an article about potential future party leaders. Mr. Bradley ran a profile about John."

She looked to Doris again. Her sister nodded.

"It wasn't unkind to John," she continued, "but in general I think John disliked the man."

She seemed to be holding back. Dan wondered if she might be afraid of revealing everything she knew in front of her sister. He took another tack.

"Did he mention someone called the Magus, by any chance?"

"The Magus? Like a wizard, you mean?" She stared blankly at him. "No, never."

Dan drained his cup and set it down. "All right, thank you, Mrs. Wilkens. I won't bother you any longer, but if you think of anything else please call me."

Dan offered her his card. When he stood, she looked up.

"If you'd like, I will go through my husband's diaries and see if I can come up with some names of people for you to talk to."

Dan smiled. "I would very much appreciate that."

The conversation was over. The sister saw Dan to the door. There was a furtive look in her eyes. She put a hand on his sleeve.

"John didn't kill himself, Mr. Sharp. It wasn't in him." She glanced over her shoulder to be sure she couldn't be overheard before continuing. "I don't want to upset my sister, but he would never have done that."

"You might be surprised by the people you would never think such a thing of who actually do kill themselves. They seem to have it all together, then suddenly something slips out of place and their lives are threatened. Everything that matters to them disappears and they take what seems the only avenue out."

She shook her head. "We had a conversation not long before he died. We — the family — were going off for the holidays. He took a moment to wish me a happy

Christmas. I told him I was sorry about what had happened. He said not to worry, because he had something that would clear his name. John wasn't going without a fight, Mr. Sharp. He said he knew who was behind it and that he had an ally who would help make things right. He would never have given up until his name was cleared."

Dan watched the emotions come and go in her face. He wanted to reassure her, but there was nothing he could say that she needed to hear. "It's good your sister has someone like you to be close to at times like these."

"Yes," she said. "We hadn't been in touch for some years. I came back at the right time."

"I'm sure she's glad you did."

ELEVEN

High Stakes

DAN LEFT THE WILKENS HOUSE and cut across the boulevard. Trees overarched the street, branches criss-crossing in a cathedral of green. The neighbourhood was an oasis of calm, tucked away from rush-hour traffic and the high towers of commerce. It was like a fairy tale, a dream of Neverland, just holding its breath and waiting for the Big Bad Wolf to blow into town. It lulled you into thinking all was well with the world, that blue skies were the norm, forever staving off the cold, grey rain. Forget your troubles, come on, get happy. All you need is money.

His cell buzzed. "Sharp."

"Hi, Dad!"

"Hey! How's it going in the land of grass and honey?"

Ked's laughter reached him from across the continent. "Don't joke! Half my schoolmates are stoners."

"Yeah, but it's legal there, isn't it?"

"Yeah, nearly. Everyone jokes about how it's B.C.'s second-biggest cash crop after lumber. Anyway, I've got my finals to worry about. I can't mess up."

"Good. Don't let yourself get distracted. So, what's up?"

"Nothing. Just wanted to be sure you're still coming for the graduation. Charlie's away, so he said you could have his room if you wanted. That way I'll get to spend more time with you."

"Of course I'm still coming. Wouldn't miss it for anything." Ked the good shepherd — it was just like his son to check up on him and make sure all was as it should be. "I might just take you up on your offer to room with you. Hotel rates are out of this world these days."

"Cool. I'll tell Charlie. So, what's going on there?"

"All good here. Nick and I are just finalizing plans for the wedding."

"Can't wait!"

"In fact, it's good I'm coming to visit while I can still afford to travel. This event will bankrupt us. I've got a case on my hands that's keeping me busy, but it won't stop me from coming."

"You're probably working too hard, as usual. You need to take a break once in a while."

"I'll do my best to relax while I'm there and not try to solve other people's problems."

"Ha ha."

It struck Dan that a short break from his routine before the wedding and the pressures of finding a new office was just what he needed. Life would be that much sweeter for a little relief, but after the wedding, he intended to take all his vacations with Nick.

"By the way, I saw Trevor last weekend," Ked told him.

"How is he?"

Dan didn't want to say that Trevor was still unfinished business to him, or that he felt it would be unfair to Nick to keep in touch with an ex who had meant so much to him at one time.

"He's doing great. No new love interests in his life, if that's what you're thinking."

"Well, that's none of my business."

"He still lives on Mayne Island," Ked persisted. "Alone. But he's happy."

"Good. I'm glad to hear that."

"It wouldn't hurt for you to call him once in a while."

Dan had an unsettled feeling, like pollywogs somersaulting in his stomach.

"I'm not sure that would be appropriate."

"Dad! C'mon! There's no reason you shouldn't talk to one another."

"No, you're right. Maybe I'll give him a call sometime."

"I told him you're coming to B.C. He seemed excited."

"Ked!"

"Don't worry. I told him about Nick. I didn't want to get his hopes up, in case you two decide to see one another while you're here."

Until Nick, Trevor had been Dan's most serious relationship. Ked had been hardest hit when they separated, asking for months afterward whether his father and Trevor might eventually get back together.

A faint pulsing interrupted the line.

"Oh, gotta go!" Ked said. "I've got another call coming through."

"Okay, talk to you soon."

"You mean *see* you soon," Ked corrected as he hung up.

Dan got in his car and headed to Little Portugal for the second time that week. Rush hour had begun, but with a little adroit driving and careful avoidance of all major arteries, he knew he could get there in half an hour. Long gone were the days when a cross-town trip lasted fifteen minutes. Now a simple journey to the grocery store took nearly that long, and all major outings had to be planned well in advance. A neighbourhood hangout you actually enjoyed was considered a real find, appreciated for its rarity as much as for its ease of access.

Hansen's house was starting to look familiar. Peter opened the door warily to his knock. The corgi butler didn't put in an appearance. Perhaps he'd been sedated and locked in a closet.

"Oh, it's you."

"Expecting someone else?"

"Not expecting, no." Peter shook his head. "But that annoying journalist has been here twice today asking about Tony's disappearance."

"Simon Bradley?"

"That one, yes. Miserable sod. I shut the door in his face about an hour ago."

"Then you heard the news?"

"What news?"

"That Tony's wallet was found in the Mount Pleasant Cemetery."

"Oh, god!" Peter's intake of breath was audible. "I closed the door on him before he could say anything."

"It was just his wallet," Dan added quickly. "There was no trace of Tony all through the rest of the grounds."

"Please, no!" Peter ran a hand through his hair. Unlike Mrs. Wilkens's grief, Hansen's was tangible.

Dan put a hand on his shoulder. "There's no reason to suspect anything worse than that at present."

"It's just —" Hansen stopped and shook his head. "I cut off his funds and I've been worried ever since about where he might be sleeping. I thought it would drive him home, but this …" He trailed off, his hands waving airily in the presumed direction of a fund-less Tony wandering in search of accommodation. "Come in. Please."

He ushered Dan into the study and indicated a chair.

"I know I asked whether Tony was in touch with John Wilkens —" Dan began.

"He wasn't, as far as I know," Peter interjected.

"John's business card was in Tony's wallet."

Peter looked up with confused gaze. "Why would he have that?"

"I don't know. I was hoping you could tell me."

"There's no reason they should have been in touch with one another."

"Okay, let me ask again. Why do you think Tony gambled away all that money? Was he trying to punish you for something?"

Peter's composure returned, along with his arrogance. "I told you before. I hired you to find Tony, not to accuse him of something. Apart from stupidity, of course, and I can do that myself."

"Then tell me what you know. What about those text messages on his cellphone? Have you thought about why this Magus would have anything to do with Tony?"

"I'm still trying to figure that out. As I said, I've heard of the Magus, yes, but nothing more."

"Nothing at all? Maybe something about how he operates? No — wait. Back up a second. Is it a *he*? Does anyone know for sure?"

Peter shook his head. "I never really wondered about it because I never took it seriously. I suppose it could be a *she*. It could even be a *they*, for all I know. It's all just rumours, nothing concrete. Mysterious things happen to damage the reputations of people in power. Not leaders, precisely, but public figures who are seen to be up-and-coming. People you might have thought were above suspicion."

"Is there anything obvious about them? A way to tell who's being targeted?"

Peter's face betrayed a moment of uncertainty. "I really wish I knew. From what I can see they all have some sort of buzz about them. You know — the next big thing."

"Did it happen to you? You said that coming out hurt your campaign chances in the last election —"

"That was my own doing," Peter interrupted. "I chose to come out. There was no threat. No one forced me to do it. Besides, I wasn't the first openly gay candidate to run."

"But you didn't win. Maybe someone was counting on that."

Peter shook his head. "Not likely. In any case, I just try to keep my nose clean and do my job. I'm not about to do something stupid that might cost me another election."

"Another election? You're running again? You never mentioned it."

Peter gave him an exasperated look. "You're not my press agent. But, yes — I'm running again. I've been told my chances of winning a seat in the legislature as an openly gay candidate are good this time. I've got the party's full backing."

"But that might be precisely why someone contacted Tony." Dan's mental wheels were spinning. "What if someone is trying to upset your campaign?"

"Before it even starts?"

"Has it started?"

"Barely. I've discussed my intentions with Alec Henderson and the premier. They've both given me their blessings. I'll make the announcement next week."

"Maybe someone got wind of it and wants to subvert your campaign."

"Why?"

"Because you're a contender. You're young, you're energetic, and everyone knows you'll grab the bull by the horns and run with it if you get in. Maybe someone sees you as a direct threat."

Peter pondered this. "So you think someone wants to skewer my campaign and that Tony is part of the picture?"

"He's your husband, so he certainly reflects on your personal life." Dan paused. "Think about it. When you're a minority, whether visible or invisible, you always have to try harder."

Peter shrugged. "I've spent my life being discriminated against as a gay man. I don't need a lecture on marginalization."

"No, maybe not," Dan said. "But maybe you need a reminder of your vulnerable points. Right now, it seems that Tony is a weak area in your profile."

Peter let out an exasperated sigh. "I've been trying to tell him that for months. If I run for a seat then we both have to keep our reputations clean. He's like me by proxy."

"Exactly. Someone may be trying to run him off course to make you look bad. Gambling is a sore point on Tony's scorecard —"

"No kidding!"

"Maybe it has to do with the money itself. That text on his phone told Tony not to worry because the money would be there."

Peter held up a finger. "You said Tony gambled away twenty thousand dollars last month. I just checked my records. That's significantly higher than what was missing from our accounts."

"That's what happened to John Badger Wilkens, wasn't it? Money went missing, but his wife insists he's innocent."

"You saw her?"

"Yes, right before coming here. That doesn't mean he was innocent, but she's denying it for all she's worth and I'm willing to give her the benefit of the doubt. John Wilkens was definitely an up-and-coming type in his party."

"He certainly had a buzz. There was talk that he could become Speaker of the House. And possibly party leader."

"So, if someone set Wilkens up for a fall, then maybe someone is setting you up as well."

"But why? Whether John was guilty or not, we represent opposite interests on the political spectrum. His party is everything I'm against — affluence, influence, position. Why would they set up both of us?"

"Maybe to help a third party. To split the vote for someone coming down the middle. Someone in the NDP, for instance."

"What can I do?" Peter sank his head onto his hands. "If they're trying to get at me through Tony, then I'm fucked!"

"Not necessarily," Dan said. "If we can find out who's doing this then we can put a stop to it before it affects your career."

Peter gave him an appraising stare. "I hope you're wrong, but I'm afraid you may be right. Despite what anyone may think of me, I really want to be a good politician. Someone who puts people first."

"I'll do what I can for you," Dan told him. "But you need to help me by telling me all you know and everything you hear. Can you promise me that?"

"Yes, of course."

TWELVE

Gun, Poison, Rope

DAN HEARD A FAINT BEEPING. It reached into his dreams, disturbing his sleep. He rolled over and looked at the clock: 3:23 a.m. Nick snored softly beside him, a mini furnace emanating waves of heat. He'd come in late from his shift, sometime after Dan had gone to bed. But that wasn't what woke him.

He looked to the bedside table, where a faint glow was just fading from his cellphone. He picked it up. It felt warm to the touch, but there was no alert for a text or an incoming message. Curious. Just then it buzzed again.

"Sharp."

He listened for a moment, then heard someone say, "Sharp."

"Yes, it's me," he said tersely, before realizing it was the echo of his own voice, like some transatlantic blip following him across the seas back to his own ear.

It was an eerie moment. He held the phone for a second longer, then put it down again. It wouldn't be the first time someone had been desperate enough to call in the middle of the night. Unconquerable fears, suicidal urges, suddenly remembered clues as to the possible whereabouts of a missing loved one. Once even a drunken request for his recipe for Chicken Marbella from a lonely friend. All reasons were valid and worthy of attention, as far as Dan was concerned.

He lay there adjusting to his surroundings, wrenched back from the images of a dream where he'd been struggling underwater. His car had gone off a bridge. The water was cold. It stopped up his mouth and lungs till he couldn't breathe. Instead of struggling, he just sat there, immobile, waiting for everything to go on. Some people lived their entire lives underwater without recognizing it. He thought of John Wilkens, who had come up for air, gasping for breath, claiming to be suspicious of irregular goings-on behind the scenes, only to lose his reputation, his job, and finally his life.

Dan crept quietly out of bed and went to the bathroom. Taped to the mirror was a handwritten note from Nick: *Left a little present in your study. Best viewed on an empty stomach. N*♥

He padded softly down the hall. It was still deep night, no incursion of day yet. The hour of gamblers, insomniacs, witches, and suicides. An envelope lay on the far side of his desk, a divide between him and whatever it contained. He slit open the flap and shook it. A pile of photos bundled together with an elastic band slid out. On top lay a single sheet of paper, folded in three. It proved to be a copy of the coroner's report on the death of John Badger Wilkens III.

Dan glanced over the findings. The verdict was suicide by hanging, just as he remembered from the papers at the time. Someone had written the word *Inconclusive* above *Suicide* then scratched it out again, initialling the corner before scratching over those initials to obscure them. Why the doubt and then the change of mind? The report stated that the rope Wilkens hanged himself with had come from the garage of his family home. A photocopied receipt showed he'd purchased it the week before Christmas. A planned death then. It also showed that Wilkens had had a blood alcohol concentration of 0.34 percent when he died. That was close to acute intoxication, even for a practised drinker. Maybe he'd been trying to drink himself to death before he realized there was an easier way.

Dan slipped off the elastic and went through the photos one by one. Here was the disgraced MPP in his final pose on a gurney in the city morgue, where he'd been photographed for the last time, still under the glare of public scrutiny.

It wasn't the way anyone would want to be remembered. The lighting was harsh, highlighting flaws and physical imperfections. He hadn't been arranged in any way to make him look better for what he'd undergone. The opposite, in fact: his eyes bulged, his tongue protruded between his teeth, with more than a hint of blue in its coloration. He looked like a man who had just had a fright or who was trying hard to give one. Like a Halloween gruesome or something out of a zombie flick.

The next shot showed the mark of the ligature encircling his neck, a raw, red burn where the rope had abraded the skin. Dan knew exactly how that rope would feel, the sharp bristling of the cord as it snapped taut and stiffened around his windpipe. The insistent pressure closing off his air, the unforgiving tension as he tried to free himself. At first the surprise would be sharper than the pain, with the sensation of oxygen being cut off from the lungs. Then would come the brain's realization it was shutting down, gravity combining with the body's weight to tighten the noose around the trachea, blocking the blood flow via the carotid artery and the jugular vein.

A sudden drop would have resulted in a neck fracture — quick and painless — but according to the report John Wilkens had died slowly, over the course of ten to twenty minutes. He'd been semi-conscious for a good part of it. Even if he'd fought to relieve the pressure temporarily, the end would have been the same. Only once he'd lost consciousness would his struggles finally have ceased and the restricted air flow resulted in strangulation. Self-slaughter was a grisly business if you didn't manage it right.

It was hard to say why people chose to die the way they did. Sometimes it depended on how and when they wanted to be found. A gun was quick, but left a mess for others to clean up. Poison could be fast or slow, but the mystery would remain: was it intentional or accidental? Could it have been prevented? He'd seen the bodies of crash victims he suspected of having purposely run their cars off the road, creating a nightmarish barrage of blood and carnage, though it had never been proved. Others he'd heard of had died in even more mysterious circumstances: the athlete who took a midnight swim from which she never returned, the experienced climber dying from an unlikely fall. But hanging yourself required effort and planning. It seemed to be a statement, but of what? And how had Wilkens managed it in his inebriated condition? It was useless to speculate. Unless there was a note, so much always went unanswered.

The next photograph showed a close-up of the neck. The flecks and fibres of nylon embedded in his flesh had been highlighted for greater clarity, like grain stubble in a field of uneven furrows. Someone had unnecessarily drawn arrows in magic marker, pointing out the fibres, as though you might miss the intent of the photograph.

The final two shots were of Wilkens's hands. Both showed the same yellow threads beneath fingernails torn and bloodied. The thumb nail on the right hand had been ripped right off. Dan sat back and stared at the photos. The word *Inconclusive* flashed before his eyes. There was nothing inconclusive here. These were the hands of a man who was grasping at life, not reaching out for death.

He turned back to the first shot, staring at the sightless eyes and protruding tongue, the words stilled forever. *Speak no more!* For just an instant, Dan could hear John Wilkens's last croaking gasp.

THIRTEEN

Posse

DAN STOOD BEFORE THE FULL-LENGTH mirror in boots, a black T, and jeans. The effect hadn't come off quite right, looking more rodeo than urban ghetto.

"I have no idea how to dress for this," he confided to Nick.

"I'd give you tips if I had a clue myself."

"Surely you've had to break up fights at rap concerts before."

Nick tried not to smile. "Sure, but I was busy watching out for knives, not studying fashion trends. Just a guess, but I'd say you need more bling. Take off those boots and put on a pair of Ked's sneakers."

The doorbell chimed. Downstairs, Donny called out a greeting.

"I'll get it. You get ready," Nick told Dan.

Donny and Prabin were seated on the couch when Dan came downstairs. Nick had brought out a tray of coffee.

"Are we doing this for real?" Dan asked.

Donny held up an admonitory finger. "Gentlemen, this is the new culture. Do not mock. I've sent the boy on ahead. He is so pumped that we are all coming to see him perform, so let's make it real for him. Our generation was nurtured on *The Rocky Horror Picture Show* and Madonna. These kids have Eminem and Puff Daddy. Not for us to wonder."

"But will we get it?" Nick asked.

"Get it? What's to get?" Donny shrugged. "Rap isn't a mystery. It's cultural empowerment. It's a protest against racism, poverty, oppression."

"It's also anti-gay," Prabin groused.

"Not all. They've got a few girl rappers and gay rappers to round out the diversity factor," Donny said.

"But queer is definitely a minority."

"Sure there's misogyny and homophobia." Donny shrugged. "There's even racism in rap. It's just racism with a black face. But that's not all rap is. Much of it's about self-esteem, which is what these kids need most. Nobody else gives that to them, so they give it to themselves."

"Then maybe they don't need an audience," Prabin said, ducking when Donny threw a pillow.

A cab arrived. The driver seemed a little fazed when they told him the address, as if he wondered why four well-dressed gay men would want to head into the battle zone. He took them to their destination, dropped them off, then turned around and zipped away as though he couldn't leave fast enough.

The club was in a ghetto, but Canadian style, meaning it was still relatively clean and orderly looking, despite having the city's highest murder rate. It was nothing Dan hadn't seen before, although in a neighbourhood like this he would normally be investigating a case, looking for one of the city's disappeared, not arriving in search of entertainment.

The giant at the door looked over the unlikely four-some with a foreboding smirk until Donny announced that they were guests of Lester Philips. Suddenly, his face lit up. He ushered them inside a cavernous space reverberating with the quickened pulses of restless teenagers.

Hip hop. Rap. Urban beat. It invoked fear in the hearts of the timid and the uninitiated, but clearly imbued a sense of excitement in the kids who were enjoying the scene unfolding around them.

The foursome did their best to blend in with the surroundings, feeling like outsiders stumbling on a strange new world. For the most part they were ignored by the crowd. The din was loud, eardrum-damage territory. Anger and aggression postured onstage as the performers proclaimed their message, seemingly just a step dividing reality from fantasy, the songs suggesting weapons could be props or lethal forces depending on the hands wielding them.

"I'm just glad I have my own police escort," Dan joked.

"I could probably arrest most of these kids right now if their stories are even half true," Nick said. "Everyone's got a posse and everyone's killed someone who dissed them."

Prabin shook his head. "I'd hate to be a kid these days trying to compete with this macho bullshit."

"It may be bullshit to us," Donny reminded him, "but just remember, it's real to them. Anyone with talent sees it as a ticket out of here."

There was a momentary lull as a well-groomed white kid took the stage. This was followed by scattered cheers as he, too, was accepted as one of the crowd. Tall and muscular, his torso framed by a sleeveless T-shirt, he towered over his bandmates. He shared the bling and the attitude with the other performers, but even from a distance his eyes flashed blue around the room. Boy-band material at its most nubile.

Dan could barely make out the words, which were intoned in a surprisingly soft voice. The boy's hands gesticulated in a way that seemed to refer variously to himself, to the crowd, and to his various body parts. It was a full-frontal come-on to the audience.

"Does the white guy qualify here?"

Donny shot him a baleful look. "Try not to make racist comments. If he's cool, the crowd will like him. If not, he won't be invited back."

"He looks like a baseball player."

"He *was* a baseball player. That's Mike Stud. Now he's a rapper."

Dan almost laughed. "He calls himself 'Stud'?"

"It means 'badass.' It means everyone wants to join his posse and get with him 'cause he's cool."

"Yeah, I can see that. Not to mention his biceps and those baby blues."

"Dude can't help it if he's pretty."

The boy finished his set and headed offstage as the sound ramped up again. Lights blazed and swivelled over the audience. In another era, they might have been searchlights scanning for signs of revolt among prison-camp detainees.

"Keep it real! Keep it real!" the MC shouted out, as though an insurrection of phoniness threatened to break out.

The next performer picked up the mic and leered over the crowd. "Money, money ... where my dolla at?" he shouted, as the band broke into a frenzied rhythm. "Money, money ... Ain't in my pocket. Whatchoo tryin' to dockit?"

Dan looked around and saw half the crowd mouthing the words along with the rapper. Others raised fists in support of his credo.

"They understand this song?" he asked.

Donny rolled his eyes. "Obviously they understand it. It's not about proper grammar. It's about communicating to the masses. It's about keeping it out of the hands of the government."

"Well, that certainly explains a lot about the world."

"Okay, smart guy. This is the beat of the street. These kids understand one another. You and me and Nick and Prabin are just a bunch of privileged gay men with voyeuristic intentions. If we don't get it, it's because it's not about us. It's the poor talking to the poor."

"Poor I understand. Where I come from, dude."

"Yeah, apart from that."

Dan smiled. "So, you're saying what we're doing is cultural appropriation. Slumming it. Crossing 110th Street for the night."

"No, what we're doing is supporting a good cause. We are art patrons."

The money-obsessed rapper left and the MC returned. "Special night, we got M-Power," he called out, as the crowd livened up. "Y'all know M-Power!"

The crowd cheered as a young man ambled onstage with a horn.

"There he is!" Donny shouted, the very picture of a proud father.

Along with Lester, the band members were a tall, thin bass player and a tiny keyboardist who looked prepubescent but played like a professional. The group's message was a mix of love and anger, more flowers than revolt. The anger was focused on self-empowerment and lending a hand to the less fortunate. Nothing about burning down the city or killing people, Dan noted with relief.

The sound was tight, the lyrics thoughtful. It was far more than just slogans and anthems, with a nod to making the world a better place, starting with "the man," which Dan took to mean one's self. A little Ghandi never hurt, even in ghetto slang.

The set lasted for three songs. M-Power retired as the final group took the stage. Within minutes, Lester was heading through the crowd toward them, high-fiving everyone. He gave Donny and Prabin a hug.

When he came to Dan, he leaned in and said, "Got someone for you to meet, Uncle Dan."

Dan's curiosity was piqued.

Lester turned to the young man at his side. Dan recognized the band's diminutive keyboardist. Up close, he looked like he might be in his twenties, if just.

"This is Taejon. He writes most of our tunes. Taejon, this is Dan Sharp, the guy I told you about."

Taejon took Dan's hand and shook. "Good to meet you."

"I like your music," Dan said. "Smart lyrics. Tight sound."

Taejon nodded. "Thanks, man. Appreciated. So listen. Why I asked Lester about you? I saw this story on TV about these government dudes. He said it's you, yeah? Trying to find some guy?"

"It's possible. I am looking for someone whose husband is in government."

"So, maybe I know something, yeah? My cousin, Sam the Brother, he was another rapper. Sam sold to them badass dudes at city hall. The mayor and them, yeah? I told him to leave that shit alone, but he got his sorry self killed. Nigga didn't learn fast enough."

"Sorry to hear," Dan said, thinking of the notorious mayor and his rampage across public morality and decorum. Outspoken, racist, and maverick, yet his popularity scored highest among the lower-class kids and immigrants he abused verbally. It took all kinds.

"My cousin's friend, he called himself D-Rap. D-Rap knew these guys. Only he ducked from the scene before he got nabbed. Then he got righteous."

"D-Rap was a badass rapper before he got religion," Lester butted in. "He was an awesome performer."

"He's still awesome," Taejon corrected. "But now all this God stuff come out of him, like he's possessed. Now he don't perform. Be like, 'I just sit at home and wait for messages from God.' Whatever, dude."

The concert ended and the crowd began breaking up. Taejon continued the tale of his dead cousin out on the street.

"When my cousin got iced, D-Rap said he might like to talk to someone about it. He told me. So now I'm telling you."

Taejon looked at Dan dead on: message delivered.

"Where can I find D-Rap?" Dan asked.

"I can put you in touch."

"Tell him I'd like to meet him."

"Then you will." Taejon nodded and left.

Nick and Prabin went to the corner to hail a taxi. Donny waited till they were out of earshot.

"You're going after the Ford brothers now?"

Dan shrugged. "If that's what it takes."

"Stirring up the wasp's nest."

"I am a WASP, after all."

"In case I've never said it before? Stay out of this one. You'll get hurt."

"Oh. I see. Like I couldn't figure that out."

"I'm serious," Donny said. "You need someone to protect you."

Dan shrugged. "That's why I'm marrying a cop."

FOURTEEN

The Other Mrs. Wilkens

THE PHONE WAS INSISTENT: *Unknown Number*. Wary client or potential stalker? It was hard to tell. Dan was busy typing up some notes. He ignored it twice, then picked up on the third time around.

"Mr. Sharp?"

"Yes?"

"This is Anne Wilkens. I'd like to speak with you. In private. It's — it's about John. It's important. I promise."

Her voice was hesitant, vaguely insistent, pleading with him to come to her home.

"When?"

"As soon as possible. I'll explain when you get here."

Dan thought of the tottering widow he'd met at the Wilkens home two days earlier. She sounded different today. Maybe she wasn't drunk yet. It was still a bit early in the day.

"All right. I'm at my Leslieville office. You'll have to give me time to get there. Say, twenty minutes?"

"Yes, thank you. I'll be waiting. And ..."

"Yes?"

"Nothing. I'll explain when you get here."

He hung up and looked out the window. The sky threatened rain, promising a dismal day ahead.

For once, traffic was good. He sped up Jarvis to Mount Pleasant and, after a few short turns, pulled into the circular drive in Rosedale. It had taken only seventeen minutes.

Standing on the stoop, he heard voices within. There was nothing he could make out distinctly, but they were animated. He raised his knuckles and rapped. The voices stopped and the door opened. There stood Mrs. Wilkens and her sister, both with guilty looks on their faces.

He'd interrupted something private. Family matters, a heated conversation. Clearly it was something too discreet for outside ears. Dan looked past the stern face of the school mistress who had barred his way on his first visit, addressing himself to the other sister.

"Mrs. Wilkens?"

The younger woman spoke first. "Forgive me, Mr. Sharp. I'm Anne Wilkens."

Dan looked from her to the older woman, who nodded.

"Please come in," Anne said. "I'll explain."

Dan entered and waited as she closed the door behind him.

"This is my sister, Doris."

The other woman — the one he'd known as Mrs. Wilkens — turned a corner and disappeared.

The real Anne Wilkens led him to the same room where they'd chatted the previous day. As they passed along the hallway, Dan looked through the open doorways. *No books*, he thought. *Is there no library in this house?*

She indicated a wing chair. "Please sit."

Dan declined her offer for tea. They stared at each other, alone in the room that time abjured. On the table, an oil lamp waited to be lit as though they were still in the nineteenth century. On the reading desk, pictures of the dead congregated like holy relics on an altar. Somewhere, a clock ticked its theory of the forward motion of time. Profanation, a heretic in the House of God.

"I'm sorry for lying to you," she said. "The media has been hounding me since my husband's death. My sister and I got into the habit of switching roles. For my sake, I mean."

"I'm sure that's very kind of her, Mrs. Wilkens."

"Please, call me Anne."

"Anne, then."

While she was less severe than on his first visit, she looked even more miserable. Perhaps due to her deception, perhaps to her widowhood. Dan was struck by his own current state of grace, sharing life with the redoubtable Nick. Loneliness was never enviable.

Anne Wilkens clasped her hands together, thumbs beneath her chin. "You're probably shocked at my deception —"

Dan interrupted her. "I'm never shocked at what people do or say, but thank you for being honest with me now."

He settled in the chair, wondering where this was going.

"It was foolish of me to try to deceive you," she began. "I wasn't sure why you had come to see me the other day.

Despite what your card said, I was reluctant to believe you were a private investigator. But I looked you up and saw your website."

She turned and glanced at the window. Lead glass, Tudor style. Outside, the rain began to spit; the diamond panes were illuminated against the slate of the sky.

"Forgive me. This is hard for me. I've been avoiding the truth. Avoiding John. I haven't even been to his grave since the funeral."

Dan thought of the photographs, the ligature marks around her husband's neck, her conviction he had not taken his own life.

"Take your time."

"I had an affair." She shook her head. "No, not really. Let me explain. We met a few times in a downtown restaurant. I wasn't worried, it wouldn't have been out of line for me to meet with a man in public. Just business."

"Is this what you and your sister were arguing about just now?"

"You heard? Yes. She doesn't want me to tell you this."

Dan watched her confusion give way to something loftier. Grief and desolation. The grief he'd thought missing on her sister's face when he'd believed her to be the widow.

"You asked if my husband felt threatened. I'm not sure he did, but something happened to me that I think you should know about."

She turned back to the window. The rain lashed against it in sudden gusts.

"At first I didn't connect it with … with what happened. But later, after I began to think clearly again, it all started to fit. It had to do with the man I met."

"Can you tell me what happened between you?"

"Nothing!" she broke in. "Really, nothing happened, but we kept in touch. He … he was sympathetic. He asked me things about John and his work."

"What sort of things? About accounts?"

"Yes … and other things." Her eyes lowered. "John had said something was awry with the books. I didn't pay much attention at the time. I never questioned his honesty, so if there were mistakes I assumed he would fix them." She paused. "I think he meant there were irregularities on someone else's part and he was looking into it."

"Does this have anything to do with the power plant cancellations?"

She looked up in surprise. "I think it does, indirectly. The money John was accused of stealing went missing later, but he said there were documents missing to do with the cancellations. Documents that might have proved the cover-up was deliberate and who was behind it. He felt it was key to the whole thing."

"And you told him about it. This other man?"

"Yes." She hugged herself tightly. "My husband and I … did not have a strong sex life. That's why … that's why it happened. This sort of thing was new to me. I was so taken by this man. Once when we were sitting together in a restaurant he reached over and took off my glasses. Then he blew on the lenses and polished them with his handkerchief while staring directly at me. It was … strangely intimate." She laughed unhappily. "That must sound absurd."

"No. Keep going."

She nodded. "My sister had just come back into our lives. We hadn't spoken for many years. You see, I stole John from my sister."

"How did you steal him?"

"He was dating Doris. She was very glamorous back then. Even though she was older, they were planning on marrying. I was so jealous that I purposely made him fall in love with me. I thought I deserved him more than she did. Doris was heartbroken." She covered her face with her hands. "I didn't realize how awful it would be for her. She's had a hard life since then. There's been nobody for her. Only I didn't deserve him. Clearly, or I wouldn't have let myself be seduced by someone else."

Dan looked past her to the rain pelting the window. He imagined the body of a hanged man swaying beneath a bridge, a bride jilted at the altar. Life was full of surprises, not all of them kind. It was harder still when you felt condemnation from the dead on top of everything else. They couldn't forgive you even if they wanted to.

"What was his name, this man? Are you still in contact with him?"

"He called himself Mark. I never knew his last name. I haven't heard from him since John died."

"Not surprising. How were you in touch with him?"

"He phoned me. The numbers were always different. I remember hearing a variety of sounds in the background. Traffic, what sounded like a children's playground. Once I heard church bells ringing. Another time a dog."

"He was using different cellphones while walking around the city." He held her glance. "Was John ever here when he called?"

"No. It was as if he knew when John was at work. Maybe he was watching the house and knew when I was on my own."

"It's possible. Did he ever come here to the house?"

"No, never. I would have panicked."

"He probably knew that. Where did you meet him?"

"It was at the dry cleaner's. He held the door open for me on the way out. It wasn't that I found him attractive — he was really very ordinary looking — but he was powerful in some way that excited me."

"Was it on your way out or his?"

"Mine. I just assumed he was a customer coming into the shop and that we had met by accident."

"And he was just going in?"

"Yes."

"Did he have any dry cleaning in his hands?"

Her mouth fell open. "No. He wasn't carrying anything. He didn't even go in. Once we started talking, he just stayed outside with me. Then we left."

"It wasn't an accident. He was following you."

She nodded. "I should have thought of that."

"He set you up. Who knows how long he'd been following you around, looking for an opportunity to meet. When did this happen?"

"It was ... about a year and a half ago. I think."

Dan was inclined to believe her, otherwise her story would have been smoother, more precise in the telling and full of solid details: times, dates, places.

"In all your conversations with him, did he ever tell you anything about himself? Anything personal?"

"Just one thing that I can recall. He told me he'd lost his

wife two years before. Of course, I felt sorry for him. What a fool I was." She smiled bitterly. "When I think back on everything we talked about, I don't even have a sense of his political opinions, whether he was rich or poor. Nothing like that. I just felt that this was an ordinary man whose life was lived outside the bullring of politics. He seemed so sincere. Someone I could unload my frustrations on and never have to worry about them being told to anyone else." She looked embarrassed. "I wasn't looking for sex."

"Did he strike you as someone who might have been in media? A journalist after a scoop? A friend of Simon Bradley's, for instance?"

"Not at the time or I would have run a mile away from him, though I've wondered about it endlessly ever since." Her brow furrowed. "I guess that's why he caught me off guard. He just seemed like a kind, concerned person."

"How did you come to be talking about your husband?"

"My ring." She held up her left hand. "It was being cleaned, so I wasn't wearing it at the time. I won't take it off now —" She caught herself. "We'd been talking for a while when I realized I might have given him the impression that I was single. I had already decided to have an affair with him and then changed my mind about three times during the conversation. I thought I had better make my intentions clear at that point. I told him my husband was in politics. He seemed interested, but only in a casual sort of way. I guess I was trying to impress him when I talked about John's position in government." She looked away. "As I said, I was very foolish."

If she wanted consolation, Dan wasn't about to give it to her.

"And you think because of this your husband was set up to look as though he had stolen from public accounts?"

"I think my husband discovered something and this man knew about it. And I confirmed it for him. Then to cover it up, they blamed it on John, ruined his reputation, and ... and killed him." She shuddered. "Do you think I'm crazy?"

"I don't think that." Dan touched her hand. "Have you told the police?"

"No." It was a whisper. "I was too ashamed."

"They should be told. It may help in the investigation. For what it's worth, I believe you. I saw the coroner's photos. His fingernails were shredded. I think your husband was fighting for his life, not trying to kill himself to evade responsibility."

She looked up. Her eyes brightened momentarily. "Do you think they can find this man?"

"Impossible to tell at this point. Maybe if you give them a description, it will help. It doesn't mean they'll clear your husband's name. They may never be able to prove what happened to the missing money."

She touched his sleeve. "Thank you for listening to me. I wasn't asking for absolution, I just wanted to tell someone, I guess. I know you're the right person. I'm not expecting to be forgiven."

"It's not my place to forgive. In any case, you couldn't have known what you were getting into. You just have to forgive yourself."

"Yes. Thank you again."

Dan stood and looked around. *No books*, he thought. *There are no books in this house.* For a moment he imagined that in all of Rosedale there were no books other than bank-account books. Ridiculous, of course.

Dan debated for a while before making the call. He hated betraying a confidence, but sometimes there were extenuating circumstances. She hadn't asked him not tell anyone about her seducer, and he had convinced her to go to the police with the information, so it would come out at some point. Still, he thought, it might help convince Will that something peculiar really was going on at Queen's Park.

He put the phone to his ear. Will answered immediately. When Dan explained what he had just heard, Will swore aloud.

"Why didn't she say anything about it at the time?"

"She was ashamed," Dan said.

"If half the people who do stupid things stopped to think about it beforehand, considering where the shame might lead them should they be caught …" He stopped. Dan thought the line had gone dead, then he heard Will laugh lightly. "They would probably still do the thing they shouldn't do, wouldn't they?"

Dan agreed. "In any case, I've convinced her to go to the police with the information."

"She has no choice, really."

"In the meantime, can you see if you can find any connection between Tony and John for me? Just to see if there's anything there at all. Tony seems to have got his hands on a large amount of money and then gambled it away. According to Peter Hansen, the money didn't come from him. There's got to be something in that."

Will sighed. "All right. I'll make a few discreet inquiries. Although I can't guarantee how far this will go once I start to dig into it. Especially now that it raises further questions about missing funds."

"I understand. Do what you can. And thank you, Will. Sorry for putting you on the spot."

"That's my job, isn't it?"

FIFTEEN

The Rapture

THE RAIN HAD LET UP, BUT THE sky was ragged with clouds. Dan fought traffic all the way back to his office, thinking about what Anne Wilkens had told him. It made sense, but something still bothered him about her story. He couldn't put his finger on it. There was the obvious fact that she and her sister had lied to him about their identities, but she at least had decided to come clean. He was still pondering the question as he pulled into the lot behind his building.

Upstairs, he made a few calls to see if Tony Moran had shown up on anyone's radar, officially or otherwise, but no one had anything new to tell him. There were still a few loose ends to clear up, including booking his flight to B.C. in a week and a half, before he could head home. Anne's story stole his focus while he puttered about, making it difficult to concentrate. He kept coming back to her tale of the would-be lover. Clearly, she believed her husband had been murdered because of her indiscretion about something he knew. Simon Bradley was adamant about the same thing, despite coming at it from a different perspective.

Still, the pieces weren't quite pulling together. Will had scorned the idea of an invisible Magus, while Peter merely admitted to having heard rumours. And yet Tony's texted conversation clearly spoke of the Magus as an acknowledged fact. Where did the truth lie?

Dan had just finished booking his flight online and was struggling to print his electronic tickets when his cell dinged with an incoming message. At first he didn't recognize the word he saw, then he realized it was a name: *Taejon*. The text from Lester's bandmate was brief, if inventive: *U want 2 meet ma cuzin's friend, yah? Can do for u. Call on the corner Queen @ Ontario in 1 hr. Come alone. Pick up the phone. It's kool.*

Dan found himself smiling as he interpreted the note. *If this generation doesn't shatter the English language beyond all recognition*, he thought, *then there might be hope for the next one to kill it entirely.*

His printer was humming nicely. He looked over the dates and times as the sheet fed into his hands: *Toronto–Vancouver/Vancouver–Toronto*. It would mean time away from Nick. The thought gave him pause. Even if it was only for a few days, they'd been attached at the hip for so long it would feel strange to be on his own again.

He turned back to the text. One hour, it said. He checked his watch. It was just past seven. He texted back to confirm.

Lester had said Taejon's cousin's real name was Javon Williams. He had had Nick look up his record in the police files. *A rapper's rap sheet*, Dan mused, *while a copper taps out the beat*. What he'd seen had been a revelation, to say the least. Nick wasn't going to like to hear he was going to meet the notorious rapper alone. He considered what to say before dialing Nick's cell.

"Hi, hubby-to-be. It's your one and only."

"I'm suspicious. You only call when there's bad news."

"Such faith you have in your beloved. I sometimes call you with the baseball score."

"True enough, but that's usually bad news, too."

"You're right. I'm calling to tell you I won't be home for supper tonight."

A loud groan came from the phone.

"I'm cooking my heart out for you right now."

"I'm sure I'll love it even more if you can wait till later."

"Angel hair pasta usually isn't good a couple of hours late."

"Sorry, I'll pick something up while I'm out."

"No, don't do that. I'll wait. What's up?"

"I just got a text from Lester's bandmate, Taejon. He's setting something up for me to meet his cousin's friend, the rapper from hell."

"Dan, are you serious? Do you want me to come? That guy's dangerous. I don't like the thought of you going to meet him alone."

They'd had prickly but inconclusive discussions on Nick's propensity to interfere in what Dan thought of as his business.

"I'll be okay. Taejon guarantees that everything's cool."

Nick snorted. "And you think that makes it all right?"

"You're right, you are suspicious and I only call with bad news. By the way, I've just come back to my office after spending almost an hour talking to John Wilkens's widow. She and her sister were playing switcheroo games on me. Turns out Doris is Anne and Anne is Doris."

"Is this supposed to make sense?"

"Not really, but thanks for listening. The weird thing, though," Dan continued, "is that Anne Wilkens — the real widow — thought she was having an affair with another man, only it turns out he wasn't interested in her. He was only interested in what she could tell him about her husband. She says John knew something about the cover-up of the power plant cancellations and when she told this man, her husband was killed."

Nick whistled. "Think she's right?"

"I think — now that I've met the real Mrs. Wilkens — that she might be onto something. I sent her to the nearest police precinct to talk to the nice man there."

"Good advice. Glad you're not trying to handle that one yourself."

"No, but it's tempting."

Nick let that hang in the air for a few seconds. "You're scaring me, Dan. You've already said people are dying over this. Please be careful."

"Always."

"And keep your cellphone handy."

"I will."

It was coming on twilight as Dan reached Moss Park. People were milling about in groups of twos and threes in the growing gloom, standing on the sidewalks and in the middle of the road, hawking their wares. Drugs, guns, girls. Dan had certainly been on better streets than these. Hell, he'd grown up on better streets, and that was in Sudbury's Flour Mill district, hardest of the hard in a bleak mining town. Around here even the convenience stores seemed to be trying to stay invisible. He would keep Nick's advice in mind and not relax his guard.

It never ceased to amaze him where he found himself digging up dirt and sniffing down cracks to discover whatever it was he might be looking for — in this case the friend of a dead rapper who knew Donny's adopted son Lester. The chain linking one person to another was often elusive and hard to grasp, but you never knew where it might lead.

Taejon's dead cousin, known locally as Sam the Brother, had grown up in Lawrence Heights in the city's northwest, not far from the nightclub where Lester's band had performed. At eighteen, Sam had joined one of the local gangs, the Gatorz. Between the Gatorz and the Five Point Generalz, their members had racked up an impressive number of the area's homicides.

Someone had interviewed Sam the Brother for an article on violence in his neighbourhood. "This ain't no organized crime centre. This here the Jungle," he said, giving the district its street name. "We at war, but it's *dis*organized crime run this place," he laughingly told the reporter. A month later, he was dead.

The dead rapper was trouble, with a career-criminal background long enough for more than one public enemy. But the live rapper Dan was about to meet was even more troubling: an African émigré who'd had a long list of charges thrown at him — sexual assault, forcible confinement —

with all but one, that for drug peddling, tossed out of court. Darkest of all were allegations of human trafficking. Out of the blue, however, the career-criminal-slash-rapper who called himself D-Rap had transformed overnight into a law-abiding, peace-loving citizen. *No accounting for strange*, Dan thought.

He got to the corner of Queen and Ontario streets just before eight. A few minutes later a nearby pay phone rang, one of the last in the city. It was like a scene from a spy movie. Dan picked it up and listened to the caller's smoky voice. The instructions were simple: walk one block to the corner of Parliament and Queen, be there for 8:15. He was to hang out on the northwest corner across from Marty Millionaire, the sprawling vintage furniture store, and wait for someone who, if they liked his look, might approach him. Oh, yeah: *And stay cool, brother!*

That was it.

Dan was naturally wary wherever he walked, but he was not, generally speaking, afraid for his safety in downtown Toronto. Having slate-grey eyes and a scar dangling from his temple eased up on the pressure to appear tough to anyone who might mistake him for prey. Tonight, however, he was very much on his guard.

The men who hung about on the streets of Moss Park were for the most part transients and homeless types, the ones you would see hanging around in the early mornings looking for casual employment outside the Followers Mission. They were mostly of the friendly persuasion. The prostitutes could be pretty harsh, Dan knew, but so, too, could the proprietors of long-time establishments like Coffee Time, whose owner had recently been arrested for selling crack along with coffee and donuts. Once again, it took all sorts.

Dan checked his watch: 8:05. Still a few minutes to kill before his would-be greeter showed himself. He took a stroll down Ontario Street. The gloom was sepulchral, the streetlights of the dimmest wattage available. Gas lamps would have provided better illumination. He understood why the residents were up in arms lately. It hadn't been long since a nurse had been shot on these same streets coming home from the hospital early one morning. Even that hadn't convinced the city to provide better lighting. Perhaps a renewed letter-writing campaign by locals would do the trick, but he doubted it.

As he emerged onto Richmond, a car slowed. Its driver looked him over. Not a pleasant-looking face. Dan felt a surge of adrenaline as the vehicle ground to a stop beside him.

Things happened quickly, as Dan would later tell Nick. A second man leaped out and came at him with a tire iron. Small and wiry, not much more than a teenager, but extremely agile. Dan's eyes were camera-like, taking staccato shots of everything: black Mazda, licence plate 239 RDC; the assailant white, early twenties; five-ten, dark hair, flattened nose, dark eyes.

He ran straight at Dan, the iron raised. The first blow missed Dan's shoulder by an inch as he dodged to the left. The second came down on his forearm. He grabbed the bar as tremors shot through his limb, but he hung on, twisting and wrenching the iron from his attacker.

They struggled for possession of the bar, grappling with it as if they were trying to get past it to reach one another directly. Dan's grip proved stronger. He shoved his attacker off balance. Having lost his advantage, the man turned and dashed back to the car. Dan ran after him, heedless of the voice in his head saying he could be carrying a gun. The Mazda was already peeling away from the curb as his assailant leaped inside and fought to close the door. Dan raised the iron and brought it down on the rear windshield with all his strength, shattering the glass in every direction. He had one last look at his attacker's face as he turned in fright. Kids, really. No professional would be so messy.

As the car raced off, Dan flung the iron after it. It bounced off the trunk and went clanging along the ground. He felt adrenaline coursing through him, his heart pounding. The entire episode had taken less than a minute. He leaned forward, hands on knees, catching his breath and panting with the effort.

So much for staying cool.

He pulled out his cellphone and dialled 911, quickly relating the details, how a black Mazda with a smashed rear windshield and two male occupants had just attacked a pedestrian at the corner of Ontario and Richmond. The dispatcher kept him waiting for a moment. When he came back his voice was skeptical.

"Sir, are you sure that was the correct licence number?"

"Absolutely," Dan sputtered.

"And you're sure the car was a black Mazda?"

"A black Mazda RX-8." Dan felt his impatience growing. "Yes, I'm sure about both."

"They don't match, sir," said the world-weary voice.

Dan felt disgust rise in his throat. *Of course, you idiot!* he wanted to scream. *Run a trace!* "Then they've switched the plates. Put out a bulletin looking for a black Mazda with a smashed back window heading west."

He hung up feeling angry, exhilarated, and frustrated all at once.

His watch read 8:13. He had two minutes to get to the corner and meet his designated greeter. It occurred to him that he could've been set up, and that maybe the attack was the only greeting he would be getting tonight, friendly or otherwise. There was only one way to find out.

He was on the corner at 8:15. Three middle-aged women milled about waiting for a streetcar. Seconds later, four teenagers spilled from the doorway of the Souvlaki Express, laughing and joking among themselves. Dan couldn't pick out a single person who seemed to be sizing him up or preparing to meet him. Then he looked across the street. A solitary figure sat in the window of No Bull Burgers, staring out at him from behind dark glasses. *Gotcha*, he thought.

Dan watched as his contact left the burger joint and crossed the street, holding out a hand to stop a car racing through the yellow light. It swerved. The figure kept on course without so much as a glance backward. Moses parting the Red Sea.

"You Dan?"

He recognized the husky voice on the phone.

"Yes."

The glasses came off, the better to see him with. "You wanna see somebody, yeah?"

"I'm here to meet D-Rap."

"Ain't no D-Rap. Not no more." She laughed, not unkindly. "He the Rapture now, see?"

Dan was not sure he did see, but he wasn't about to leave. She looked at his torn lapel.

"You had some trouble?"

"Yes, I did have some trouble. Two guys in a black Mazda attacked me with a tire iron."

"They not our people." She shook her head sadly, as though someone had just littered the sidewalk. "Ought not be bringing this shit down on the neighbourhood."

Her eyes seemed to take in the sad high-rises, the dilapidated storefronts up and down the street, as though the area were an oasis of beauty and tranquility. Still, peace and security were not to be sneezed at in any borough when you called it home.

"Some good people live hereabouts. We got our community gardens over back of that lot." She pointed to a spare bit of ground. "We also got community days when we all get together and share what we grow. We even have a public pizza bake, you dig? This ain't no place to be hurtin' people."

"You should tell the guys who attacked me. What's your name?"

"Serenity."

She replaced her sunglasses and ducked down an alley. Pausing for a moment, she pulled out a lighter, flicked it, and motioned him forward.

So, here he was on his way to a meeting with someone called the Rapture, after being attacked by two thugs wielding a tire iron. A woman named Serenity was leading the way wearing sunglasses and carrying a cigarette lighter. The whole thing was beginning to take on the overtones of a very goofy Hollywood thriller. Could anything else surprise him tonight?

He followed her unexpectedly quick footsteps to the back door of a high-rise. They stepped inside. Someone had smashed the bulb in the entryway. By the flickering light he saw that the stairwell was littered with garbage and the walls covered in the usual splashes and slashes of graffiti. In his day it had been *Johnny loves Jean,* or at worst *Dan loves dick.* Now it was a world of colourful whirls and swirls, like being stuck in a kaleidoscope. It felt like a place that had seen many inhabitants, but had been loved by none. He wondered how many drugs and guns were run up and down these stairs. A promising young football player, a local hero, had been shot to death in one of the nearby buildings not long ago, Dan recalled. The sad thing was that no one really knew why. But then murderers didn't usually announce their reasons, at least not publicly.

"Does the Rapture live here?" Dan asked, as much to make conversation as to keep himself on track.

Serenity turned and held up the lighter to see him better. "That like asking where God live. Nah, he don't live here. He just come to meet you. He a big deal, you know."

"I gathered that. From his name and all."

"The Rapture be like the real thing."

Dan wasn't sure what that implied — maybe not Coca-Cola — but whether she meant he was a true representative of God, a celebrity in the rap world, or just a big deal in the urban ghetto remained to be seen.

They passed a couple of small boys playing with matches on one of the landings between floors. Serenity gave the kids a weighty glance and they scurried off.

"You nasty," she called after them, waving a finger in admonition. "Don't be killing people with that fire."

They exited on the ninth or tenth floor — Dan had lost count — and stopped in front of a door with a portrait of a blindfolded woman painted on it. The figure held a flame in her hands and seemed to be fading in and out of the dusk. Dan looked at his guide and thought he saw a likeness there.

Serenity rapped once then turned the handle. They entered a room lit by dozens of candles, outfitted with rattan rugs and fabric hangings like the tent of a visiting sultan. A melody floated ethereally through the air, borne aloft on unseen currents. An irregular grey shape stretched across a far wall. Drawing closer, Dan guessed it was a hippopotamus skin, cracked and wrinkled as a dry riverbed. It emitted a rank smell that reminded him of potent hashish.

The only incongruity, if it were an incongruity, was the Harley-Davidson perched dead centre in the room. Five hundred pounds of customized chrome, steel, and rubber, with a pair of tusks adorning the handlebars like the bull horns he'd seen on truck hoods in the American south. They were placed as though on an altar, some obscure deity represented by their presence.

Serenity turned a corner into another room where a large man lay sprawled on a sofa. He was shirtless, in a feathered vest, with black-and-orange ankara pants. A bright blue fez sat on his head. The man's eyes turned to Dan. His lips rippled lightly. A smile, not a smile.

"Mr. Marlow, I presume. You've come upriver to see about the rivets?"

It was an educated accent. The voice seemed to emanate from a blob of jelly.

"I'm not —" Then he caught the reference: Conrad.

"No matter," said the man. "Try not to choke, just my little joke. Ain't no yolk been broke."

A jester, then. He nodded to Serenity. "Thank you, my dear."

There was silence for a moment. The door closed behind them.

"My intended," said the man.

Dan took a step forward. "I'm Dan Sharp," he said, unsure whether to offer a hand. At the last moment he decided not to, nodding instead.

The man on the sofa watched him intently.

"Dan the man," he intoned. "I am Dan, Dan I am. You be, I be, we be Dan." He laughed suddenly. "And I am the Rapture. The Rapture capture Dan the man. Welcome, Dan I am."

He gestured slowly with one hand, as though offering Dan to partake of all he could see. On his chest, the outline of an eagle spread its wings. *Always a frigging eagle*, Dan thought. *Why never a cockatiel or a lowly sparrow?* On his forearm, tattooed strands of barbed wire encased the verses of Psalm 23. Enlightenment in chains. It seemed the whole world was angry these days. Dan could relate.

The Rapture followed his gaze. "You are my guest. Be at rest, ain't no test."

It was feeble rhyming, little more than the linguistic tricks of Dr. Seuss. If that was the extent of his rapper schtick, Dan thought, it wouldn't hold a candle to the names on the world's stage.

"Sit."

Dan glanced at one of several footstools. Sitting would have placed him several inches below the Rapture. There were no other seats in the room.

"I'll stand, thanks."

"As you wish. I understand you've come about a certain question of … law."

"In a manner of speaking. I was told you know something about the death of a man named Sam the Brother. I understand he was your friend."

The Rapture regarded him intently. "What of it?" he asked abruptly.

"I'm looking for a man named Tony Moran who seems to have gotten himself in trouble. It's possible that Sam had something to do with the men who are looking for Tony, possibly to harm him."

The Rapture continued to stare. "I did the dance with Death, but she went away bereft, 'cause I won the con-*test*."

He waited to see if Dan caught his meaning.

"You outsmarted somebody," Dan ventured.

"Indeed. Know this. The Rapture don't dance when he ain't in a trance. Ain't none but the King make him do that thing, make the Rapture sing like a shing-a-ling. You dig?"

Dan nodded. "I dig. Someone asked you to do something you didn't want to do. You refused. Are you afraid of them?"

He seemed affronted. "I fear no man nor devil."

"Then you're either very brave or you're a fool."

The Rapture's lips parted with scorn. "You be your own invention, ain't no prevention. You choose your own reality inside the vanity. This life no man can ever know, 'cause they only see the woe, nowhere to go in this political show."

He bared his teeth in what passed for a grin. "The man with the yellow collar, he loved him the dollar. The immigrant man, he ain't got no thing, but the immigrant no swing from the bridge like bling."

Dan thought about John Wilkens hanging from the coiled yellow rope. "That's impressive," he said.

The Rapture eyed him. "So you understand what we are talking 'bout?"

"Yes," Dan said. "I understand. Who was it came to you?"

For a moment, Dan thought he saw a trace of fear betrayed on the Rapture's features.

He shrugged. Not worth losing sleep over. "They knew about my drug charges. Said they could get me off and that I'd get a thousand. D-Rap, he need the money. They put the bills in a bin and walked away. There was a gun with it."

"Who left it there?"

Another shrug. "Said he'd protect me. Said he knew people high up in government. Called himself the Magus or some shit like that. Ain't no rapper name."

"Do you know who he is?"

"Don't know no names. Names not important. They come to the Rapture when he still D-Rap, see? They say, kill us the man in the stone house. But God say, 'No, D-Rap, you don't do this thing. You no more D-Rap, you the Rapture now. You stay true to my word, I be true to thine.' So they went to another name of Sam the Brother, and say, 'Do this thing. Here plenty of bling, if you make the man swing.' So he did and now we know, he down in the ground, ain't make no more sound. Sam the Brother is gone. Let that be a lesson to all who folla the dolla."

The Rapture let out a cackle, his flesh jiggling.

Dan heard the door open behind him. Serenity had returned. His interview was almost at an end.

"And you?" Dan asked. "What do you follow?"

"Me?" The Rapture laughed again. "I follow the Lord. The Lord provides, even here in the ghetto."

"And that's all you need now?"

The Rapture nodded. "I ain't got much, just a roof over my head. But let this be said, it no matter because …" He held up a finger and stared at Dan intently. "Mistah Kurtz — he ain't dead."

SIXTEEN

Dirty Little Secrets

NICK WAS SITTING AT THE kitchen table. The word *glower* came to mind when Dan saw his expression. And probably not just because the angel hair pasta had wilted. There was definitely a scowl.

"Glad to see you back," Nick said. "Alive, I mean."

Dan had updated him by phone about the attackers on his drive home. It had mostly been a one-way conversation, with Nick's silences filling the void.

"I am indeed alive," Dan replied, rubbing his palms together. "And starvin', Marvin."

"Not to mention cocky. I was hoping for a little remorse, but instead you're cocky."

Dan tried to look contrite. "Just trying to lighten the mood a little. Sorry."

"Sorry and ...?"

"Yes, definitely sorry. I don't think I caught the second bit."

"How about, 'Sorry and I will definitely take you along next time I do anything dangerous'?"

"I'm sorry. I will definitely take you along. I promise."

"That's better."

Nick got up to throw more noodles into a pot of boiling water.

"Though in all honesty I wasn't expecting it to be dangerous," Dan said.

Nick sighed and turned back to him. "Then that just makes it worse, Dan, because you knew you were going to meet someone who is a part of the underworld."

"Formerly part of the underworld."

"Formerly. Whatever. You should have anticipated danger."

"Right. I'm sorry. Again." Dan tried for a smile. "Don't worry. This isn't my way of getting out of marriage. For the record, I have every intention of being around for the wedding."

"Oh, the good intentions clause. That's reassuring. Not." Nick glowered again. "And also for the record, I have no intention of spending all that money on a funeral for you instead of a wedding."

"I would hate for you to do that, but you might want to put that suit to good use."

"You really are infuriating." He caught sight of the bruise discolouring Dan's arm. "That's going to need looking after. Did you at least find out anything useful?"

Dan recapped the bizarre interview he'd had, struggling to describe the man who seemed to want to pass himself off as a modern-day Kurtz. Nick listened in silence, shaking his head when Dan related how the

Rapture said he'd been offered a gun to kill John Wilkens.

"They tried to coerce him on the basis of his drug charges," Dan added.

"Not uncommon with this type. So it may actually turn out that someone really is trying to fix elections?"

"Not elections. Reputations. To ensure that certain people cannot win their campaigns. That's what Simon Bradley thinks."

"Same thing, isn't it? Fixing elections before they get started?"

"Well, technically yes. But killing someone is different than sabotaging a reputation. John Wilkens's death could turn out to have been for entirely different reasons."

"Fair enough. But what do you intend to do about it? I mean, it's not your case, really. You're not being paid to look into this."

"True, but I can't just ignore what I know." Dan shrugged. "I've tried talking to several people, including an old friend at Queen's Park, but no one seems to want to take me seriously. Until now, only Simon Bradley and Anne Wilkens have believed that something is going on."

"Remind me again — what was that about the sisters' secret identities?"

Dan smiled. "Conspiracy theory three hundred and ninety-seven. They went out of their way to convince me that the older sister was married to John Wilkens when in fact it was the younger sister. Anne, the real Mrs. Wilkens, told me later how she stole John from Doris. Practically left her jilted at the altar, by the sounds of it. Apparently they hadn't spoken for years till Doris came back into their lives last year."

"And Doris still stands by Anne? Impressive, I'd say." He caught Dan's eye.

"Meaning?"

"Meaning they lied to you once. Who's to say they won't lie again?"

"I'm not sure what they would have to gain."

Nick shrugged as he drained the pasta, then tossed it in a marinara sauce and placed it on the table.

"Well, as an officer of the law, I feel I ought to remind you that people who lie once will always lie."

"And when you were in the closet living with your ex-wife, weren't you lying about who you were?"

Nick screwed up in his mouth. "That's different. It was for my survival."

"Ah, the exemption clause. Everyone else should tell the truth, but I have an excuse."

Nick punched him on the shoulder. "Smartass. Shut up and eat."

The paving stones were cool and wet beneath his feet as Dan reached down to grasp the morning papers. It was a headline in the *Scene*, the city's alternative paper, that caught his eye: *Queen's Park allegations spreading.* The byline read *Simon Bradley*. He brought the paper inside and read quickly. The allegations of the cover-up at Queen's Park had snagged others, with investigations into missing emails and charges of hard drives wiped clean for the purpose of obscuring evidence. There was a mention of John Wilkens's involvement as the one who first cried foul. If this was all true, then Simon did have his finger on something, after all. It was the article's final sentence that made Dan stop: *Police also are questioning the late MPP's widow about her relationship with a man in connection with the financial scandal associated with her husband's office.*

He threw the paper down and grabbed his phone. It was Doris who answered.

"Good morning, Doris. This is Dan Sharp. I'd like to speak to Anne."

Her intake of breath was abrupt.

"Haven't you done enough damage?"

"Please put her on the line."

A hand was held over the receiver while a muffled conversation ensued. Finally, Anne Wilkens came on the line.

"Yes, Dan. This is Anne."

"Forgive my asking, but did you go to the police, as I suggested?"

"Yes, but it … hasn't turned out well, as you probably know. I wouldn't have gone if I'd known they would release the story to the press."

"Are you sure it was them? Did you tell anyone else about your affair?"

"No. Just you and then the police."

"And the police assured you confidentiality?"

"Yes, but … well, it hasn't turned out that way." She paused. "I'm sorry. I have to go. I have things to attend to."

"Wait. Just one more thing."

"Yes?"

"Did you speak to the police on the phone or in person?"

"I went down to the station and spoke to them in person, as you suggested. I really should go."

"All right. Thank you. I'm sincerely sorry for what's happened."

Dan thought back. Three days ago, Simon Bradley had appeared on the scene at Mount Pleasant Cemetery minutes after a call from Nick alerted Dan that Tony Moran's wallet had been found. Two days ago, Anne Wilkens told him of her so-called "affair" with another man. She'd assured him that no one but she and her sister knew of the affair, and clearly her sister wanted to leave it at that. Now, suddenly, it was public knowledge of a very embarrassing sort.

Coincidence? Not bloody likely, thought Dan.

Dan had the back of his phone off in seconds. When he couldn't locate anything other than what should be there, he opened a drawer and pulled out a magnifying glass. Still nothing. But that didn't mean much.

He pieced the phone back together and dialed Simon Bradley's number. Simon's voice answered, smoothly assuring the caller he would return the call as soon as possible. Dan left a curt message, then dialed Will Parker's number.

"Stupid question, Will," he said when his old friend came on the line, "but that matter we discussed the other day … about John Wilkens's widow. Did you mention it to anyone?"

Will hesitated. "If you're asking whether I tipped off anyone in the media, then no. Absolutely not. I saw Bradley's piece this morning and I've been fielding questions about it ever since. But I did speak about it with one of my higher-ups on the understanding it was completely in confidence. I doubt he'd breach that trust, Dan."

"Who was it?"

Will hesitated again.

"Come on, Will. I need to know."

"It was the Attorney General. Given the gravity of the subject I had to reveal what I knew. Hardly a likely source for scandal-mongering, if that's what it was."

Dan persisted. "Did you speak to him on the phone or in person?"

Will's lawyer side kicked in. "I don't mind answering your questions, but what is this about, Dan?"

"It's about me trying to determine whether my phone has been tapped. I was the sole source on this outside the Wilkens family until two days ago. Nobody else knew about this but me. And you are the only other person I told."

"Oh, brother!" Will said. "In that case, we can rule out my phone because I spoke to the Attorney General in person."

"Then it must have come from my phone or my office."

Will sighed. "Don't get paranoid, Dan. It could have come from elsewhere. The article mentioned the police."

"I advised Anne to talk to the police."

"Well, then. It could have come from a cop with loose lips."

"Possibly, but Simon Bradley has surprised me before with the information he's had access to."

"He's a radical journalist, so it's no surprise. There's no telling where his sources come from. I warned you about him. He's a slimeball. But how would he have tapped your phone?"

Dan thought back to the night they met. He'd briefly left his phone on the table in the diner while he paid his bill, but that was hardly enough time for Simon to take it apart and plant a bug. Then it struck him. The colossal stupidity! He'd downloaded an app to access Simon's article. Once it was downloaded, Simon could have sent a simple command putting Dan's phone under Simon's control. He recalled waking in the night and seeing the light fade on his cell, the phone warm but with no trace of a caller or message. That had to be it. What had been unthinkable spyware fifteen years ago was now in the hands of every parent monitoring their kid's communications. Without even touching Dan's phone, Simon could make it send and receive any kind of data: email, voice messages. It had been done easily enough to the royals, so it had probably been done to him.

"I downloaded an app he sent. All he would need is my number to forward an SMS from his phone to mine and he could control it without my knowing."

"Those are pretty serious charges —"

"If I can prove them. Which I probably can't."

"I still say someone else could have found out."

"I'd like to believe that, but it's not the first time he had access to information that only I knew."

"Try not to get worked up, Dan. These things happen in politics all the time."

Dan felt his blood pressure surge. "I'm not in politics, Will."

"You are now."

"In that case, it's time to pay Mr. Bradley a visit."

Nick had just come down to the kitchen and stood watching him.

"Who deserves a visit?"

"Simon Bradley."

"The journalist with the famous father?"

"Grandfather. I think he's been tapping my phone."

Nick put up his hands in protest. "Wait! This is getting way too serious. Why do you think that?"

"Remember how he just happened to show up at the cemetery after your call about Tony Moran's wallet? Simon always seems to know things he shouldn't about what I've been working on."

"If he's after a scoop, he could be listening in on the police radio. That's bad enough. But if he's tapped your phone, that's highly illegal."

"Yeah. It's also not very polite."

"Still cocky, I see."

"Occupational hazard. In any case, suspecting him is one thing, but proving it is another matter. I'm not some high-profile celebrity who merits a big investigation."

"You're hardly Prince Charles and Camilla Parker Bowles …"

"Or Sir Paul McCartney."

"Dunno … I've never heard you sing."

"You wouldn't want to. In any case, there's not much I can do about it at the moment."

"I can get someone from work to check out your phone. They're pros. The best there is."

Dan shook his head. "Bradley's never been near the house, so it would all have been done from afar. Nothing that can be traced easily. Still …"

"I would remind you of last night's conversation. Don't do anything I wouldn't do," Nick advised, gently rubbing the bruise on Dan's arm.

"No, I wouldn't do that."

"For the record, you worry me sometimes. Right now, you worry me a lot of the time."

"Admit it. It keeps you on your toes."

Nick watched Dan put on his coat. "Don't miss supper tonight."

"I promise."

SEVENTEEN

Simon Says

THE SCENE'S WEBSITE PROUDLY boasted about its independence from mainstream media. It had the whiff of puritanical zealotry: *We the knowing. We the free-thinking. We the upholders of truth.* From a free street corner rag, it had grown in over a decade to include a video news production house that made minor stars of people like Simon Bradley. The only problem, Dan found, was this sort of maverick political correctness did not respect individuality, but merely offered another kind of conformity. *Be like me,* is what it really said. *Think like me.* Somewhere, always, someone wanted to be the new messiah.

He found the address. The *Scene* was part of a complex on King Street East. By the time Dan got there, morning traffic had congealed like cholesterol in a meat-lover's arteries. It never failed to surprise him how people drove as though they were still living in the Toronto of thirty years ago, where in reality it was more like the Manhattan of thirty years ago, still far from good. It took fifteen minutes of crawling, barely containing his fury each time someone tried to bypass him in a side lane, to reach one of the underground Green-P parking lots. This was followed by another five minutes of circling till he found a free space.

The Confederation Life Building was a marvel of two-tone red sandstone and Romanesque Revival, one of the city's remaining treasures after the great fire of 1904. As downtown addresses went, it was one of the most desirable. Dan stood on the sidewalk looking up. *Must be nice to be a radical these days*, he thought. *I'd love to relocate here, though I probably couldn't afford it in about, oh, a million years.*

The directory sent him in search of the elevators, which ejected him onto the fourth floor. His footsteps were nearly soundless in the spacious corridors. The doorway was grand, opaque glass with a rippled texture and an oversized slogan: *The zine that's always on the* Scene! It looked like the headquarters of a multinational corporation. He entered and looked around. The room was full of over-earnest thirty-somethings with colour-streaked hair and ardent expressions. *Save the world and get famous doing it!* Someone bumped into him. He turned and caught a pile of papers before they tumbled to the ground.

A young man glared. "Dude, could you not stand there?"

Everybody had rules.

"Right, yeah. You're welcome."

At a counter to his left, a receptionist glanced up with a bored expression, as though challenging him to be interesting enough to make it worth her while. He'd barely finished asking for Simon when the reporter's head popped up from behind a divider. The hair was still cool, but the clothes were a little more casual today. His face showed surprise and fear.

"Dan, how ... well, how incredible to see you here. To what do I owe the pleasure?"

"I think you already know." He walked over and tossed the morning's paper on Simon's desk, dropping his cellphone on top. "I'm just wondering how you manage to know what I'm doing before I do half the time."

"I'm not sure what you mean."

"What do you think would happen if I turned my cellphone over to the police and asked them to find a link between the data it's been sending out to another number and yours?"

Simon smiled nervously. "Very little, I assure you."

Dan didn't know if he was more impressed or angered by the fact that Simon smiled as he said this.

"Do you think that will stop me from trying?"

Simon blew him off. "You're welcome to do whatever it takes. I hope you're not suggesting I'm guilty of such an offence. It runs counter to my moral beliefs, putting me on par with some sort of Axis of Evil. Metaphorically speaking, of course."

Dan leaned in close.

"You have been tapping my phone. That is a federal offence. Keep your nose out of my business or I'll break your fucking neck. Metaphorically speaking, of course."

Simon glanced around the office. "You realize you are threatening me in front of a roomful of witnesses."

Dan glanced around at the faces staring in open curiosity. These were the people, he knew, who would be front and centre during mass disruptions at any G12 convention. They'd be directly involved in attacks at the protests or, if not hands-on, then ready to report any goings-on. They would know their legal rights to a T and be as quick to use the law against anyone who stood in their way as they were to flaunt and disrupt it. A hotbed of rebellion and anarchy in the making. *And more power to them*, Dan thought. *Just not on my turf.*

"That's so you know I'm serious."

Simon shook his head. "Your allegations aside, instead of castigating me you should be co-operating with me." He lowered his voice. "Don't you wonder why Tony Moran disappeared? Ask yourself: what's the man's weakness? Answer: his husband."

"So?"

"A little convenient that he disappeared right before an election, don't you think?"

"How?"

"Dan, please. Tell me you don't still think John Wilkens's death was suicide." When Dan didn't contradict him, Simon relented. "Come with me."

Dan followed him to a small, private interview room. All eyes were on them as they made their way across the office. Dan wondered what Simon's co-workers made of Simon. His grandfather's reputation would not have done him much good here. Though groundbreaking in his day, Simon Bradley Sr. was old world and, therefore, status quo. Dan bet that this crew was against anything that smacked of hierarchy and privilege. Here Simon would have to prove his mettle. Dan felt a grain of respect for him. He looked again: he was just a kid, really. A kid with a big ambition to do better than his forebears. But there was danger in hubris.

Simon closed the door and gestured to a chair. Dan sat.

"It's a simple matter here at the *Scene*," Simon said proudly, nodding toward the outer office. "We're the little guy. We're independent. You may be aware that nearly all the news generated in North America is owned by one of six major news sources: News Corp, Viacom, CBS —"

"Spare me the lecture. I know the stats."

Simon looked disconcerted. No doubt he was used to being the expert when it came to radicalism. *We the free-thinking* ...

"Okay, then. You'll also know that apart from small independents like us, there are only a few people who decide what actually becomes news. That's why our work is important. We go against the grain of what's considered acceptable for public consumption. We dig in the dirt that others avoid."

"Some call it muckraking," Dan reminded him.

"I disagree. It's only after we expose anything of interest that the larger papers barge in with their muscle and money and try to take over. It's the David-and-Goliath syndrome. In this case, I've found what I believe to be a verifiable breach of just about every law and rule of government you can imagine. Politics is dirty business."

"'Power, corruption, and lies.' Isn't that what they say? So, why has no one else barged in until now?"

"Because John Wilkens's so-called 'suicide' stole the headlines. No one bothered to keep digging. No one but me. A year ago he was raising hell over a possible cover-up that turned out to be true, then he's suddenly accused of padding an expense account to the tune of tens of thousands of dollars. John was already a very wealthy man. It didn't make sense."

"As you said, politics is dirty business."

"Ask yourself who benefits most from Wilkens's death."

"His life insurance beneficiaries. That's probably his wife."

Simon shook his head sadly, as though the answer disappointed him. "I don't mean financially. Who benefits politically?"

"You tell me."

Simon looked past Dan's shoulder, out the window where his colleagues had their noses buried in computer screens. "The night John Wilkens died, he called me."

Simon held up a hand when he saw Dan's skeptical look.

"True. I swear. He was going to tell me what he knew about goings-on behind the scenes at Queen's Park. He never showed up. I didn't believe it when his death was declared a suicide two days later. I still don't believe it." He paused. "So ask yourself — who benefits?"

Dan shook his head.

"His opposition in government, that's who."

"Alec Henderson?"

"Yes, him. Wilkens was a rising star. He was becoming too well known and too powerful for them to ignore. If his allegations came out, it would have ruined Henderson."

"Oh, come on! You can't expect me to believe he was killed so Henderson could win the next election. That's fucking ridiculous."

"No. I'm saying he was killed him because he found out something that would have brought the whole government down. The cover-up was far more extensive than anyone knew. First the missing emails and now the hard drives wiped clean. What's next? You can't find what doesn't exist. But John found something. I think he found a paper trail. And I think it leads back to Alec Henderson."

"So?"

"Listen, I pored over most of the emails that were made public. There were thousands."

"And what did you find?"

Simon smirked. "Nothing. It's not what's there, but what's not there. Who's not named. As you said earlier, the premier and the energy minister conveniently retired from politics. But who didn't get fingered? Who is still in politics? That's what I want to know."

He glanced out the window at his virtuous, truth-chasing colleagues again. Never give your scoop away.

"John knew that someone had cost the province millions of dollars. Henderson worked on that portfolio as an adviser. He was tough and ambitious. He was trying to make his mark. Then along comes the scandal to the tune of nine hundred and fifty million dollars, and he goes quiet. Right after the premier resigns, there's an election. Lo and behold, Henderson gets a seat and he's whisked over to educational reforms and comes up all shiny and new. Just like Mr. Clean. Someone obviously had plans for him."

"Then why not just expose it and be done with it?"

"John was trying to, but they smeared him to make sure no one would listen to him. First it was a cover-up, then it was a frame. And then it was murder. There is a force out there, whether it's a man, a woman, or a group of people, who believe they can manipulate the way politics are run in this country. I can't prove it yet, but I will. And Tony Moran is going to lead me to it."

"Why Tony?"

"Because Tony has been in contact with the Magus." He paused, looking like the cat who swallowed the mouse who ate the cheese. "And I have been in touch with Tony."

"You spoke with Tony?"

"Yes. Twice."

Dan thought of the text exchange on Tony's cellphone. "Where is he?"

"He won't tell me. He phones only when he thinks it's safe to talk. He's afraid of the Magus."

Dan shook his head. Will had warned him about this sort of thing. Scandal-mongering, ludicrous conspiracy theories. "It's too far-fetched. If this were the U.S., I might believe it, but this —"

"But this is Canada. Yes, I know. And we're all wide-eyed and innocent. But we are next door to the biggest, most manipulative power broker in the world. Okay, except maybe for China. Who knows where this shit ultimately leads? But it still stinks. Think about it — are we going to stay naïve and foolish forever? It's time Canadians woke up to the political realities of the twenty-first century. It's time we started choosing our allies a lot more carefully than we've been doing. Peacekeepers of the World be damned. These are major powers, and there are people out there who are not going to let us be led down what they see as the wrong path. Do you really think none of those countries have considered our size, our resources, our proximity to the U.S.? Get real. You're the one who's dreaming, if you think I'm making this stuff up."

"Where's your proof?"

"I don't have it. Not yet." Simon shook his head. "Think about it. We know China has been spying on us for years. North Korea, Russia, too. It's in all the papers, not just the *Scene*. Provincial politics is the testing grounds in Canada. We're one step from federal politics, the people who run this country. There's a federal election coming up. My guess is that Henderson is going to be running for a seat in parliament."

"What does that prove?"

"Just think about it. Who is the most powerful person in the country?"

"The prime minister."

"Wrong." Simon shook his head. "The most powerful person in the country is the person who stands beside the prime minister. The chief of staff. The one who whispers in the prime minister's ear about the way things should be run. I think Alec Henderson wants to be that person, and I'm convinced someone has chosen to make it happen for him."

Dan considered this. "You realize you sound like a crazy person?"

"I admit it sounds crazy even to me, and I've been dealing with this crap for a decade now." He glanced at the window where his colleagues were diligently fact-checking and cold-calling. "In any case, I've heard a rumour."

"A rumour?"

"We'll call it that for now."

"Between gentlemen, as it were?"

"Forget about gentlemen. Between you and me, I think politicians are fucking arseholes. But it's the faces behind the scenes I don't trust. They're smart. They stay out of the spotlight, where the glare could expose every move they make."

"You seem to enjoy the spotlight, Mr. Bradley."

He snickered. "True, but as long as I'm still standing in it all is well. The moment I disappear you should start looking for whoever is behind a missing nine hundred and fifty million or so." Simon leaned his chin on his fist. "The thing is, Dan, you wouldn't be here if you didn't believe what I'm telling you. Don't let anyone tell you otherwise."

"Meaning?"

"Your friend Will Parker knows a lot more than he lets on."

Dan's eyebrows rose. "That's his job. I've known Will a long time and he's one of the good guys; he's on our side. If he were twenty years younger, he'd be working here with your lot."

Simon shrugged. "Nevertheless, there are forces at work in Queen's Park making things happen behind the scenes in ways we can only guess at. So, please, I'm begging you. I know your reputation and I know I can trust you. Give me a chance to prove the same thing to you in return."

"Would you trust someone who bugged your phone calls?"

For once, Simon had the decency to look embarrassed. He rallied quickly. "I can help you find Tony Moran."

"I'll think about it."

Dan opened the door and went out, bypassing a roomful of eager young people doing their best not to stare.

He stepped out into the street and looked around at the bustling crowds, the swirling traffic. Everywhere, people were going about their daily business, earning money to better their lives, heading out for coffee or to lunch assignations, meeting up with colleagues, worrying about picking up the dry cleaning and getting home on time to feed the kids. He, on the other hand, was concerned with phone taps and allegations of criminal conspiracy and government corruption on a world order.

And the day had just begun.

EIGHTEEN

Guns and Flowers

DAN'S NEXT STOP WAS CHINATOWN, an address on Spadina Avenue. Nestled between the stands of flowers, fresh fruit, and vegetables was the entrance to L.B. Electronics. They were, as Dan knew, the best retailer for the modern criminal, great and small. With the right word spoken in a tongue known only to a select few, tucked away in a security-proof basement could be found illegal DVDs, counterfeit software, cable TV decoders, radar scanners, lock-picking tools, wire-tapping devices, traffic signal changers, GPS jammers, odometer modifiers, and — best of all, in Dan's estimation — untraceable pay-as-you-go cellphones.

After perusing a few options, he selected a small Asian-built model devoid of English lettering, pulled out a wad of bills, and walked out a happier man. The airwaves were free and clear once again. At least for the moment.

He cursed, upon reaching his car, to find a bright yellow invitation to contribute to the city's overpaid parking division tucked neatly beneath his windshield wiper and thought yet again that if there were a way to dispense with personal vehicles — like moving to a country with no roads — he would seriously consider it. No, nothing was really free and clear.

He got in, pushing the ticket to the back of the glove compartment along with all the other unpaid slips, and unwrapped his new toy. Unlike so many other cell users whose memories of simple things like numbers and addresses had faded, he could still recall all the contacts he regularly dialed. He felt triumphant, like a virtuous hold-out from the digital age. A Wi-Fi mutineer, an AI rebel, an analog saint. Maybe even the second coming of Walden. Then he turned on his cell and dialed.

Not alarming Donny was sometimes a game and sometimes an occupational necessity, one he practised often, for his long-suffering friend had a habit of worrying and then nagging him unnecessarily.

"You're lucky I picked up. I'd pretty much given up answering unknown numbers."

"No need. You're a married man now."

"There's always radio-show giveaways. And to what do we owe the pleasure of this exchange?"

"I'd like you to use this new number for the next little while," Dan replied. He could hear his friend's thoughts humming over the line.

"Why?"

"I lost my cellphone."

"So, if I am to use this number just for the next little while, should I conclude that you expect to find your old cellphone?"

"Stranger things have happened."

"I smell a rat. But I will obey your wishes till I am otherwise advised."

"Thank you. One day when we reach the Promised Land all your good deeds will be rewarded."

"I've been to Provincetown. And believe me, nothing is free."

When Dan stopped in at Queen's Park in the afternoon, Simon Bradley's allegations were still running through his mind like a virus in a fresh bloodstream. He hadn't quite formulated a plan of action, but he knew something would present itself. He called Peter Hansen to ask permission to speak to Alec Henderson, trying to frame the questions he'd like to ask about Tony. Peter snorted at the suggestion.

"Absolutely not. You can't disturb the minister."

"It might be helpful if I could talk to him, just to see if he has any thoughts —"

"No. The option is closed."

"Just a few words. This isn't a parliamentary debate. I'm not tabling a bill."

"Dan, just forget it. I can't have you upsetting the minister. He has a very heavy schedule today."

He hung up.

Dan walked over to the reception desk. A sign announced the next tour starting at 2:15. Dan checked his watch — it was just getting on to two o'clock. He could wait.

When the guide saw him, she smiled. "Back again?"

"I couldn't resist. Your tour was compelling."

"Thank you!" She beamed, his own best pal.

He was prepared to do his disappearing act again, but in fact he didn't have to. Outside the council chambers, a crowd of reporters had gathered. Cameras, microphones. Something was brewing. Dan could tell his guide was particularly excited today.

He leaned over to her. "What's the scoop?"

Her eyes darted around. "I'm not supposed to say."

"I promise I won't tell a soul."

That was all it took to loosen her tongue. "A minister is announcing his resignation today."

"Who?"

"Alec Henderson, the minister of educational reforms."

"Resigning?"

"You'll see."

A moment later the door opened and out came Henderson in a casual three-piece. The reporters tensed, moving in for the right angle. Where once they would all have been men, today more than half were women, all jockeying for position with an elbow here and a foot there, as yesterday's friendly weather girl went shoulder to shoulder with men who looked more like dissolute linebackers.

The minister held up a hand in greeting, appealing to the reporters like an old friend, despite the fact that any of them would have turned on him for a headline scoop. Once they had quieted down, the minister of educational reforms blithely announced his resignation from the provincial cabinet. He would stay on, however, to see the controversial sex-ed bill through.

"And after that?" someone cued him, like the straight man in a comedy team.

"After that I will be running for a seat in the federal election, which we all know is going to come up sometime next year."

There was a smattering of applause from a handful of men and women from Alec's inner office, who looked as though they would willingly support a campaign for a marathon sled race around the north pole if he'd announced that.

The minister looked around for more questioners. Dan held up his hand.

"Yes. Over there."

"Is there any news on Tony Moran, the missing husband of your special assistant?"

Henderson's face took on a look of regret. "Unfortunately, not yet, but we are still hopeful that Tony will be found safe. It's been a trying time for my assistant, Peter Hansen, and all of us. We're a close-knit group. I've got a personal promise from the chief of police that he is doing everything in his power to find Tony."

Henderson's eyes roamed the crowd in search of a more promising question.

Dan spoke up again. "Do you think the power plant contract cancellations will hurt your chances of winning in the election?"

Alec looked confused for a second, then put on a brave smile. "Not at all. I wasn't directly involved in the cancellations."

"Were you aware, sir, that Tony Moran and your former opposition critic, John Wilkens, were looking into irregularities involving your former ministry at the time of Wilkens's death?"

Henderson's face blanched. He shook his head. "No, I wasn't aware of that. John Wilkens was a good man and a good politician. This has nothing to do with me," he said, waving to the crowd to indicate the session was over.

Other reporters pressed in to ask further questions, but the press secretary waved them aside. "That's all the minister has to say at present. Thank you for coming."

Dan slipped away from the crowd. Once outside on the steps, he pulled out his old cellphone. Bradley answered on the first ring.

"Dan! What's up?"

"I owe you one," he said. "Alec Henderson just announced his resignation to run in the federal election next year."

At three he closed his office and headed to the gym, decidedly a luxury when he was busy but a necessity the older he got and the more his joints fought back. Dan knew he wasn't going to win over his body with a show of force, but he refused to let it take him down with a surprise attack.

On leaving the gym, he saw there were four missed calls from Nick. That was unusual. He tried Nick's cell. When there was no answer, he called home. Still no answer. Something felt wrong. He pressed his foot on the gas.

Nick's car was in the drive. It was all Dan could do not to run up the walk and into the house. He fought with the key until it turned. The bolt shot back.

A moment of silence then, "Nick? Everything okay?"

Shuffling sounds from the kitchen.

"I'm … yeah."

Nick sat at the table staring out the window.

"What's going on? Everything all right?"

A bottle of Dewar's rested on the table before him. Nick avoided his glance as Dan picked up the glass and sniffed. Not to verify the smell, but to give himself time to think. In all their time together, neither of them had touched a drop of alcohol without the other being present. They both knew that the possibility it would happen one day was strong. In fact, it was highly probable, given their histories. Dan had dreaded this moment, but never once had he fooled himself into thinking it might not happen.

When they met, they'd seriously discussed their mutual problem with alcohol, each acknowledging a long-term dependence and his decision to steer clear of it. In both cases it related to their sons. Dan's drinking had stopped at Ked's insistence, once the boy had grown old enough to recognize his father's problem. Nick's had started with the loss of his son to leukemia at age five. Both had suffered a decade of abuse where alcohol tore their lives apart. Neither wanted to go back to those dark days. They had that in common. Now here was the wolf at the door once again.

"You've been drinking," Dan said. He struggled to keep the accusing tone from his voice. "Drinking alone, I mean."

Nick's head was down. "Drinking, yes. Alone, yes. I'm not drunk."

"Why are you drinking?"

"I didn't know where you were."

Dan sat back. "You're blaming this on me?"

He shook his head, keeping his eyes on the table. "No, Dan. There's no blame. I had a problem and I needed something to steady me. You weren't here and you weren't answering your phone. I made an adult choice and had a drink. One."

Dan looked at the nearly full bottle. It was down a fraction.

"Can you look at me, please?"

Nick lifted his face. The afternoon light showed bruising around his left eye.

"Oh, shit! What happened?"

"What it looks like. I was in a fight."

"With someone you were trying to arrest?"

"No. With another cop. In my office." Nick reached across the table and picked up an envelope, tossing it to Dan. "This was taped to my locker today."

Inside was a card: BEST WISHES ON YOUR ENGAGEMENT. Pink frills, hearts, and flowers. Dan opened it to a photograph of two naked men kissing, their erections pasted over with guns.

"No way!" Dan exhaled slowly. "Someone at your division did this?"

Nick nodded.

"Was it the two guys at the cemetery the other day?"

"I haven't a fucking clue. I decked the first guy who laughed. Guilt by association is how I figured it."

"Did you hurt him?"

"I sincerely hope so. I'll find out when I go back. I've been suspended for a week." He shook his head and smiled. "Stupid thing is, I don't even know if it was supposed to be funny or insulting. You can never tell with cops. They can be such assholes even when they're trying to be your buddy."

Dan laughed lightly. "And I caused a stir at Queen's Park today," he said, relating his recent adventure. "So I guess we could both use a drink."

"I've had mine. You go ahead."

Dan twisted the top off the Scotch and filled the glass partway, tipped it to Nick then swallowed. He made a face. "I forgot how this stuff burns."

"Don't get used to it, okay?"

Dan thought for a moment. "Will it be hell when you get back to work?"

Nick nodded. "Probably. Word will get out. I'll be shunned for a while. At least by the worst ones. There are a few who are okay, but they'll probably avoid me for a while. If someone is cool with me then it will be read that he's also a fag. It's like high school there. It was all right when I kept it to myself, but now everyone will know."

"I don't envy you," Dan said. He looked at Nick's black eye and laughed out loud.

"What?"

"Thing is, you look pretty hot right now."

"There's always a bright side to everything."

NINETEEN

Sharks

A PHONE WAS BUZZING. DAN looked over. It was his old cell, lying on the dresser beside the new one. Will Parker's name flashed on the screen.

"Hello, Will. What's up?"

"Good morning, Dan. I know it's abrupt, but I need to meet with you. Say, an hour from now?"

Dan looked over at Nick, who had rolled over and covered his face with one arm.

"Sure. What's it about?"

"In the interests of ensuring our privacy, I suggest we leave that till we meet in person."

Later, Dan realized it had felt more like a summons than an invitation. *Your friend Will Parker knows a lot more than he lets on*, Simon Bradley had said. Had he known then what was behind Will's request, he might not have gone.

The CN Tower was the single most prominent building on the city's horizon, rising 553 metres above abandoned railway land, yet its actual whereabouts remained shrouded in mystery to many. Getting there was like finding the end of the rainbow. But it wasn't North America's tallest phallic symbol Dan had come to visit. Rather, it was an aluminum-clad labyrinth of aquatic showcases he was headed for. By chance, Ripley's Aquarium made its home right next door, its entrance within easy shooting distance for any skilled marksman from the tower's observation deck. Muzzle to target, rifleman's rule. He got in line to buy his ticket.

Will was just laying a knife and fork across his empty plate when Dan arrived at the cafeteria. He pressed a napkin to his lips, looked up, and offered a cautious smile.

"Thought I'd take the opportunity to have a bite while I was waiting," he said apologetically. "I never know when I'm going to have a free moment."

He glanced up at the balcony circling the rotunda. "Lot of kids here today. How's your son, by the way?"

"Good. I'll be seeing him in a week."

"Send my regards." Will nodded and pushed his plate aside. "Have you been here before? Wonderful place, whether you're an adult or a child. Let's take a walk."

Dan followed him into a maze of glowing glass walls, the schools of fish turning and flashing under the lights.

"It's a good place to talk," Will was saying. "The kids get so excited you can barely hear yourself. No one else would be able to overhear you if you didn't want them to. We're also underground, so our phones won't work."

"And I thought I was secretive."

"I need to be wary. Every day of my life. I know things that would blow apart the lives and careers of some of the best-known people in the country. I can't afford to slip. The Cold War is alive and well in the political system. Remember those Russian Matryoshka dolls?"

Dan nodded.

"Politics is like that: secrets concealed within secrets. Open one and you find another concealed inside. You never know when you get to the bottom of anything. There could still be something else hidden within." Will looked over at Dan. "But you already know that, don't you?"

"I've guessed from time to time."

"I have to cover a lot of things up. Messy things. Other people's mistakes. Mostly things I can't talk about."

"Even when they involve murder?"

"Especially when they involve murder, Dan."

The shushing of the water surrounded them, all but drowning their words. They stepped onto a moving sidewalk taking them past the largest displays.

"So, are you telling me this Magus exists?"

"I'm not telling you anything, officially or otherwise. I'm just talking. What if I said he exists? Or she? Or them? What would it prove? Publicly, I would still tell you it's all nonsense, that such things can't happen in an enlightened country like Canada. But this is politics and it's a dirty business at the best of times."

A wolf eel watched them through the glass. Its jaws gaped as though it thought the two men might be food.

"So, what are you telling me?"

Will fixed him with a stare. "I'm telling you that you're playing with fire. You need to watch out for the power behind the throne. It's never the king who carries the dagger. It's always the Iagos and the Brutuses. They're the ones to watch."

"And the Simon Bradleys?"

Will made a dismissive gesture.

"The Simon Bradleys of this world are nothing compared to the people who want power, Dan. The people who want to take the country in a particular direction. Our current prime minister is a good example. He'd like to align us with the Americans and move us all to a more conservative place. Never underestimate him. He's a smart man with powerful backers who stay well-hidden behind the scenes. That's why he's dangerous. So far, he's carried off his agenda very successfully. There's an election coming up. If he gets another five-year mandate, there's no telling what he'll do. We've all seen what's happening. In the decade he's been in power, we've gone from peacekeepers to war-makers. That should tell you a lot. We are slowly but surely becoming a satellite of the U.S. Some would say it's inevitable, but we've managed to maintain a healthy distance for nearly a century and a half."

The sidewalk carried them along, past a million and a half gallons of water, the glass arching overhead as though they were at the bottom of the ocean. Captain Kidd. Jules Verne. The Titanic. A hammerhead shark drifted silently past, its dull, predatory eyes scanning for prey. The dark wings of a manta ray unfolded softly nearby, the two sea sisters strangely within striking distance of one another.

"I appreciate the confidence, Will, but surely that's not what you brought me down here to discuss."

"No, it's not."

They had reached the heart of the aquarium. Will stepped off the sidewalk. Dan joined him. Others passed on the conveyor, oblivious to the pair's temporary defection.

"I love the sound down here," Will said. "It's like the pulse of the world."

He turned to watch as two more sharks floated overhead.

"Have you ever noticed how often the feds refer to us as 'the taxpayers of Canada' these days, as though that's all we are to them now? Just a source of income to run the government. It's telling."

"But surely this Magus is a far step below all that. We're talking provincial politics —"

Will interrupted. "Daniel, I know you. You're not naïve. Where do federal leaders come from? The testing ground is the provinces. We make young leaders here."

"Like Alec Henderson."

"Like Alec … and others. We are forging the future. Canada can no longer remain unaffected by the rest of the world. If there is a Magus — and I say *if* — then the Magus will be watching carefully to see who is coming up that ladder. If anyone is capable of making big waves in future then that person is going to be closely observed. Accidents are not allowed to happen. We can't afford a false move on the chess board of politics."

"Let me guess. You think I've just disrupted that process by fingering an up-and-coming federal candidate with my questions."

"I'm saying you've annoyed some powerful people and they won't let you continue doing it."

A group of schoolchildren drifted past, looking up in hushed awe as a giant turtle propelled itself gently above.

"So you are talking about the Magus."

"Officially, the Magus doesn't exist. Just rumours, a bogeyman to scare the impressionable into behaving."

"But unofficially? Just curious — is it a single person, a group? How exactly does it work?"

"Even if I knew, I wouldn't be able to tell you, Dan. This is the heart of darkness as far as politics are concerned." He glanced over his shoulder, concern shadowing his face. "I'm afraid this is out of my league. You may never trust me again after today, but I had to consult someone else on the matter. He wants to speak with you. He insisted, in fact."

"Who?"

Will made an apologetic gesture. "He'll be here in a minute. Just — please forgive me for this. If you can."

"Forgive you? Who the hell are we talking about? The Attorney General?"

"No. I'm sorry. Due to the allegations you brought me, I've had my hand forced. I hope you understand." Will nodded at someone over Dan's shoulder. "He's here."

He held out his hand. Dan looked at the hand, but declined to shake. Will shrugged apologetically and stepped back on the moving sidewalk. Dan watched as it carried him away.

A figure came up and stood quietly beside him. It was Steve Ross of the Canadian Security Intelligence Services.

"Surprised?" Steve asked.

He wore a casual shirt, a burgundy sweater, and loose-fitting flannel trousers. Just another middle-aged dad. Grey tipped his short-cropped hair. Dan recalled perfectly the last time they'd met. He'd put on fifteen pounds and started balding on top since then, but he was still as ordinary as they came. Someone who could blend into the woodwork. Mr. Nobody at your service. Perfect spy material.

"I suppose I shouldn't be," he replied.

"It seems you've come to our attention again, Mr. Sharp. You certainly do get around."

"I could say the same for you. Only I was invited."

"Yes, you were. By me, in fact. You've been stirring things up again. You know how territorial we guard dogs are."

"Well, I'll back off then. I have no intention of snooping around in CSIS territory."

"Too late, I'm afraid. You seem to have found something of interest to us."

Dan shook his head. "I don't know what I found, but it seems to be what got an MPP killed."

"You seem awfully sure it was murder, after an esteemed colleague of mine declared it suicide."

Dan thought back to the scratched-out *Inconclusive* above the coroner's verdict of suicide. "Call it a hunch," he said, "but most disgraced politicians don't hang themselves from the underside of bridges."

"A pity. I wish more of them would. Do you know why he was hanged?"

"To send a message, I would guess. To anyone else who might look too closely at whatever is going on in the provincial legislature."

"But hanging? Surely there are easier ways to kill a man."

"You would know."

Steve shrugged. "Who do we hang? Public enemies, traitors, horse thieves. Not too many of those around any more. Who else? Speakers of the House."

"He wasn't a Speaker," Dan said.

"Not yet. Perhaps someone wanted to prevent him from becoming one."

"Maybe. The odd thing is he was murdered and no one seems to give a damn except his wife."

Steve watched him shrewdly. "What is she paying you to look into this?"

"Nothing. I'm not officially looking into it."

"Well, now you are, it seems. We would like you to help find the Magus. We'll pay you well for whatever information you bring us." He stroked his chin and looked at Dan. "Welcome back. It's good to be working with you again."

"No. This isn't going to happen."

Steve managed to look surprised. "I'm afraid it is. Whatever made you think you had a choice?"

"You think I'm bluffing?"

"You'd be doing your country and democracy a big favour."

"Democracy — right. Remind me again. Wasn't Adolph Hitler democratically elected? George Bush, the ex–coke addict and born-again Christian? Let's not forget our own mini-fürher, Stephen Harper." Dan shrugged. "What good is democracy when the people who vote are idiots?"

Steve smiled slowly. "What's it like to be so cynical?"

"You tell me. You're the spy."

"So you won't help us?"

"Won't help you, can't help you. Forget it. I helped you before and look where it got me. I'm just lucky I wasn't the one who ended up dead."

"You refuse?"

"I refuse."

"Remember the Security of Information Act, Daniel."

"You can stuff it."

Steve smiled. "In fact, I can have you stuffed *with* it. You did sign a non-disclosure agreement, as you may recall."

"Yes, well, I believe that pertained to a different case."

"There will be consequences."

"Threats work both ways, Steve … Paul. Whatever your name is this week."

"I could arrange to have something incriminating planted on your laptop."

Dan rolled his eyes. "Child porn is so yesterday."

"I was thinking more of a direct link to ISIS. Didn't you have a child with a Syrian-born woman?"

Dan felt as if he was looking into the flat, soulless eyes of a shark. He shook his head and turned away. From behind him he heard Steve's voice.

"Ten thousand dollars."

Dan stopped and turned back. "What?"

Steve was checking his cellphone. "Is that really what he paid you to find his husband? You must be good." He shook his head in mock dismay. "We'll pay you twice that for whatever you can tell us about the Magus. Think about it."

A small furor arose as a group of schoolchildren rushed by. Steve looked past them, then turned his gaze to the glass ceiling above. "Be a real mess if this thing ever sprang a leak."

TWENTY

The Good Book

DAN DROVE STRAIGHT BACK TO his office, unlocked his door, and reset the alarm. His Day-Timer was in its usual place on the desk. It served merely as an appointment reminder, and contained no valuable information, so he had never seen the sense in locking it at night. Even if someone had been through it, however, he doubted there would be any fingerprints on it but his own. CSIS would never be so clumsy. In fact, he doubted he'd find even the smallest indication that anyone had been in his office searching for information about his affairs with Peter Hansen or anyone else.

He turned to the page where he'd written Hansen's name on the day of his visit. There was the entry, *$10,000 CASH*, underlined beneath the time of Peter's unannounced visit. Easy enough for any semi-competent burglar to discover. He *had* been foolish to leave it lying about. Better start locking up everything at night then. With CSIS, there was no telling when there might be a next time. Still, it said nothing about Tony Moran. The only document Dan had in writing about Tony was a CV with various addresses for gambling dens, yet Steve Ross had known exactly how much he'd been paid and for what. Good sleuthing? Dan certainly couldn't imagine Hansen volunteering information to CSIS about hiring a private investigator to look for his missing husband. He'd been far too concerned with discretion.

He tried to recall if he'd had a phone conversation discussing Hansen's payment. He couldn't think of one. There was Nick, of course. They'd talked about it while watching the evening news. Dan couldn't recall if he'd stated the exact figure, though he hardly suspected Nick of betraying him. So, if not his phone, then where was the leak?

He ran his hands under the desk and along the drawer edges. Nothing. He pulled out a chair and stood on it to examine the light fixture. Lots of dust and more than a few dead moths. Nothing had been disturbed there recently. Picture frames, ditto. Same with the filing cabinet, the other likely place to conceal a bug. The only thing of interest he found was a long-dead bourbon bottle stashed behind some empty file folders, a remnant of his drinking days. He tossed it across the room, snagging the bin with a dour clank.

Try to think like a surveillance operator, he told himself. *Where would I hide a bug?* If it was extremely small, there was little chance of locating it without sophisticated debugging equipment. Maybe he should take a trip to the Spy Depot and stock up on some of the latest gadgets.

Bookcases flanked the doorway, volumes leaning against one another in companionable disuse. Windows took up most of the space on the two outside walls, while the fourth wall, on his left, separated him from an adjacent office.

Funny how he'd never seen his next-door neighbours.

His fingers thrummed on the desk for a second, then he pulled out the bottom drawer and selected a tiny pick, rubber gloves, and a ski mask. He slipped the mask on and went out to the hall. The only sound was the padding of his shoes on the linoleum. It paid to be on the top floor away from the traffic.

One door down, soft light rippled through opaque glass interrupted here and there by an ornate gold script: *R.L.G. SUPPLIES.* Silence emanated from inside like darkness in an empty crypt.

Dan paused and tried to recall how long the company had been there. Not long, was the best he could come up with. No memory of a recent move-in came to mind. While that might have seemed odd it was not entirely unusual in a building where businesses came and went quickly. One floor down, a bustling movie production office had come and gone within a month, taking the circus with it when it left.

Maybe he should pay these things more mind.

He set to work. The door was different from his own, the lock more sophisticated in its design. Exactly what sort of supplies did the R.L.G. people deal in? He managed to ease it open in less than a minute. To no one's surprise but his, he'd become an expert in breaking and entering over the years.

The door swung inward. There was no camera or surveillance system in direct line of sight. And thankfully, no alarm. A simple desk and fold-up chair sat to one side, turned away from the window. Granted there wasn't much of a view, Dan thought, unless you enjoyed looking at other people's garbage bins and back alleys. Still, most people would have made the most of the light. Unless they didn't want to be seen from the street.

The desktop was clean, with nothing but a green blotter. No papers, no pencils. Who used blotting pads these days? He pulled the drawers forward slowly, one at a time. They were empty except for a couple of Sudoku books, a copy of *Why Everything You Know About Soccer Is Wrong*, and a stack of coupons for *One free medium hot beverage — available at participating McDonald's restaurants*. He still had a hard time calling them restaurants. No matter. Clearly, someone had too much time on his or her hands.

Apart from the desk and chair, the only other items in the room were a coat rack with three bent wire hangers and a brand-spanking-new filing cabinet. He went over and yanked the handle. It yielded a few thin hanging folders with a handful of unused order forms inside. Not a booming business, then. He pushed the cabinet away from the wall and looked behind. Again, nothing.

Someone had stacked a dozen unopened boxes against a far wall. The label read *R.L.G. Supplies* and the street address. Well, they had to supply something. He hefted one of the boxes. Good, solid weight. Something shifted inside. He slit the top open. Copies of the Holy Bible in soft black cover. Fifty or more. With real pages and everything. A chill ran down his spine. *R.L.G. Supplies*. Short for *Religious Supplies*. Bible wholesalers next door to his office? Since when?

He turned to the common wall, feeling for irregularities, imperfections, anything that might conceal the smallest of devices. Once again, nothing. He could spend hours and still not discover how they spied on him. Worse, they might come looking for him if he stayed too long.

Time, gentlemen.

His new cell rang as he stepped back into the hall. For a moment, he felt a hit of paranoia. Then he saw the name.

He slipped back inside his office and closed the door, pulling off the ski mask. "How's the wedding planning business?"

"Atrocious." Donny's voice was strident. "Have you any idea how much photographers charge?"

"No. I thought that was your department."

"Unbelievable!" He was preparing for a rant. "Whoever invented these rites and rituals should be … should be strung up from the gallows. By his scrotum."

"Sorry to hear I've been ruining your week," Dan said.

"You're oddly apologetic," Donny said. "What's up?"

"You probably wouldn't believe me if I told you."

"Try me."

"Well, for one thing I seem to have neighbours next door to my office whose business is selling bibles."

"Okay, that's ominous and strange. What else?"

Dan lowered his voice. "I think they may have bugged my office."

"You're being bugged by Bible-thumpers? That's going to limit the conversation. Should I hang up now before I say something irreligious?"

"You could at least tell me how things are going first."

"I'm terrified to say a word. Who could be listening in?"

"This is my new phone, so probably nobody," Dan replied. "Or it could be just a bunch of second-rate journalists. Thanks for giving me the opportunity to insult them."

"You're very welcome." There was a moment of suspicious silence. "Does Nick know about this?"

"Actually, I just figured it out. I need you to promise you won't say anything to him yet."

"Cross my heart and swear on a Bible kind of promise?"

"Yeah, that kind."

"Then no, I won't. And I strongly advise you to tell him now before he finds out later that you've been holding out on him with important secrets." He spluttered. "Why wouldn't you tell Nick? He's a cop, for god's sake."

"Actually ... you're right. I should tell him."

"Okay, you're being very peculiar. First you apologize to me and now you're agreeing with me. What gives? Have you been cloned by the pod people?"

"No, I think it was the Stepford Wives. I agreed to get married, didn't I? Wouldn't you say that's the oddest thing I've done lately?"

"Hmm ..." Donny pondered. "Can't say I disagree. But you will tell Nick about this? Cross your heart and hope to die?"

Memories of the photographs of John Wilkens's body laid out in the city morgue flashed before Dan's eyes.

"Yes — at least the cross-my-heart part. I'm not hoping anyone else dies."

Dan closed his office and took his Day-Timer with him. Telling Nick was not going to be easy. The fact that he was a cop was one thing. That Nick had already warned him about the risks he took would only make matters more complicated. But knowing CSIS was now involved in his case, however tangentially, only made it that much worse.

Dan came and stood just inside the kitchen door, watching as Nick went back and forth from the kitchen to the dining room.

"Hey! You're actually on time for dinner."

"Smells good."

Dan continued to stand there watching. Nick looked over from sorting the table settings.

"What's up?"

"Something I can't tell you about."

"Is this a guessing game?"

"Sort of."

"Because?"

"Because I signed official papers saying I couldn't discuss the matter with anyone."

Nick straightened and stood very still. "That would be the Security of Information Act. Is CSIS involved in this?"

Dan nodded. "That would be a good guess. If you were guessing."

"Enough with the charades, okay? What can you tell me?"

"Nothing."

Nick's eyes flashed. "Oh come on! You can't think that answering questions in our own home is going to jeopardize anything."

"I'm not sure that's a conclusion we can draw at this moment."

Nick's mouth opened, but no sound emerged. He motioned for Dan to step out onto the back patio.

Once outside, he said, "Okay, what's going on?"

Dan dropped his voice to a whisper. "I think my office is bugged and possibly this house."

"Great. What you're saying is that whatever we do might be heard by someone from Intelligence Services."

"Possibly. I don't want to get too paranoid yet."

"Well, let me know when to start."

"I'm not entirely sure what's going on. For now we have to be careful. I don't want to involve you more than I have to."

"In case you haven't noticed, I am involved."

"I know. And for the record, I am worried."

"Of course. That's what CSIS does. They worry people to death when they should be out hunting ISIS. Just tell me as much as you can. Legally, I mean."

Dan thought back. He saw a woman's classical features traced in the air, a face with slender cheekbones, a knife-torn throat.

"I saw someone murdered once. I'm not allowed to talk about it."

"Because it would endanger national security?"

"Because some might say it would."

"Whoever was murdered must have been important."

"It was … *she* was someone important." He paused. "I was approached again today. I refused to help. I don't think I can tell you any more than that."

Nick stared at him.

"It's to keep you safe," Dan said.

Nick's expression said he doubted that.

"In any case," Dan said, "I just wanted you to know they've become involved. Unofficially so far."

"Unofficially? They are the least unofficial organization in the country. CSIS doesn't do 'unofficial.'"

"Well, whatever it is they're doing, they haven't formalized anything yet."

"Let's hope they don't, but that's unlikely given the fact that they've already approached you."

"I just wanted to let you know so you wouldn't worry."

"Well, too late for that. Did you really think I could *not* worry?" He paused. "I hate to say it, but I really think you're in this over your head."

"Yes, you're right. Sorry again."

TWENTY-ONE

Knock, Knock

THERE WAS NO FURTHER WORD from Steve Ross for the next few days, no sound or presence of any obvious sort on the other side of his office wall. Maybe the bible sales-people worked only on Sundays. Dan hadn't spoken to Will since being handed over to CSIS. He wasn't sure he was willing to forgive his old friend for the transgression, regardless of whether he'd had his hand forced or not. For the moment, he was determined to have no further involvement with Queen's Park.

Once Nick's probationary week was up, he returned to work. Glad for the return to normalcy this provided, Dan forged ahead with his efforts to locate Tony Moran. Then Nick went on evening shift, leaving Dan more time alone to think and plan.

In the meantime, he'd come up with an idea that required Donny's help. They met at Starbucks. *What place could be less worthy of electronic snooping?* Dan reasoned, as Donny eyed him skeptically over the tabletop. The room reverberated with the echoes of conversation and the insistent treble of whiney pop singers. Miniature laser lights flashed patterns of green and red, marking the floors, the walls, and the customers. A tiny spot caught Donny's cheek, twitching and crawling across his face in a series of dimples. A marked man caught in the sharpshooter's sights.

"You really think this is a good idea?"

Dan shrugged. "I can't find the bug in my phone or in the office. If I'm right, it's the best way of finding out if someone is really listening in."

Donny made a show of shivering and looking around the room. "They could be anywhere. They might be listening right now."

Dan smiled and glanced at the late-afternoon shoppers and high school students ordering iced macchiatos. "An unlikely crowd for it, but then again, you never know."

"Okay, so let's see if I got it right. You want me to ask Prabin to call you on your office line and pretend to be Tony Moran suggesting a meeting time and place."

"That's it. Neither Tony nor Prabin has ever called my office phone, so Prabin's voice will be neutral. But make sure he uses a public phone. I don't want anything traced back to him or you."

"Then what?"

"Then we sit back and see who turns up. Not the real Tony, of course, since he won't know anything about it."

"Won't this be putting you and Nick in danger?"

"Nick is on nights. He's not going to know about it."

Donny rolled his eyes. "Oh, that's great. Not only are

you putting yourself in danger, you won't even tell the one person who could protect you."

"I can't involve Nick in this," Dan said. "There's too much at risk here."

Donny sighed. "Why can't I have normal friends?"

"Because they're boring?"

"Yeah, that. Please tell me you will be careful."

"Of course I'll be careful."

Donny's shoulders slumped. "That doesn't mean very much though, does it? I mean, you can be careful all you want but who knows who you're really dealing with?" He searched Dan's face for reassurance. "Wait a second. You do know who you're dealing with, don't you?"

Dan held up a hand. "Don't ask, okay? I can't tell you any more than I've already said."

"And that's supposed to make me feel better?" When there was no answer, Donny went on. "Should I just knock you on the head and be done with it? Put you out of your misery?"

"It won't help."

"You're right. It never has before." He looked resigned. "When do you want this done?"

"Tomorrow. Then just forget we ever had this conversation."

"Or what? You'll have to kill me?" Donny gave him a gloomy look. "This is getting really out of hand."

"That's what Nick thinks. Please just do this for me."

Dan smiled when Prabin's message showed up the following morning. It was perfect. Prabin sounded realistically nervous, but not over the top. Anyone who didn't know him would believe it was the real Tony Moran claiming to want to meet Dan in person, saying he had sensitive information to pass along. And if anyone cared, he would be by the office at nine o'clock that evening.

Dan played it through twice, glad that he'd kept his old answering machine when everyone else had ditched theirs, then pressed *69 and waited while the operator's voice told him the call came from a Bell pay phone that did not take incoming calls.

He sat back, taking stock of his surroundings. It wasn't the dreary sort of private investigations office depicted in movies and noir fiction, not all dust and despair. Maybe it was the gay gene, but Dan couldn't do without the personal touch. Like the art. And the books. His shelves were full. Someone might have done a survey of World Literature here. A handful of thrillers, a few homegrown titles among them. "Death by snowshoe" was how one wag put it when it came to suspense in Canadian crime fiction. All this would come with him, as would the photographs and carpets, of course. But he'd miss the wide floorboards, the old-fashioned lead-frame windows, the tin ceilings — which reminded him yet again that he still hadn't found a new office to call home.

Nine o'clock, the appointed hour, came and went. He stood at the window looking down on the street. There was nothing unusual in the slow passing of cars, the occasional pedestrian dressed in airy summer garb. The neighbourhood was mostly a throughway to other parts, not a destination where people stopped after close of day. The city lights were interrupted briefly where they met the dark flow of the Don, the divide between east and west, then lit up again on the far side of the river.

Dan thought of the bibles and sudoku books in the empty office next door. In the daytime, noise from the street filtered in, the lively conversations of passersby lit up the interior, while footsteps one floor below might sound as if they were right outside his door. But at night, he always knew when the place was deserted. The building was an echoing mausoleum, humming with the current of the electrical grid and the scratching of mice in the walls. Perhaps he should have been better prepared for whoever might show up. He doubted the call would fool Simon Bradley. If Simon had told the truth about talking to Tony, then Simon would know Tony's voice. On the other hand, Prabin's call might have alerted whoever Tony was hiding from, someone dangerous. The security camera would catch anyone entering the lobby, but that was no guarantee of safety. A baseball bat lay hidden in the bottom of the filing cabinet. Dan retrieved it, leaning it against the leg of his desk.

He replied to a few emails as he waited. If nobody showed up then either his plan had failed or the message hadn't been heard by anyone concerned with his recent activities. Or maybe, just maybe, no one really cared about Tony Moran's whereabouts. But he doubted it.

At 10:37 his phone rang. He picked up the receiver, identified himself, and caught the sound of wind whistling on the other end. He identified himself again, but no one spoke in return. The line went dead. A crank call. Possibly. Outside his door, he heard the tread of someone coming along the carpeted hallway. Dan waited, his body tensed.

Footsteps approached and passed his office. He opened the door. At the far end of the corridor he could make out the figure of the building's regular cleaner bending down to plug in a vacuum.

It had occurred to him that anyone watching would wait to see who arrived before coming up to the office, but he hadn't wanted to get anyone else involved in his little prank. No bystanders or background performers.

Frankly, he was surprised not to hear from Simon Bradley. Maybe their confrontation at the *Scene* office had put fear into his heart, though he thought he'd made up for it by letting him know he'd been right about Alec Henderson's resignation.

At eleven, Dan stretched and lifted his feet from his desk. It didn't pay to get too comfy on the job.

At eleven thirty, he locked his office and headed downstairs. Outside, the sidewalks were deserted. From a distance came the clattering of a streetcar. The accordion doors opened and shut again after ejecting a single figure. A woman. Tall, older. She turned and went into the convenience store without even looking in his direction.

Dan steeled himself when a slim dark form emerged from an alley and headed his way. He caught the haunted look in the youngster's eyes as he reached out a hand.

"Can you spare some change, sir?"

"What do I get for it?"

The question seemed to startle him. "I'm hungry," came the reply.

"We're all hungry, son."

Dan fished a toonie from his pocket and dropped it into the outstretched palm. The look he caught was disappointment. *Tough*. In this neighbourhood you'd be lucky not to get a boot for your troubles. The boy slipped the coin in his pocket and left. No contact.

Dan made his way slowly home along Queen. Once or twice he felt the hair on the back of his neck rise as others approached, singly or in pairs, but nothing further happened.

Junk mail and flyers spilled out of his mailbox like weeds in an untended lawn. The porch light was off. Dan sifted through the advertisements, squinting to read the names: *Occupant; Resident; Lucky Winner!* And one for his neighbours two doors down. He tucked them all under his arm and unlocked the door. Ralph came up for a quick pat on the head then returned to his cushion. Steadfast Ralph. And Nick, the other steadfast in Dan's books, was on night shift. There was no sound in the house.

He opened a tin of spiced kippers, grabbed a fork, and turned on the radio, eating straight from the can. Bachelors' habits die hard.

Done, he rinsed the can under the faucet, tossed it in the trash, and washed his fork. It was garbage night. He grabbed the bag — surprisingly light, thanks to Nick's insistence on eating fresh whenever possible — then toted it downstairs to the basement and dumped it into the recycling bin. Next, he flattened two cardboard boxes Nick had carted his dinnerware over in and tied them up with string. A good citizen. Then again, the grumpy sanitation engineers refused to touch anything not properly bundled and presented. Soon they'd be wanting it wrapped in bows and ribbons, with politely worded thank-you cards. Everyone was a Martha Stewart.

He was about to head back upstairs to take his carefully packaged refuse outside when something caught his eye. The window over the washer was ajar. He examined it carefully. It was open an inch, but even an inch meant it had been left unlocked for who knew how long. He couldn't recall having opened it any time in the past week. Had Nick been airing out the basement for some reason?

Ralph would have howled at the first sounds of an intruder, but with the basement door closed he wouldn't have been able to get downstairs. Presumably no one would come up and face an angry dog, even if they'd known he was geriatric. Howl all he might, however, there would be no one to hear Ralph sound the alarm.

Dan tensed, keeping his ears and eyes alert. No sounds came to him. Basements could be surprisingly quiet. He closed and locked the window and turned back to the room. Gripping a flashlight — it would come in handy as a weapon, if need be — he began a through search, trying to hold his paranoia at bay. The problem was, there were so many places to hide. Behind the furnace, for one, though cobwebs were his only find there. Slowly, he let himself inside the tool room, keeping the light trained dead ahead. The switch dangled from a string an inconvenient five feet into the room. He'd always planned on moving it closer to the door, so why the hell hadn't he?

His beam swept the space. Nothing hiding behind hammers and saws carefully hung on the walls, the drills and pliers silent in their slots. Basements might be spooky in general, but at night they became veritable haunted houses made all the worse by an overactive imagination.

Ten minutes later, satisfied he was alone in the house, Dan hauled the recycling out to the curb. Feeling wide awake, he took advantage of Nick's absence to watch the late-night news. It featured the usual showstoppers, including more political spill-out from the revelations at Queen's Park. There was no further mention of Anne Wilkens's involvement in her husband's affairs, he noted. And for that he was genuinely glad.

The weather report followed. Even that had been whipped up into a tantalizing drama of portending storms. Had no one heard of summer rain? Dan leaned back against his chair and closed his eyes, lulled into a light sleep. He realized later, on reflection, that he'd heard the shot but it hadn't registered till Ralph lifted his head and whined.

He was instantly alert. "What is it, Ralphie? What's wrong?"

Ralph struggled out of his basket, making a low and ominous growling sound. A moment later he broke into full-fledged barking and bounded for the door, forgetting for a moment that he was an old, arthritic dog.

Something slumped against the front entrance, but the sound was drowned out by Ralph's ruckus.

"Who's there?" Dan demanded.

No answer. Slowly, cautiously, he reached for the handle.

"Who's there?" he called again. Still no answer.

Something was propped against the door. Dan opened it a crack till he could make out a pair of legs lying across his front step. Gently, he eased the door inward, crouching down and cradling Simon Bradley's head with his hands. He felt for a pulse. It was faint.

Dan looked around. The yard lay in darkness. The shooter could still be out there. He grabbed hold of Simon by the armpits and pulled him carefully into the living room. He looked back to see a long trail of blood on the carpet.

A gurgle came from Simon's lips. Dan leaned in.

"Magus." It was a choked whisper.

"The Magus did this to you?"

Simon was struggling for his pocket. Dan put a hand in and felt the compact curves of a cellphone.

"Okay, try to relax. I'll call for help."

The phone lit up at his touch, but it was password-protected. He dropped it on the couch and reached for his own, giving the operator explicit instructions. Dan heard a whimper and saw that Simon was trying to sit up. He grasped Dan's arm. His grip was incredibly strong for a second or two, then relaxed suddenly.

"Don't talk," Dan said, but he was the only one who heard.

He sat there on the floor beside the body till the wail of sirens cut through the night air like streamers.

Dan answered the knock, identifying himself as a private investigator to the wary-looking officers. Then he deposited himself on a chair to endure their questions, keeping Ralph tightly leashed beside him.

Who was the dead man? That was easy: Simon Bradley, the journalist.

Why was Mr. Bradley here? Not so easy: he didn't know.

Did Dan know who had shot him? Even more difficult: not a fucking clue, in fact.

They asked all the obvious questions, plus a few he hadn't expected.

What was his relationship with Mr. Bradley?

None.

Was there anything personal between them then?

No. Otherwise he would have acknowledged the relationship.

Did he, Dan, live alone?

No, not that that was any of their business, though he was reluctant to name Nick as his partner, particularly when dealing with Nick's colleagues. In fact, Nick saved him the bother when he showed up ten minutes into the call.

"I heard the address on the radio," he told Dan quietly as he took in the officers swarming over the house. He glanced down at Simon's body. "Who is this guy? How did this happen?"

"It's Simon Bradley, the reporter who called asking to meet me after the news brief on Tony Moran."

"The snoop? The one who's been tapping your phone? What the fuck is he doing here?"

One of the officers looked over with interest. Nick waved him off.

"Nothing. Just a private conversation."

The cop came over, a scowl written large on his face. "How do you two know each other?"

Dan let Nick take the lead.

"I live here," Nick said quietly.

The officer took this in with barely a change of expression. "You the guy who was on suspension last week?"

Nick nodded.

"Huh."

He noted Nick's badge number, writing it in a notebook before turning back to the room and Simon Bradley's body.

The forensics testing looked like it was going to go on for some time. In the meantime, Dan and Nick arranged to go to Nick's condo, giving enough contact info to the investigating officers to satisfy the most ardent of enforcers.

"Sir, please make sure you are available at all times in the next twenty-four hours," one of the officers told Dan. He looked to Nick. "I'll hold you responsible if I can't reach him."

"He'll be available," Nick said.

With an overnight bag over one shoulder and Ralph pulling him onward, Dan followed Nick to the car.

Nick was silent as they drove across town to Queen's Quay. Even Ralph seemed alert to the unspoken tension, keeping his head down where normally he'd have been up sniffing at the windows, waiting to have them opened for him.

"I'm sorry," Dan began. "I never wanted this to land in your lap."

He went over all that had happened in the lead-up to Simon's death. Nick's expression hardened at the mention of his faked call to draw out the eavesdropper.

"I know it was reckless," Dan admitted. "But I couldn't involve you because of what we discussed."

Nick stared straight ahead. After a moment he said, "I'm starting to feel as though I don't know you."

"That's unfair. We've been over this before. This is my job. Sometimes I have to take risks, just like you. I'm sure there are plenty of things that happen to you in the course of a day that I never get to hear."

"Maybe. But even I wouldn't muck around with CSIS."

"What do you expect me to do? Just ignore it? I didn't ask for a corpse to end up on our doorstep."

Nick's jaw tensed. "Sometimes it's better just to do nothing, but you don't seem to get that. You better be prepared for what's coming."

"That sounds ominous."

"You know as well as I do this isn't over yet. Not by a long shot."

At the condo, they went to bed without a word. After half an hour, Nick picked up his pillow and went off down the hall. Dan heard the guest room door open and close.

TWENTY-TWO

Ten Thousand Reasons

THEY WERE WAITING FOR HIM at his office the next morning. Some were metro cops, but Dan could see immediately that at least two were not. CSIS, he guessed. A warrant was shoved under his nose. He let them in and sprawled in the visitor's chair as they went through his files and desk drawers. Steve Ross's words came back to him: *There will be consequences.* He thought of phoning Nick for advice, but they hadn't spoken since their discussion last night.

One of the cops turned to him. Dark, muscular. Shaved head. Attitude to burn. He'd just missed out on being Vin Diesel. The officer glanced over at the safe.

"We'll need the combination, unless you want me to break into it. Sir."

Dan unlocked it. The envelope with Peter Hansen's retainer lay on top. The cop grabbed it and rifled through the bills, whistling.

"That's a lot of money. Do you usually have so much on hand?"

"No."

No paper trail, Hansen had said. Could there have been more to it than that? It all seemed very convenient at the moment. Convenient for Hansen.

"Care to tell us why you have so much money on hand, sir?"

"No. I'll wait till I speak with a lawyer, if you don't mind."

"Sure, if you prefer. If you think you have reason to need a lawyer." He counted through the bills slowly, fanning them on the desk like a gambler laying out a winning hand. "Then again, I can think of ten thousand reasons about now."

Another officer came over and flipped through a pocket notebook. He looked up at Dan. "I see your partner is a police officer."

"Is that a question?"

He looked at the money on the desk. "We'll get you to sign for that, but I think you better come down to the station for questioning. If you want a lawyer present, you should call one now."

Dan was about to say he didn't like lawyers and therefore didn't have any to call, so a public defender would be in order, when he suddenly remembered one lawyer he was on speaking terms with. Or at least had been until recently.

They were in a small, grey, windowless cell masquerading as an interview room. Dan, Will Parker, and the officer who'd asked him to come to the station sat around a desk that was covered in small scars and scratches. Torture chamber might have been a better fit, Dan thought.

Will gave the cop his best don't-fuck-with-me look. "Is my client to be detained after this question period is over?"

The man scowled, obviously not prepared to be on good terms with any lawyer representing a potential murder suspect.

"That depends on whether he confesses to anything."

"My client hasn't done anything he needs to confess to," Will said, with a look at Dan as though to confirm the statement.

"A man was shot to death in his living room last night —"

Will interrupted. "A man was shot on the street outside his house and ended up on Mr. Sharp's doorstep. Mr. Sharp brought him into his home in an effort to save his life, potentially risking his own while doing so. He had no reason to wish harm on Simon Bradley."

"That's not what Bradley's colleagues tell us," the officer said, thumbing through a pad of handwritten notes. He turned to Dan. "It says here you were overheard threatening Mr. Bradley in his office a week ago —"

"They were not credible threats," Will interjected. "Mr. Sharp had no reason to wish harm on Mr. Bradley."

The officer picked up the envelope with Hansen's money. "You don't call this reason enough?"

"Mr. Sharp has already indicated the money you found in his office safe is —"

"A substantial amount of money."

"As you keep repeating, Officer Boychuk. And, as Mr. Sharp has explained, it was being held in safekeeping for his client, Peter Hansen, as a down payment for finding Mr. Hansen's husband. It has nothing to do with Simon Bradley."

"We haven't been able to reach Hansen yet to confirm this." Boychuk gave Dan a skeptical look. "Do you always get paid that much money for a search, Mr. Sharp? Hell, I'll leave this dump in a second and come and join you if you do."

Dan shook his head. "It was an advance. I told Mr. Hansen it was too much."

"Then why not just give it back to him?"

"He'd already gone by then. I didn't look in the envelope till later."

The officer feigned confusion. "Don't you normally sign contracts with your clients?"

"Normally, yes. He showed up at my office without warning. When I said we needed a contract, he refused one."

Boychuk looked pleased, the cat catching an unobservant mouse. "How could you tell him there was too much money if he was already gone?"

"I called his cellphone."

"I see." He shrugged. "Did you at least offer him a receipt?"

"Yes. He refused that too."

"Funny kind of client."

"Tell me about it. I said I would hold the money in my safe until I had concluded the job and we would work out the details then."

The officer harrumphed. "Must be a rich guy, this Mr. Hansen."

"I couldn't say. I get hired by poor people, too. My terms are on my website. Mr. Hansen told me he'd read them before approaching me. As I said, he dropped the envelope on my desk and left before I counted the money. I hadn't formally accepted the job. I told him I would think about it and let him know."

"You have an awfully casual attitude to what you get paid, is all I can say."

Will's hand came down on the desk. "My client hasn't denied having the money. What you think of it is your problem. Unless you have any further questions …?"

Boychuk picked up his notepad and stared hard at Dan. "Don't leave town till I say you can."

They were on the sidewalk outside the police station. Traffic rushed past and pedestrians eyed gaps between cars, calculating the risk of jaywalking. A few of the spryer ones managed, the others heading for the crosswalk.

"Thank you for rescuing me," Dan said.

Will brushed it aside. "I'm just glad you're still talking to me after the other day."

"I thought about it. I realized I put you in a delicate position. Still, I have to say I was a little taken aback when Steve Ross showed up."

"He insisted. He said he was an old friend of yours."

Dan managed a smile. "'Friend' is the last word I'd use. We were acquainted once upon a time."

Will nodded. "You'd probably be more surprised to know just how far his reach extends. Especially when it comes to government matters."

"Maybe, but I won't be so naïve next time. It won't happen again, I can assure you."

"For your sake, I hope not. Anyway, that's in the past. We have other fish to fry, as they say." He gave Dan a searching look. "Any idea why Hansen would pay you so much money and insist on doing it in cash?"

"Are you suggesting he planned on killing Simon Bradley and then pinning it on me?"

"Maybe not, but it certainly makes you look suspicious. I don't like it."

"I can't help that. Hansen thought he was buying discretion with that money, which is funny considering he's a public figure and news of his missing husband is all over the media. And that had nothing to do with me either, in case you're wondering."

"I wasn't wondering, Dan. I know you better than that. Unless you've changed a lot in the last decade."

"I'm still gullible, it seems."

Will smiled for the first time since he'd arrived at the station. "I always thought you were too trusting. You believe in human goodness. It's what I remember most about you from when we worked those help lines together."

"Is that such a bad thing?"

"Not necessarily, but I'd overhear you trying to convince callers they weren't as bad as they said they were. In my experience, when someone tells me not to trust them or does anything that makes me wary, I don't try to argue them out of it."

He pulled out a cigarette. Dan thought of Donny, glad to know there was at least one other person in the city who stuck to his convictions, no matter what.

Will took a drag and nodded at Dan. "Do you think Hansen will deny giving you the money?"

"If he does it's his word against mine, but I doubt it. He's running for office next year. I don't think he'd want a public fight over something like this. It would make him look too shady."

"Whereas if he gets publicity for having hired you to find his husband, it would make him look like a guy who'd do anything for family." Will gave him a knowing look. "Not a bad bit of publicity, when it comes down to it."

Dan stared at him. "You don't really think … you don't believe Hansen set me up for a publicity stunt, do you?"

"There you go being all naïve and conscientious again. But no, I don't really believe he could have foreseen all this. Even if he killed Simon Bradley himself —" He stopped. "Let's not go down that road. Politicians may be liars, but they're usually not murderers."

"Simon Bradley wasn't convinced of that. He believed John Wilkens was killed to prevent him from hurting Alec Henderson's career prospects. He knew Henderson would be running for a federal seat in the next election before it was announced. Do you think there's even a remote chance Henderson had Simon Bradley killed?"

"Not a credible theory, Dan." Will pulled on his cigarette, exhaled, and watched the smoke disappear. "Look, leave Henderson alone and don't mess around with CSIS. Believe me, you will not win. If they say John Wilkens killed himself then that's the story we're all going with right now. Maybe sometime in future …" He shrugged. "I'll get you out of this. I promise. Just don't make things worse. And I can get your money back fast. No need to wait on it."

"The money is the least of my concerns," Dan said. "It's not like I have plans for it. I was just going to let it sit in the safe till I found Tony. Ironically, I'd already tagged it to go to the catering bill for the wedding, if I earned it."

They both managed a laugh.

TWENTY-THREE

The Trophy

DAN GOT WILL TO DROP HIM back at his office. He entered carefully, looking around at the piles of paper that had been sifted and abandoned on chairs, his desk, the floor. What they expected to find was anybody's guess. Years of filing had been done with meticulous care, so if they were looking for irregularities, they had only to check the records by date or client number and match them up with his archives of appointment ledgers, not to mention his income-tax claims. Except for Peter Hansen, of course, who had demanded anonymity. Which, Dan now saw, was working against him. But if Hansen had planned it for that reason, he wouldn't get away with it. He still had the notation of Hansen's visit in his Day-Timer crammed in among so many other things, like the note to call another caterer. That it didn't look as though it had been added later solely to substantiate his claim would add to his credibility. He'd also discussed Hansen with Nick the very same day. So, there was that going for him, too, if it came down to his word against Peter's.

He picked up the phone and dialed Hansen's number. When there was no reply, he waited for the beep.

"Peter, it's Dan Sharp. I want you to know that the police were at my office today. You may already have heard that Simon Bradley was shot outside my home last night. If not, then you have now officially been informed. My problem currently is an envelope with your ten thousand dollars in it. Despite my promise of confidentiality, I told them it was from you, so you can expect to be answering further questions about it. I hope you will do so clearly and truthfully."

He hung up, wishing yet again that he'd never heard of Peter Hansen.

On the far side of the room, a potted palm had been lifted from its base and set down again beside it. He restored order, matching pot to base. Prints and photographs hung askew on the walls. He straightened them, then turned to his desk, where a colourful ceramic parrot, a gift from a one-time admirer, lay on its side with its beak cracked. It had been a pricey item. German antique. He'd never liked it. He picked it up and dropped it in a bin.

Dan was on his knees, shifting his desk into place when he heard a throat clear behind him. He looked up to see a boyish figure standing in the open doorway.

"Mr. Sharp?" The voice was hollow, almost out-of-body sounding.

Dan had never seen a real ghost before, but this man was about as spectral as they came.

"Sorry for disturbing you. Quite a mess you've got here."

"That's all right. As you can see, it was a helluva party in here last night."

"Really?"

"No. My office was ransacked by the police. I believe it had something to do with your husband. If your husband is Peter Hansen, that is."

"Yes, I'm …"

"Tony Moran," Dan finished for him. He stood and wiped his hands on his pant legs.

Tony looked nervously about. He was the least secure, least confident-looking person Dan could recall ever having met. He was reminded of a schoolboy nabbed for a minor insurrection and silenced by the fear of being blamed for larger faults through association with the wrong school chums.

"How did you find me?"

Tony's face lit up. Simple questions seemed to be his forte. "Oh, that was easy."

"That's never good."

"No, I mean I found your address online. Simon Bradley told me about you. He said if I ever got in trouble I should talk to you."

"Simon said that?"

Tony nodded. Dan recalled the gentle face in the photograph on the dresser in Tony's bedroom, thinking of the contrast between Tony and his husband. There was a fragile beauty to Tony's features that hadn't been captured in the picture. He could see why someone as powerful as Peter Hansen might be entranced by him. Entranced enough to marry him and drag him into public life, willing or not, believing Tony would help improve his image.

"Is it true Simon was killed? I mean at your house."

"Not exactly," Dan said. "He was shot coming to see me. I don't know why. I found him on my doorstep. He died in my living room. Did Simon think someone wanted to kill him?"

Fear eclipsed Tony's features. "I … I don't know. He never said anything like that."

And he wouldn't have, Dan knew. Simon may have been milking Tony for information, but he wasn't going to do anything to scare such a meek little rabbit.

"I was about to make myself a coffee. Would you like one?"

The offer seemed to cheer Tony up. "Sure, yeah."

Dan went into the hall and fiddled with the Faema, one of many things he would soon miss about his office.

They sat across from one another and sipped from their cups. Tony's clothes were shabby and he had dark circles beneath his eyes. Sleeping rough, Dan thought.

"I decided to meet you because of the news story. Simon told me …" His voice trailed off. "You found my wallet, right? In a cemetery?"

Dan shook his head. "Not me. It was turned in to the police."

"That's not what Simon …"

"Were you sleeping there?"

"Just one night." He paused and blinked at the light. "Simon told me you found it. He said he talked to you there."

"I did talk to him there. I didn't find your wallet. A homeless person did."

Tony's face betrayed his confusion. "He said you did. He said you knew everything about what was going on. That you had access to all the information. Why would he lie?"

Dan was taken aback for a moment. "I don't know. Maybe he thought I knew more than I do." *Or maybe he wanted you to believe that so you would come to me if anything happened to him*, Dan thought.

Tony shivered. "It scared me when I heard what happened to Simon."

"Who is the Magus, Tony?"

"I don't know. I never met them."

"Them?"

"I think so. I was never sure." He gave a nervous laugh.

"Does Peter know you're okay?"

Tony looked away. "I don't know if he wants me back. He kept saying I was a liability."

"A liability to what?"

"To getting elected."

"Why did you marry him?"

"He said he'd help me get a better life. He helped me with my gambling addiction and this is how I repay him."

Your husband pitied you, but now he thinks he married beneath himself, Dan reflected. *Since when do politicians marry for pity?*

"I was dirt when Peter met me. I guess I was supposed to behave like a trophy wife."

And with those boyish good looks you might have been ideal, Dan thought, *but for the poker-playing fly in the ointment.*

"I don't know what to do," Tony said.

"Why not just go back home? What are you afraid of? These people who call themselves the Magus? What have they got on you?"

"Nothing!"

It was the most unconvincing answer Dan had ever heard.

"I don't even know who they are." Tony's voice rose to a whine. "I thought they wanted to help me. Now I don't know."

"Help you what?"

"Just … help me get my life together."

"When did you last hear from them?"

"Yesterday. They keep texting me to ask where I am and what I'm up to."

"What do you tell them?"

"I don't tell them anything now that Simon's been killed."

"And John Wilkens? Did the Magus have anything to do with that?"

"How did you — ?" He put down his coffee and looked nervously around. "I shouldn't stay here. They can find you. They know how to track you down."

"How?"

"Cellphone. I left my old one at home, but they tracked my new number."

At that moment, Dan would not have bet a dollar that Tony Moran wasn't a certified mental health patient. He could have been holed up at CAMH with paranoid delusions for the past three weeks, for all he knew.

Dan's phone rang. Peter Hansen's name flashed on the screen. "It's Peter."

Tony looked terrified. "How does he know I'm here?"

"He doesn't. I left a message before you arrived." Dan put the cell to his ear. "Sharp."

"Hansen here. I just got your message. What on earth is going on?"

"Thanks for returning my call. Listen, I've got ..."

But when he turned to look over his shoulder, his door was wide open. Tony had vanished.

"You've got what?" Hansen was demanding in his querulous voice.

Dan shook his head. "I've got questions for you," he replied. "Lots of questions. Let me call you back."

TWENTY-FOUR

Like Father, Like Son

By the time Dan got to the street, Tony was out of sight. He looked in all directions, tried to make out faces in the backs of two cabs passing by, but there was no sign of him. He'd vanished again.

Back in his office, he sat staring at the phone, feeling like a failure. Calling Hansen back and relaying how he'd had Tony in his office but then let him slip away did not go over any better than he expected. At least he'd convinced Peter that knowing Tony was alive and reasonably well was better than nothing.

And on top of everything else, now he had to tell Ked he wouldn't be coming for his graduation after all. He went online and cancelled his reservation, then picked up the phone again, trying hard to imagine the words that might lessen the blow: *I'll make it up to you; we'll get together in a few weeks; don't worry, I know you've done really well.* He replaced the receiver. Letting his son down was something he hated doing. It had to be done, but he would pick the right time.

He made his way back home and stood on the sidewalk outside his house. The grass was green, the flowers waved in the wind. Nothing at the front door or along the walkway suggested the sort of tragedy that had occurred there less than twenty-four hours ago. It was as though in the face of death there could be nothing permanent.

Ralph came scrabbling across the hardwood to greet him when he turned the key in the lock. That meant Nick had returned. Time to face the dragon. Dan was prepared to apologize, though he'd begun to resent that he was always first to back down. He noted ruefully that he had never dated anybody more stubborn than himself. Until now.

"Hello, house?" he called out.

He glanced into the living room. Empty. A lover of order, Nick had put everything back in place. All appeared more or less as it had been, except for the blood stain on the carpet. That would take professional cleaners. But where was Nick?

He hadn't long to wonder. His partner looked up from the bottle of Dewar's planted in the centre of the kitchen table. This time it was down considerably more than one drink.

"I brought Ralph back."

Dan's gaze shifted to a suitcase standing off to one side. "What's going on, Nick?"

"I came to get a few things. I'm going to stay at the condo for a while. Till you sort yourself out."

"What? You're bailing on me? Can we talk about this?"

"I'm not bailing. This is only temporary."

"Until what? Until the wedding? The wedding you want?"

Nick put a fist to his head. "I can't do this right now. Things are very difficult. I'm under a lot of pressure. I had a talk with the chief. He advised me to maintain a distance from you for now." He looked up and caught Dan's angry expression. "I'm sorry."

"Your boss advised you to split up your family in a time of crisis? Why? Because you're gay and gay families don't matter the way other families do?"

"That's not why!" Nick's face hardened. "Sometimes I have to act like a cop, Dan. I don't always get to have feelings."

"I'm glad you can just turn them off and on. Because I can't."

"That's unfair."

Dan felt a moment of remorse. "I can talk to the chief of police for you."

"No!" Nick looked panicked. "I can't go over my boss's head. That's not how it's done."

"Then how is it done? By running out on me?"

"I'm not —" He glared at Dan. "This is cop stuff. You wouldn't understand."

"Try me."

They stared each other down for a moment. A horn blared outside.

"That's my cab."

"You can't just leave."

"I have to. Look, I'll call you later. I was going to leave a note but …" He got unsteadily to his feet. "I have a job to protect and my being here is clearly jeopardizing it."

"You're gay and you're a cop. Are you even happy with either of those things right now?"

Nick's expression darkened. "I was very happy with both of those things until you walked in that door a minute ago. And I am telling you, for the sake of my job and this relationship, that I need to leave right now."

"Right — your career versus our life together." Dan glanced at the bottle. "And you're turning back into a drunk."

"I needed a drink." Nick glared. "Do you think this is easy for me?"

Dan picked up the bottle and shook it. It was past the halfway mark. "Looks to me like it was pretty easy."

Nick headed toward the door. Dan put up a hand to bar him.

"Don't go like this. I'm begging you."

"Please, Dan. I have to —"

"I'm asking you not to leave!"

Nick grabbed Dan's arm. Dan tensed, pushing him backward. Caught off guard, Nick stumbled, hitting his head against the doorframe. Time stopped for a moment, then pitched recklessly forward.

"I'm so sorry …" Dan reached out to help, but Nick pushed his hand away.

"Don't touch me!" Nick brushed a hand against his forehead and looked down at the blood. "Like father, like son."

"Nick, I'm sorry. I didn't mean —"

"Shut up!" He stumbled to his feet, pushing his way past Dan and grabbing his suitcase. "We're done here."

The door slammed closed. For a second Dan was tempted to run after him, but he knew it would do no good. A fist fight on the front lawn to stop Nick from getting into a cab was not going to resolve anything.

He sat at the table as the walls contracted around him. The room was suddenly empty of Nick, empty of their life together. He picked up the bottle of Dewar's. The rust-red liquor bewitched as it swirled and clouded. *Looks to me like it was pretty easy.*

He poured a glass and sat gazing into its depths. Without even tasting it, he could already feel the burn. If he followed his old routine of drinking till he couldn't remember, it could take him anywhere. There was no telling where he might wake up or what he might have done in the meantime. It was a dark door behind which stood the unknown. Like an old friend, it had let him in many times before. It never refused his knock, never failed to open to him. His own heart of darkness, it was a river leading him wherever he wanted to go. He saw himself boarding the gangplank, going up on deck, watching as they lifted the rope and pushed off. The current growing more rapid, the river widening and …

He picked up the glass and pitched it at the cupboard. It dented the wood, splashing its contents around the room, then fell to the floor. Splinters of glass flew in every direction. *Whose fault is this?* he wanted to scream. *Who is in control here?* But there was no answer, no one to hear. There never was.

He'd had a lover once whose previous lover had died not long before he and Dan met. The man's arms and chest had been covered with burn marks. He'd described how he placed the lit end of cigarettes against his skin to cauterize his despair. Asked if it helped resolve his feelings, he said no, but that it made him forget his other pain for a few moments. You could scream and scream and hit all the right notes, Dan knew, but it still wouldn't work out.

He turned to the mirror over the sink, tracing the outline of the scar on the side of his face with a finger. A therapist once told him that until he could forgive his father he'd never learn to trust his emotions or have a functional relationship.

"I don't know if I can do that," Dan had replied.

And now he'd done the unforgivable: inflicted harm on the man he loved most in all the world. He had no doubt who he had to thank for that.

His father had been a violent man, with no sense of who or what he was other than the functionary of a mining company. The sum total of his life was to be a miner. What discipline he could be said to have had was simply waking on time for his designated shifts, and these always underground, whether he arrived in the early morning, in the bright mid-afternoon sunshine, or the appropriately named "graveyard" shift. It was only later, as an adult, that Dan wondered when it had all begun to wear thin for him, at what moment Stuart Sharp the man must have stopped to take stock, realizing he would always be a man journeying between house and hill, stepping inside an elevator chugging endlessly up and down, and knowing that one day the journey would end permanently underground. It wasn't a life anyone would envy. Add to that a bored, philandering wife, a woman who could not be relied on to be at home when he returned from his long day's labour, and then you might begin to understand why he'd turned to drinking to relieve some of the boredom, a bit of the anxiety, and all of the heartache.

At a distance, at least, it helped explain the terrible things he did, first to his wife, when he locked her out in the snow one night and woke to find her shivering on the doorstep, only to lose her within the month to pneumonia; and later to his son, slamming him into a door frame, angered by his late return from school. Explain, yes, but never excuse.

When Dan's father died, Ked had gone with him to the cemetery. Dan hadn't been sure whether to bring him, but his Aunt Marge had insisted. They stood looking over the rows of monuments, Dan, Ked, his Aunt Marge, and his cousin Leyla.

"You're all we have left now," Marge told him, making him promise to stay in touch with her and Leyla as she'd once made him promise not to lie, drink, or swear.

And now she was gone, too, though he kept his promise and still called Leyla from time to time.

With hindsight, Stuart Sharp's only son stopped hating his father and began to pity him. With a little more hindsight, and a good deal of experience, Dan finally thought he understood his father. But he always knew forgiveness might not be within his grasp. He'd stood at the graveyard that day, watching the first shovelfuls of earth tossed onto the coffin. *You had a miserable life, you old bastard. I feel sorry for you. I wish I could say I loved you or missed you, but I don't. The only reason I still think of you is because every day I look in the mirror and see the scar you gave me. You probably didn't intend to scar me, but you did. Physically, at least. I don't intend to let you have the last word emotionally. At least I've learned how to love. Maybe you did or maybe you didn't, but I can't let that hold me back. You gave me physical life, so thanks for that, I guess. But as for what I've done with that life, you had nothing to do with it except inasmuch as you taught me a lot of things I never intend to be. So, maybe thanks for that, too.*

The relief he had felt leaving Sudbury at seventeen was different from the relief he felt after his father's death. Back then there had been a sense of elation on facing the unknown, the prospect of escape. Later, wiping his hands at the grave, it was simply a sense of getting back to his everyday existence, and to his son, who stood waiting for him like a solitary lighthouse on the other side of the grave.

If Kedrick was the best of what he might be said to have given to the world, then Nick was the best of what he'd given to himself. Dan felt an ache thinking of Nick's leaving: *We're done here.* In his mind he heard the door slam again, like some terrible tide withdrawing and taking everything with it. And that was that. Love would never be a problem again. Not for him.

He pushed the bottle away and sat back. Something buzzed in the living room.

He ignored it, but the sound persisted. He followed it to the couch, reached beneath the cushions, and pulled out a small, cold object. At first he couldn't think whose it was. There was a bloody stain on it. The fingerprints of a dying man.

Simon Bradley's cellphone.

TWENTY-FIVE

Eyes on the Ground

HE WOKE TO THE TASTE OF grit and metal. Maybe it was the indigestible memory of his fight with Nick or maybe it was the acrid dreams he'd endured all night long. When he was drinking, he might wake without remembering the events of the previous night, or even the company he'd kept, but that seemed a long time ago. Now when he woke it was often with the memory of something he'd prefer to forget. Like the blood-stained cellphone on his bedside table. Simon Bradley's. He knew he'd have to hand it over to the police, but a voice inside him said not just yet.

Ralph looked at him questioningly as he entered the kitchen, as though hoping for news of Nick or just reassurance that all was well. He'd always watched over Ked and now he was watching out for Dan. He pushed his cold, wet nose against Dan's arm. It was comforting, but even Ralph wouldn't be around forever. Dan patted him on the head and put food in his bowl.

"We'll be okay, Ralphie boy."

Ralph gave a hesitant wag of the tail. It was the best either of them could manage at that moment. The house was going to feel oddly empty without Nick to greet him when he came home, to cook breakfast for him, to rub his back and commiserate with him over the malfeasances of his daily grind. It suddenly struck him just how many roles one person could fill. After Nick had left, he'd waited up for hours, but there was no word from him. No message of regret, no call expressing remorse and asking for time to think things over. And there might never be, he realized. In one instant a giant wave had swept over his life, washing away everything.

There was a message from Will on his phone, a burst of sunshine amid the gloom. "I've got good news for you, Daniel. I have your money. I can drop it off or you can pick it up here today, if you like."

He returned Will's call, grateful for the excuse to fill the house with the sound of his own voice. The exchange was brief, just letting him know he would pick the money up in person.

"I'll be over for it this afternoon. And thanks."

He briefly considered telling Will that he had Simon Bradley's cellphone. As Dan's lawyer, Will should know, but the last time he confided in Will, he'd had CSIS dropped on top of him like a ton of bricks. It could wait till a more convenient time. More convenient for Dan Sharp.

He had just erased Will's message when he remembered he still hadn't called Ked. There was no point in putting it off any further. His son needed to know he wasn't going to be there to see him graduate. On top of everything else … He stopped dead. Yes, there might be a way. Why not? It would be risky, but it was worth a try. He picked up the phone and called.

"Hey, Ked. Slight change of plans."

His son's voice was hesitant. "You're still coming, aren't you?"

"I'm still coming," he said. "Just a different flight. I need to make alternate arrangements."

"Phew! I was afraid for a moment you might be cancelling because of some case or something."

"Not a chance. I'll let you know the new flight info when I have a moment to figure it out."

He sat and shovelled some food down, barely tasting it, then got in his car and headed to Queen's Park.

Dan knocked on Will's door. A cheerful voice called him in. Will was at his desk finishing up a phone call. His voice was serious and soothing, while his eyes rolled to the ceiling. The conversation ended.

"Where are the great men of today? Or the great women, for that matter?"

"Sorry," Dan said. "I can't help you there."

Will smiled and tossed an envelope across the desk. "How's that for fast work? I had my secretary get onto it right after I dropped you off."

"Very impressive, thanks."

"That's a lot of money, as the good sergeant kept reminding us. I hope you do something worthwhile with it."

Dan hefted the envelope. It would nicely cover his expenses when he attended his son's graduation. But he was keeping that to himself for now.

"Part of it will go toward paying your fee, of course."

"Keep your money. It was good practice. Let's just hope I don't end up having to defend you in court. I had a chat with the boys at the precinct this morning. I think this will all be sorted out quickly. As I said before, just stay out of trouble in the meantime."

Dan gave him an ironic look. "What does 'stay out of trouble' mean again?"

"I'm not falling for that one, Daniel. You know as well as I do what it means. Besides, you live with a cop. He'll keep you on the straight and narrow." Will gave him a shrewd look. "How is this sitting with him, by the way? It must have come as a bit of a shock."

Dan shrugged. "Sure. Nick's good. Nothing fazes him."

"Good to hear."

"In any case, let's say I owe you one. Maybe supper one day soon?"

Will gave him a non-committal smile. "I'll ask Susan about an evening off. She's pretty busy. And then there's always the kids. I never quite manage to see enough of them."

"No worries," Dan told him. "If not supper, then just a coffee when you can spare a moment. We really need to catch up on old times."

"I'd like that very much."

Dan had one more task to fulfill, perhaps the thorniest and most contentious of his day. He called ahead to be sure he was welcome. The door was unlocked when he arrived. He let himself in and followed the sounds of laughter and gaiety. Donny and Prabin were eating lunch on the balcony.

Prabin stood and wiped his mouth on a napkin, pulling out a chair for Dan.

"I'll get you a bowl of soup. It's sweet potato–coconut."

"Sounds great, thanks."

Traffic noises burbled up from the street. The question mark was visible in Donny's eyes, but he let Dan taste the broth without rushing him. Then Dan set his spoon aside, made appreciative sounds, and launched into it. They were rapt as he described Simon's murder and the ordeal of the police search. By the time he reached the events leading to Nick's departure, they both looked grim.

There was much shaking of heads and concern as Dan finished, but none more so than when he explained that he intended to proceed with plans to travel to Ked's graduation.

"I'm not asking you to understand," he said, his eyes mostly on Donny, though he glanced over at Prabin from time to time.

"You're just asking us to accept what you're saying," Donny suggested.

"Pretty much, yes."

"Blind faith, as it were," Donny added.

"Is there any other kind?"

"Not a time for semantics."

"No, I guess not."

"So, then, as your friends," and here Donny looked to Prabin, "we accept what you're saying. But I want you to know that accepting is different from approving."

"I know what this looks —"

Donny held up his hand. "Let me finish. I said I accept. However, I am not at all comfortable with the fact that you hit Nick. And now you're running out on him."

"I'm not running out on him. Nick ran out on me. He already had his suitcase packed when I got home. And I didn't hit him. I panicked when he tried to leave and I pushed him to make him stop and listen to me. He fell and hit his head on the doorframe."

"Did you apologize?"

"Of course! Nick wasn't really in the frame of mind to consider an apology at that point. I think we were both a little shocked at how it just seemed to come out of nowhere."

"Rage doesn't come out of nowhere, Dan."

"Yes, okay. You're right. I was angry that he was leaving me. Fear does that, too, but let's not go into my violence-tinged childhood and sexually damaged adolescence. A therapy session isn't going to help at this point."

Donny looked out over the city as he lit a cigarette. He took a drag and turned to Dan. "So, are we to assume the wedding is off?"

"I don't even know if he's coming back. I doubt it, to be honest. I don't know if I would in his situation."

Donny sat back. "I knew you'd fuck it up," he said at last, exhaling with a finality that matched his words.

"Hey!" Prabin interjected. "That is not called for."

Donny looked at his partner. "It is called for. I've known Dan for twenty years and he has managed to screw up every good relationship he's gotten into. Not that there've been that many good ones, so in that sense it's even more of a shame."

"Well, thanks for getting that out in the open," Dan said. "And just what would you suggest?"

"What would I suggest?" Donny stared him down. "Getting in touch with Nick might be a good start."

"I've tried. His voicemail is full of my messages. He doesn't want to talk to me."

"Then go over there and wrestle him down until he listens."

"I hardly need to tell you that's not the sort of tactic to take with Nick."

"And you think leaving town after being told not to by the police is a better one?"

"Nick won't know. Anyway, there's no sense in staying if he's not going to talk to me. I promised Ked I would be at his graduation, so I'm going."

"On a false passport."

"Not a passport. Just false ID."

"I'm sure that must be some sort of federal offence."

"Only if they catch me."

Donny shook his head. "That's not even remotely funny and you know it."

"How are you going to pay for things while you're away?" Prabin asked Dan. "Won't they track you down with your credit cards?" He turned to Donny. "We should lend him one of ours."

"No need, but thanks," Dan said. "I'm using cash. The cash Peter Hansen paid me to find his husband."

Donny sighed loudly. "Of course you are. And that makes us feel so much better to know that." He stubbed out his cigarette in a little flurry of sparks. "So, what is it you are asking us to do in order to aid and abet your decision to ignore a police order?"

"I want you to be my eyes and ears while I'm away. Plus I need you to look after Ralph."

"You want us to be dog sitters?"

"I can't very well ask Nick to do it."

"What shall we do if the police storm our condo and torture us into admitting your whereabouts? Do you expect us to jump off the balcony to elude capture?"

"That would be a bit drastic. Can't you just deny all knowledge of me?"

"By the time you come back, we may be doing just that."

"I won't blame you for it. Oh, yeah. There's one other thing." He placed Simon's cellphone on the table. "Can you get this to Lester? Ask him to download the contents for safekeeping. Once he's done that, tell him to try to override the password and unlock it if he can."

"Should I ask why?"

"Probably not."

Donny picked up the phone and hefted it as he considered the request. "I take it this is important or we wouldn't be doing this?"

"Not just important," Dan said. "It's crucial to the political future of the country."

"Grand. Thanks for leaving it in our hands."

TWENTY-SIX

Leaving It All Behind

THE ROCKIES REACHED UP, luminous in the pre-dawn light, the last great gasp of nature before the continent fell away into the ocean. It was a glorious sight. At least James G. Moab thought so.

The woman next to him was awake after having snored away the last three hours. She turned to him now, speaking as though to a kindly friend. Lonely, perhaps, or disoriented with that just-awake befuddlement common to people who sleep in public places. Moab kept his face turned to the window, even though his rational mind knew she wouldn't recognize him from Adam.

He'd had the same qualm at the airport every time someone had clocked his presence, but of course they were simply registering a striking man with grey eyes and a scar, rather than someone about to make an illegal and unauthorized exit from the city. Relief washed over him as the plane taxied along the runway, tilting up to the skies, the thud of the wheel casing snapping into place beneath them.

A steward came by to collect the remains of a breakfast so unmemorable it was forgotten before it was finished. Free to roam, Dan staggered to the back of the plane and checked himself in the bathroom mirror. He caught the face of a stranger, desperate and wary, and knew what a wanted man felt like.

In the airport, his son greeted him with such force he thought they might both capsize.

"Dad!"

His hair was long, his beard full, like a twenty-first-century beatnik. Dan stood back to take stock of the changes. For now, it was enough that they were together. He would take his time to explain the events of the past seventy-two hours, beginning with the death of Simon Bradley, followed by the raid on his office, then segueing gently over to the rather difficult issue of his physical con-frontation with Nick — best not to call it a fight — and the likelihood that their relationship was over. The thought made him heartsick. It was the closest he'd come to accept-ing the relationship's demise, which in his mind was what it was now approaching.

He thought all of this while watching the joy flooding his son's face on his arrival. Dan smiled and hugged him back. Yes, better to leave the telling till later. Mixed mes-sages were never good things.

It was definitely a students' flat, Dan thought as Ked showed him around the spartan space. All the minimal comforts of home with few of the luxuries. In the sitting room, a candle stub squatted atop a wine bottle, the wax halted in a confusion of colours where it dripped onto a battered coffee table. An avocado pit sprouted in a pot on a window ledge, while framed leftist protest posters hung on the walls. Mislaid memories for Dan, irony for a twenty-something. Ked was cooking chili for lunch. More student chic. Dan still remembered being a student and having to do without, though he couldn't imagine doing it now.

Ked hesitatingly introduced him to his absent roommate's quarters. A duvet had been thrown over the lumpy bed, a pile of laundry pushed beneath it with a stray shirt sleeve sticking out.

"This is Charlie's room," Ked said. "He's kind of a slob, but he did his best to hide the mess. Fresh linen, at least."

"No worries. I never question a free bed."

Dan looked over to the window sill where a healthy-looking cannabis plant was in bloom.

"Charlie's," Ked said with a shrug. "His name's Sidney. The plant, I mean. Charlie wanted to hide him in the closet, but I said you were constitutionally against hiding things in closets."

Dan laughed. "I guess I can share the room with a pot plant named Sidney for a few days."

"I'll leave you to unpack. Lunch should be ready in five."

Dan unzipped his suitcase and hung his jacket alongside a smattering of T's and jeans in the closet Sidney had been bound for before Ked's reprieve. He glanced over the bookcase. Charlie seemed poised somewhere between a Marvel superhero fan and an aficionado of pornography. His DVD collection displayed titles proudly: *The Graduate:*

Sex Education of a Sophomore. Dan smiled wryly. *You'll know a man by his books and his DVDs*, he mused, and wondered if Charlie hid them in the closet with Sidney when his mother came to visit.

Ked was in the kitchen stirring the chili when Dan entered.

"So, the ceremony's on Sunday," he said. "We have to wear the cap and gown thing and all that, but nobody really minds. We're looking at it like it's some sort of costume drama — well, costume comedy — so it'll be fun." He looked over and caught his father's expression. "Everything okay? I've been babbling non-stop since you got here."

"It's okay," Dan chimed in. "Just a bit … jet-lagged."

"If it's about Trevor, you don't have to worry. He won't insist on seeing you."

"Of course I'll see him."

He thought of Trevor's gentle features, his curly brown hair. Narcissus crossed with a Botticelli angel. Apart from a genuine affection, they had shared a taste for horror films and for staying home on Saturday nights instead of going out on the town. But, ultimately, Dan's choice of profession and Trevor's nerves had separated them, sending Trevor scuttling back to his corner of the world.

"Mom will be here tomorrow," Ked announced, interrupting his reveries.

Dan looked over with a blank expression.

"You better tell me," Ked said. "I can see something's up."

"I guess I better begin at the beginning."

Dan went over the events of the past few weeks, beginning with the search for Tony Moran and ending with Nick's departure. When he was done he sat back. Ked nodded.

"I could tell something was wrong. You should have told me it wasn't a good time for you to visit."

"This isn't just a visit. This is your graduation."

"Still. I don't like to think you've done something illegal just to be here for me."

"It's a grey area. We'll worry about it when the time comes. My lawyer says this will all blow over very quickly."

"I hope so."

Everything was going to be okay, Dan reminded himself. And even if it wasn't, there was no use worrying about it.

"I'm also here for me. I'm proud of you. You're my greatest achievement, don't forget that, either. That's why I've tried to give you everything I didn't have."

"Ouch! Heavy. What if I don't want it?"

"I'm not talking about material things. I'm talking about love, security. A feeling that life is worth living without having to wonder why for even one single day."

"If you have any doubts, then I want you to know I have all those things. Because of you, Dad. And Mom. That's why I was able to come here to study. It was hard, but leaving home was one of the best things I've done. There's a whole world of grown-upness here. Though …"

"Though?" Dan prompted.

"I guess … at least at first … I thought you were pushing me away when you told me I should come to B.C. Not being from a traditional family, I always felt I had to be near you and Mom for us to be together. Now I see it's not like that. I can roam and still be loved. I'm cool with it."

"It's been hard for us, too," Dan said. "I miss you not being there. Maybe more than I've ever missed anybody.

But I'm proud of you for not returning home before you finished your degree just to make me feel better. I hope you understand that."

His son nodded. "I understand."

"Good. Now — tell me about Trevor."

TWENTY-SEVEN

Retreat

From the top deck of the ferry, Dan watched the shore approach. Rain battered the waters of the strait with invisible hands, then disappeared again. The waves sparkled, a dazzling road of fairy lights, while the sun played hide and seek with the clouds.

Dan thought of Trevor's chalet-style cottage, the up-thrust roof that resembled a ski slope. If you tried a slalom off it, though, you'd come crashing down into the red cedars surrounding it. He recalled the excitement he'd felt coming to see Trevor for the very first time all those years ago. "My Mayne Island hermit," he'd called him.

Dan waited impatiently for the ship to berth alongside the piles before heading down the stairs. Trevor was there to meet him, waving and smiling. He looked good from afar. Up close, he looked even better. Still lean and muscular. It seemed as though no time had passed since their last encounter, a long night spent disentangling the reins of their relationship before they parted.

They hugged one another and stood back to assess. Like women, Dan thought, gay men will always compare. Compliments rained down. *You look terrific … Great to see you again … I've been looking forward to this.* All true. None of it truly necessary to put in words, though the intuitive, unspoken bonds between them had lessened over time.

They waited for the stream of cars and pedestrians to pass, islanders returning from the mainland satisfied once again there was nothing in the big world — that other world — that they were missing. Then Trevor took Dan's bag with that oh-so-familiar smile, hoisting it onto his shoulders, and they began the half-mile hike to his part of the magical isle.

The fire crackled. Night was approaching, misting the chalet's windows. Dan recalled how it always seemed to be misting whenever he was there, and how he'd been amazed to discover the island's trees had a permanent coating of moss, a gossamer wrap.

They'd been speaking of the past, dissecting old emotions, treading on dangerous territory. Trevor brought out a chilled bottle, poured two glasses, and handed one to Dan. They touched rims and sipped. Dan checked the label: a 2004 Viognier. The same vintage Trevor had served on his first visit. Was this going in the wrong direction?

Instinctively, he put on the brakes.

"Ked felt I should see you."

Trevor smiled. "Ah, it's duty, then."

Dan was embarrassed. "No, I didn't mean it like that. Of course I wanted to see you. I just wouldn't have had the audacity to presume if he hadn't suggested it."

"You know we've kept in touch since he moved here?"

"Yes, he told me."

"I hope it doesn't make you feel uncomfortable." Trevor lifted his glass, the firelight dancing in his eyes.

"Not at all. I was thrilled that he stayed connected with you. After all, he has no family here." He paused. "No *other* family, I should say. He still thinks of you that way. And I'm glad."

"Me too. If things had turned out differently …" Trevor's words died out. "Well, let's just say there would have been a child like Ked in the picture for me."

"If you'd found the right partner, you mean?"

"I thought of doing it on my own, hiring a surrogate and all that. But it seemed too much for one person to do all alone out here."

Dan smiled.

"What?" Trevor asked. "Oh. I guess that's pretty much what you did, isn't it?"

"If I'd known then what it meant, I might have had pause, but I had no choice. Ked was on the way and some-one had to look after him."

"Well, you've certainly brought him up right, Daniel. He's a beautiful boy, inside and out. You couldn't have had a better kid."

"Thanks, I agree. There were some difficult times, of course."

"No regrets, I hope?"

"None."

They lifted glasses and clinked again.

Dan looked out the window to the rocky walls of Pender Island across the strait. The conversation died. He was suddenly aware of the tranquility, the pervasive silence. From somewhere in the distance came a loon's quavering cry.

"I think I was destined to be a monk," Trevor said, as if reading his mind.

"It's a beautiful monastery you've got here."

"None better. As long as this monk is allowed his wine rations, I'll be fine."

For a second, Dan felt he could give it all up for this sense of peace that surpassed understanding. It was, in fact, sublime, though he knew it wasn't meant for him.

The conversation revived. Trevor gave Dan a run-down of his work, how he'd geared it toward the outdoors, designing landscapes for a college in Vancouver. Dan caught him up on mutual friends in Toronto. There was so much they no longer knew about one another. Eventually their words brought them back to their time together.

"I always felt you were trying to rescue me," Trevor said. "I think it was your sense of duty. You'd save anyone who asked you for help."

"Is that what I do?"

"It was when we were together. But you never let me help you in return. I wanted to, but I never knew how. Instead, I worried about you."

"You might be right."

"Forgive my saying so, but I don't think you ever learned to trust. You demanded it from others without giving it in return. For me, it was natural. I come from a loving family. I don't spend my life searching for trust in others and fearing it won't be there when I need it."

"And you think that's what I do?"

"Well." Trevor smiled gently. "I don't pretend to know everything about you after all these years, but it always struck me that you saw yourself as someone born to be alone."

Dan felt the unwelcome sting of recognition. He tried to recall if he'd ever taken anyone fully into his confidence, or if there was ever a time when he'd felt completely free of loneliness.

"Don't get me wrong," Trevor said. "Nobody ever gave my life as much depth and meaning as you did. It was great, but you made it so hard to love you back. It was like you were afraid to need anybody."

Dan looked out the window where the wind was gently blowing the trees back and forth. *What's the point in needing somebody?* he wondered. They all left in the end. His father to drink himself to death, Nick to protect his job, Trevor because of his fears. Even Ked left, going off to school: *There's a whole world of grown-upness here.*

"What's the point? Everyone leaves eventually." He caught the look on Trevor's face. "Sorry, I didn't mean it like that."

"It's okay. I did leave you, after all."

"I always felt I let you down."

"Not at all. You're a born rescuer. And you convinced yourself that you needed to save me. Because that's your job." He waited a moment. "What about you? Don't you deserve saving?"

"Me? I don't need saving."

"We all need saving. Even you, Dan."

Dan thought of Nick, how lost he felt without him. He saw now that he had it wrong, and had always had it wrong. It wasn't simply finding the right person that was difficult, it was learning to love through disappointment and doubt, and trying to stay the course, accepting that the other person loved you despite all the many reasons you believed deep down inside that he should not. That was where he had failed.

"It was just too hard to watch the many ways you made yourself suffer," Trevor continued. "So I ran away. And I'd do it again. Don't think I could ever come back."

There it was, the unspoken question.

"I wasn't —"

"It's okay, I didn't think that was why you came. But I'm glad you're here. Maybe old loves are the best." He held up his glass. "You need someone as hard as you by your side, though. Someone who forces you to let him in. I couldn't do it. Maybe your policeman can. I hope so, for your sake."

TWENTY-EIGHT

The Graduate

DAN CAUGHT AN EARLY FERRY from the Mayne Island terminal. He found Ked sitting in the kitchen of his flat when he arrived, a look of trepidation on his face.

"Um … the police were here this morning asking questions."

Not a great way to start the day. "About me, I take it?"

"They wanted to know if you were here. I said no and they asked if I knew where you were."

"I'm sorry you had to lie for me," Dan said, feeling sick that his son had had to do that for him.

It reminded him of the excuses he used to make to his Aunt Marge about the whereabouts of his father. *Out with friends.* How many times had he said that particular untruth? His father didn't have friends, only drinking buddies. *Fetch him home from the pub*, his aunt would say with a world-weary sigh and a shake of the head. And off young Daniel would run, hoping he'd be let into the bar despite his age so he could find his father, cheerless and remorseful, sitting over in a dark corner, working on his seventh or eighth drink. And all the time praying he wouldn't find him, not wanting his father at home.

"I didn't lie," Ked said. "The truth is, I didn't know where you were. You could have been on Mayne Island, but you might have been on the ferry coming back by then. And it looks like you were." He grinned. "I also said I spoke to you in Toronto last week and that I was flying home soon to see you there. All true."

"Did they see the pot plant?"

Ked shrugged. "Probably. I didn't try to hide it. It's like having a tulip growing in your window here. I doubt they'd even notice."

They both laughed. Then Ked turned serious again.

"You don't have to come to the ceremony …"

Dan shook his head. "I'm coming. Just try to stop me."

"I called Mom and told her not to wear anything too flashy, not to attract attention if you were with her. She agreed."

"You even think like a sleuth."

"Hey, you trained me well."

The crimson fingers of a trumpet vine climbed the red-brick auditorium in bright warning. Blood on blood. Dan looked for signs of a police presence as they reached the campus. There was nothing obvious, but then what would be the point of trying to catch a fugitive while making yourself easy to spot?

Kendra met them outside the convocation hall. True to her word, she'd dressed demurely, but she was all the more stunning for it. Dan had never seen her so lovely. A Syrian beauty. Well, after all, she'd captured his interest long enough to produce a son. And though neither of them could have foreseen it at the time, here they were twenty years later, proud of what they'd shared in creating.

She took Dan's arm. "What's this I hear about keeping a low profile? You're on the lam? Let me know if there's anything I should do or not do."

"You're doing all the right things," he told her as they entered the auditorium along with all the other excited parents.

"Can you believe we're doing this?" she asked, shaking her head in disbelief at what parenthood had brought.

"Whether we believe it or not, we're here together and we deserve a big reward for what we've accomplished."

She smiled and squeezed his hand. "Yes, we do."

"Trevor sends his love, by the way. I spent a day with the Mayne Island hermit. He looks really happy."

"I'm glad to hear that." She paused. "I hate to ask, but what does Nick think about all this absconding from justice?"

"Nick will have to adapt," Dan said, feeling a twinge in his chest. It wasn't getting easier, but rather worse each time he contemplated a life without Nick by his side.

He grabbed her by the arm and steered her toward their seats.

"C'mon. It's starting."

†

Kendra had tears in her eyes by the time the ceremony was over. Dan, too, was moved, as were the other parents. Only the graduating students seemed lighthearted, sighing with relief to think their studies were over and real life had begun. *If only they knew*, Dan thought.

The crowd spilled out onto the lawn in front of the auditorium and stood there blinking in the sunshine. *All these proud parents with their progeny*, Dan thought. It was refreshing to see people rejoicing in something for once, rather than pushing their way past one another or complaining and resenting each other for no good reason. Kendra had met a lesbian couple who introduced her to their daughter, a young woman in a wheelchair. Somewhere else, a signer's hands busily interpreted for a deaf family. This mass of humanity, varied and unique, each limited in his or her way, didn't for a moment let anything distract them from the pride they felt that afternoon.

Dan motioned for Ked and Kendra to stand before the backdrop of the Rocky Mountains, the sky blue and open. As he framed them with his camera, he found himself taking stock: the boy he'd raised to the best of his ability was standing on the threshold of manhood, looking out and contemplating what his own life would bring.

The shutter clicked. Time folded in on itself, never stopping for a moment as life rushed busily onward.

They were at the airport saying their goodbyes. Dan opened his wallet and removed one of Peter Hansen's thousand-dollar bills. He'd just spent another on a return ticket. No skimping. This time he was flying business class.

He held the banknote out to Ked, who looked at him in awe.

"Dad, that's a lot of money."

"To some people. To others it's a little. It's how you spend it that counts. Spend it well."

"Thanks." Ked pocketed the bill with a wistful look. "I was waiting to tell you that you're a hero to me, but now you'll think I was bribed into saying it."

Dan laughed. "I'm not a hero. I'm only doing what I'm paid to do. Heroes go beyond the norm."

"Okay, maybe not a hero, but you're the best dad ever. Seriously."

Dan hugged his son so tightly he thought his heart would break. "I'll see you in a week, okay?"

"Deal."

As the plane took off, Dan thought of his beginnings. His father had been a sad, broken man, his mother a frivolous woman whose dreams had exceeded her grasp. The soil his roots were nurtured in hadn't seemed fertile, but now those roots extended to a new generation for his son to carry on.

He looked down over Canada's westernmost edge, a thousand kilometres of indented fjords and islands, sandwiched between the Yukon and the forty-ninth parallel. It occurred to him that his life was like that, a vast coastline stretching far into the past and disappearing somewhere far up ahead.

A smiling steward came down the row. Dan took the newspaper offered and settled in for a long flight. It wasn't till he turned the page that he found himself named as part of the ongoing investigation into the murder of Simon Bradley, his current whereabouts unknown.

TWENTY-NINE

Big Bang Theories

It seemed ages since Dan had walked up the front steps of his office building. In fact it had been just four days. He kept his eyes peeled for undercover officers, but no one looked likely to perform the public duty of arresting him.

The warehouse was a hive of activity, a swarm of busy bees buzzing in and out of the premises on their way to lunches, trysts, hair appointments, business meetings, and whatever else constituted the workaday rhythms of the successful young entrepreneur.

Some of them, Dan knew, might turn out to be tomorrow's leaders, captains of industry running the show, the country, and even the world. He only hoped they wouldn't turn out as jaded and self-centred as his own generation. The sellouts. People who'd given up on bettering the world in favour of bettering their own standards of living.

He liked these new go-getters, likening them to big bang theorists always on the lookout for a formula to create the new world order. Ked had explained to him how scientists no longer believed the universe began as a massive explosion rushing outward to fill a void, but rather as a blast constantly expanding space itself, where future events were occurring simultaneously on multiple horizons. Due to the speed of light, however, some of those events hadn't yet reached us, like a letter lost in the mail, and in fact might never reach us.

Perhaps if he'd stepped aside from his father quickly enough that fateful day on returning from school, Dan thought, he might not now have the scar that stretched down his temple. On the other hand, while it made him feel a bit of a Frankenstein, more than one boyfriend had confessed to finding it sexy. You could never tell. One man's deformity was another man's turn-on. More importantly, maybe there was a place in the galaxy where he had not yet pushed Nick against the doorframe, ending their once-enviable relationship. The thought sobered him.

He stopped at the front desk to check his mailbox. The secretary glanced up, a pretty young woman with a vacant expression. Her eyes glazed over as if she'd never seen him before. If she'd read the newspaper article about his absence, clearly it hadn't registered. Or maybe she just wasn't paid enough to care.

After buying the property, the building's owners had dropped the personal touch. The previous secretary, Sylvia, had used to greet Dan by name and bring him baked goods. No more. Dan had seen the writing on the wall when the new management took over, but it only truly hit home with the eviction notice. He'd been approached by two other long-term tenants who asked if he was interested in fighting it, though they all agreed it would do little more than postpone the inevitable. Dan told them he'd be leaving along with all the rest.

They'd shaken their heads woefully at him. "Sad tidings," one told him. "End of an era," the other said.

Dan wasn't sure the era amounted to all that much.

Now, he pulled his mail from the box and headed for the stairs. He'd called in for messages on the way back from the airport. The first three were from the police, each more insistent than the previous one, demanding that he call back. The fourth was from Will Parker, asking Dan to get in touch as soon as he got the message. The final message was from Nick. Dan felt his heart leap at the sound of his voice, but it was cut short by Nick's tone: *Dan, it's Nick. I've got a murder investigation unit breathing down my neck looking for you. What the fuck are you playing at?* And then a loud hang-up. So much for love's fevered whisperings and tender messages of regret.

He continued up the stairs. Someone passed him hurriedly on the landing between the second and third floors. Young, sullen, and scruffy beneath a woolly toque. Not the sort of face he'd really want to remember, but it struck a chord of some sort. He looked for a glint of recognition in the other's eyes, though it was hard to say what he saw in those depths. If indeed there were depths to plumb.

They passed each other by.

Dan continued to the top floor, where he shared the space with the invisible bible salespeople. He wondered what their recent sales count might be. Perhaps he should ask the good folks at CSIS.

His cell rang just as he reached his door and stood fumbling with the keys. Donny's name flashed across the screen.

"Ah, the wanderer returns," came his friend's voice.

"Guilty as charged."

"It's about time. You've got half the country looking for you."

"Not quite a quarter by my count. But, yes, I've heard."

"Nick called twice to ask if I knew anything. I felt like a bastard lying to him."

"Sorry for putting you on the spot. He called me, too, and left an angry message, if it's any consolation. How did Lester make out with the phone?"

"Yeah, right — that. He didn't. He says it's password-encrypted in a way that after three wrong attempts it will erase the phone's contents. He didn't want to proceed with it. What the hell is on this thing?"

"I wish I knew." Dan dropped his keys and bent down to retrieve them. "I thought Lester was the sort of kid who could get around that kind of stuff."

"Normally, yes, but this is an iPhone. Lester says even the FBI can't do what it takes. They're trying to force Apple to invent software to break its own codes and get behind the firewall, stating terrorist concerns, et cetera. Predictably, Apple refuses, knowing the technology will eventually end up being used to spy on everyone. He's here if you want him to explain it to you."

"That's okay," Dan said, sorting through the keys while balancing the mail in his other hand. "I'll thank him later. I just thought it was worth a try."

"Can't you force the phone's owner to tell you what's on it?"

"He's dead."

"I didn't need to know that."

"No, probably not."

Donny harrumphed. "No clues as to what it might be? Any last words of advice before he died?"

"Apart from always making sure I brush and floss? Nah. I thought he was asking me to call 911 with it." Dan flashed on Simon's dying struggle to hand over the phone, his final breath implicating the Magus as his murderer. If only he knew who … but no.

He had the office key in hand and bent to insert it. In the back of his mind, something registered a problem with the lock casing, but that vanished as a piece of the puzzle fell into place. A future event horizon had just arrived with all the subtlety of an atomic blast.

He left off fumbling with the key and stood upright. "Wait. Of course! I'm stupid! Put Lester on …"

Lester's boyish treble came over the phone. "Hi, Uncle Dan."

"Lester, hi. Listen to me very carefully. You're only going to try this once. If it fails, leave it alone. Understood?"

"Sure."

"The password is a five-letter word. Magus. M-A-G-U-S."

He waited, holding his breath till Lester yelled in triumph. "That's it!"

"Okay. Very carefully, copy whatever is on it. I'll come and pick it up when you're done."

Donny came back on the phone.

"You're a genius, thanks for that," Dan said.

"Whatever I did."

Dan bent down and saw the gouging on the lock cover.

288

This time it registered solidly. Someone had been trying to break into his office. Someone sloppy and poorly trained, when it came down to it.

An alarm went off in his mind. His thoughts floated back down two floors to the face he thought he'd recognized. The scruffy cheeks, the woolly toque.

"Hang on a sec," he said into the phone.

Dan took the stairs two at a time, his feet tripping over one another. His heart was thumping out a warning as he reached the bottom and grasped the railing to steady himself. He couldn't remember the last time he'd been so physically reckless. Yes, he could: it was the night he'd chased the black Mazda with a tire iron.

There it was again far down the block. The car peeled away from the curb just as he raced outside.

"Fucking hell!" he screamed, startling several passersby.

A squawking came from the phone. He put it to his ear.

"What is going on over there?" Donny demanded.

"Sorry, I —" Dan began, just as an explosion ripped through the air.

He looked up. His office belched flames and black smoke into the sky three stories up.

"What's happening?"

"I think my office just blew up," Dan said.

"*What?*"

"Correction," Dan said, staring up at the flames. "I know my office just blew up. Call you back."

It took nine minutes. Dan timed their arrival and watched as the emergency response team poured from the three

EMS vehicles parked at crazy angles outside the warehouse. A crowd had gathered to stare, blocking the street. The team ushered people aside, urging them out of harm's reach in case of further explosions. Dan gave particulars to a red-headed EMS driver without stating his real name or mentioning the scratches on his lock. Those he would save for a later date, a more pertinent audience.

The driver left. Dan called Donny back.

"What the *fuck*?" came his friend's expletive. "This is what comes of hanging around with these deviant types."

"I might remind you the 'hanging around' part is not exactly voluntary. And I should also point out that nothing yet confirms anything of a suspicious nature. It could be a gas leak for all we know."

"Well, let me know when you get to the 'suspicious' part and catch up with the program. I'm sure it won't be long." Donny sighed. "Quite the homecoming. Just like you, Dan."

A young fireman came over to Dan. "Sorry, sir, but I need to ask you a few questions."

"Gotta go," Dan said into the phone. "There's a good-looking fireman who wants to talk to me."

He'd just finished that conversation when a figure crept up next to him, watching the smoke coming from the window.

"Isn't that your office?"

Dan looked over. Tony Moran stood beside him.

He shrugged. "It's okay. I was moving anyway."

THIRTY

Official Secrets

THEY WERE IN TONY MORAN's borrowed flat. Borrowed from a gambling buddy who was currently out of town. Gamblers, like addicts, know that favours are meant to be returned when you need them most. They store them like canned food in case of emergencies. You never knew when you were going to need an extra tin of something, a free sleep on a sofa. Tony's friend's flat was one of those returned favours.

It was in an old warehouse at King and Parliament. The ambience was hipster: exposed brick walls, original tin ceilings, and heating ducts painted bright pink. Things ripped back to what previous tenants had tried to hide. Frames hung crookedly, enlarged posters of famous black-and-white movie stills providing atmosphere and nostalgia: Humphrey Bogart, Mary Astor, Jimmy Cagney, Myrna Loy, Peter Lorre. Celluloid heroes and villains. It was just glitzy enough to impress a jaded TV designer, but still rundown enough to be considered chic.

A coffee table held a wealth of self-help books: *Help Yourself to Wealth, Help Grow Money in Your Pocket, Help for Winning Poker Strategies*. But nothing on how to help your gambling addiction, Dan noted.

A fire escape led past the kitchen window to a third-floor landing. Rumour had it the flat was once the lair of a notorious mafia don who ran his criminal activities from behind closed doors. But the don had died in a hail of bullets while sitting on the patio of a gelateria in Little Italy, celebrating his daughter's engagement. Not the best choice of times to make a public showing. Currently, it served as the pied-à-terre of a chronic gambler who kept the property secret from his third ex-wife so she wouldn't take it from him.

It hadn't taken much to get Tony to come with Dan. A mention of the Magus, a reference to gambling heavies who knew his name, and he was putty in Dan's hands. He suspected there was also a bit of voyeuristic interest on Tony's part, a boy-meets-daddy sort of appeal that Dan was only too willing to exploit.

Tony sat cross-legged in the middle of the floor. His hands shook as he spoke in half-finished sentences. His eyes kept darting over to the liquor cupboard. Maybe gambling wasn't his only addiction.

Dan got up and grabbed a bottle, poured a tumbler and passed it to Tony, who took it and drank quickly. After that, his speech came more freely, his tongue moving trippingly as he described his recent ordeals.

Realizing Peter had cut off his credit, he'd spent a few nights on the streets before getting in touch with some old friends who put him up at various places around the city, this location being the last rung on the ladder to a more rarefied place. Wherever he was headed.

"I'm still trying to figure out what to make of your connection with John Wilkens," Dan said, looking up as though the answer might miraculously appear overhead.

"It was the Magus," Tony replied. "They wanted me to talk to him, to be on his good side."

"But why?" Dan pressed. "What possible use could you be to him?"

Tony opened his mouth to speak then closed it again. "They never really explained it."

He was shaking again. Not from drink this time.

"The money you gambled away that night ... you said you stole it from Peter?"

"Borrowed. I only borrowed it."

"The money you borrowed then. The only problem is, Peter can't figure out where it went missing from."

An anxious look came over Tony's face. "I've been very secretive."

"When I told him how much you lost, he said you couldn't possibly have taken that much without his knowing it."

"Then he doesn't know where to look."

"How did you manage to keep it from him?"

Tony cast a fearful eye around the room. "I'd rather not say. I mean, I don't want to implicate myself any further."

Dan stood. Tony's eyes were glued to his every move.

"Where are you going?"

"I've got to go out and meet someone. I'll be back in a couple of hours. You should be fine here till I get back."

Dan glanced at the window and down to the street. "As long as you don't leave."

"No, I wouldn't do that," Tony said hastily. He checked himself. "And then what?"

"And then we'll see what we see."

Lester met him on a downtown street corner. He handed Dan the phone as though it contained nuclear secrets. For all Dan knew, it might have.

"Everything copied and safely stowed away?"

"Completely."

"Sorry for the secrecy," Dan said.

"Yeah, my dad would never have let me come if he knew I was meeting you."

"So let's not tell him, okay?"

"I'm cool."

"I have to go now."

"Wait."

Dan turned.

There was a pleading look in Lester's eyes. "Is there anything I can do for you? Anything that might … I don't know. Help in some way?"

"Lester, you are a remarkable young man. But I would never allow you to do anything that might endanger you or Donny or Prabin. Thank you."

"It's okay." He smiled. "I never knew your work was so cool, Uncle Dan."

"It's not. It just looks that way from the outside."

Dan turned and pocketed the cell. His next destination was just a few blocks away.

From outside it looked like an ordinary office, even though the country's best-kept secrets were locked behind its iron doors four floors underground. Dan called first to make sure he would be admitted, then showed up half an hour early for his appointment. Right before he arrived, he texted a number retrieved from Simon Bradley's cellphone. Then he stood and waited. Two minutes later, he saw Steve Ross come sailing through the front door and head up the street.

Right on time, Dan thought.

He went in and caught the elevator down. The doors opened onto a nondescript lobby. An attractive young man sat at the desk. He looked up.

"Can I help you?"

"I think you can," Dan said. "My name's Will Parker. I'm afraid I'm a bit early."

"Yes, sir. Mr. Ross is expecting you. He asked me to tell you to wait for him. He had to step out for a moment. Something unexpected came up."

Dan was sitting behind his desk when Steve returned from the wild goose chase he'd been sent on. Steve gave a little laugh. He did his best not to appear flustered, but his angry tone gave him away.

"Where is Will? How did you get in here?"

"Will's not coming. Your secretary let me in. Very cute, by the way."

"My secretary," Steve said, his wrath rising, "would have told you to stay in the waiting room."

"He forgot that part."

"I could have you arrested."

"For what? Sitting in your chair?"

"For jumping the terms of your release."

Dan did his best to look perplexed. "Really? How do you figure I did that?"

"We have a man by the name of James G. Moab on camera in the airport. Buying a ticket to Vancouver with cash. He looks an awful lot like you even with the baseball cap."

"Popular destination this time of year. Must have been someone else."

"You're a wanted man."

"I know that. I read about it in the paper, so it must be true."

"What do you want?"

"I don't want anything from you. I have something to give you."

"What's that?"

"The murderer of John Wilkens and Simon Bradley."

Steve eyed him curiously. "Who is that?"

"I don't actually know yet. You'll have to show up and see who drops by when I spring the trap."

"Is this some kind of joke?"

"Not at all."

Steve fingered a photograph on his desk. "I recently had two resident aliens arrested on charges of conspiring to derail passenger trains at Union Station. Not long ago, we had a group of eighteen — *eighteen!* — young militant Muslims discussing the best ways to blow up the stock exchange. There would have been massive destruction and untold loss of lives. I don't have time for this! No one killed John Wilkens. He hanged himself. As for Simon Bradley, it sounds like he was snooping where he shouldn't have been. We can't protect everyone."

"You think you've got problems? My office was just blown up with me about fifteen seconds away from being in it. Nevertheless, you asked me to help you find the so-called Magus. Well, I've been doing that. I think the Magus and the murderer are the same person."

Steve paused to let this sink in. "And how exactly are you going to catch this supposed murderer?"

"By using Tony Moran as bait. He's been in the thick of this since the beginning. Someone paid him to stay away from his husband, only he blew the money gambling. I want to see who wants Tony badly enough to try and take him from me."

Steve regarded Dan coldly. "This is a very dangerous kind of game you're playing."

"Well, let's hope I win. I'm betting a lot on the hand I hold right now."

"When and where does this all take place?"

Dan stood. "Tonight. I'll text you the details once I leave here."

Steve reached a hand to his desktop telephone. "I could have you arrested and held without notice."

"If you stop me now, we'll never know who it is."

Steve picked up the phone and held it to his ear. He looked out the glass partition to where his secretary was seated at his desk. The young man answered.

"Matthew, please see Mr. Parker out."

Dan left the office, wondering if he'd be arrested before he got to the street. He let out a sigh of relief as he went through the front door. Out on the sidewalk, he stopped and checked the photo he'd lifted from Steve Ross's desk of Steve with a friendly-looking woman, a boy, and a massive Doberman that looked as if it would swallow Ralph whole. Not a family pet. And not a wife and son either, Dan knew from past encounters. Possibly a sister and nephew, or maybe just a woman paid to pose as a cover.

He scrolled through Simon Bradley's phone until he found the number he wanted. He typed: *If you're interested, I'll be at 498A King Street East this evening. Come around 9. I've got something you want.* For good measure, he took a shot of Tony's photo that Peter Hansen had given him. Hesitating for just a second, he pressed SEND.

Next he sent the details to Steve Ross. Finally, he texted Nick's cellphone: *You told me not to try this stuff on my own, so I'm letting you know about it now.* He capped it with a few particulars, hoping Nick would at least respond, even just to tell him he was crazy and never to bother him again.

THIRTY-ONE

The Devil You Know

TONY EYED DAN WARILY WHEN he returned. During his absence Tony had closed all the curtains and moved a wing chair as far as possible from the windows. The bottle sat on his lap. It was down considerably. Dan was right: he had more than one addiction problem. All the better to make him pliable and keep him in hand until this ordeal was over.

"Is everything okay now?" Tony's voice sounded high and nervous.

"Everything's fine."

The room was drowned in soft shadows, the furniture partially submerged in darkness, a corner of a couch and the peak of an armchair jutting up midstream. Dan snapped on an overhead light, illuminating Tony like a performer spot-lit on a stage.

Tony put a hand up to his face. "What's going to happen?" He sounded sheepish, like a child whose hiding spot has been uncovered.

"We've got a meeting tonight. Here."

"With who?"

"I don't know." Dan shrugged. "That's what I still can't figure out. I thought you might know. So I texted the Magus a while ago. I gave him this address."

Panic lit up Tony's face. "Why did you do that? What were you thinking?"

"Just baiting the trap. And it seems to me you're the best bait I've got."

Tony's gaze flitted anxiously around the room, as though seeing imaginary forms in the gloom. "That was totally irresponsible. You can't do this to me."

"Too late. I've done it. Who is it we should be expecting?"

"I told you, I never met them." His voice was a whine. "I have no idea."

"Okay, I'll believe you, then. Care to tell me where you got all the money you gambled away that night in Little Vietnam?"

Tony began to hyperventilate. "They gave it to me, okay?"

"Who?"

"The Magus. It ... the money was directed into my account."

"So you could gamble it away?"

"What? No." He shook his head. "It was so I could live away from Peter."

"But you lost it instead."

"I — I couldn't help it. It was so much money at once."

"But where did it come from before it ended up in your account?"

His eyes were evasive again. "I don't know. They just diverted it from one account into another and gave me access to it. I wasn't supposed to spend it all so fast."

"Am I right in thinking the money showed up around Christmas last year?"

Tony shivered. "Simon was right — you do know everything."

"You figured out that it came from a portfolio John Wilkens was managing. That's why you were trying to get rid of it when you gambled it away."

"Oh, god!" Tony said softly.

"You told John you would share information with him about the power plant cover-up. Then you reported what John said back to the Magus. That's why they're after you now."

Tony's eyes flitted around the flat. "I didn't know they would kill him."

"Who?"

"I don't know!" He glared at Dan. "I really don't."

"Then I guess we'll just sit tight and find out." He paused with the light still on Tony's face. "On the other hand, you could just get up and leave. I don't want anyone saying I kept you here against your will. But I suspect you're safer in here with me than out on the streets." He gestured to the window. "You never know who's out there."

"You set me up, you bastard."

"And someone set John Wilkens up. I'm just trying to even the score."

Dan pulled a chair to the centre of the room, stood on it and twisted the bulb till it went out. Then he went over to the wall switch and turned it to the off position.

Tony watched him without speaking. Dan sat in a leather recliner next to a low table with a lamp pointed down toward the floor. He tossed a magazine to Tony.

"You might want to keep yourself occupied. We could be here a while."

He checked his cell. There was still nothing from Nick. Dan would discount him, then.

Tony picked up the magazine, then let it fall with a splat. He turned to the bottle and twisted off the top. His hands shook as he poured.

Dan watched him. "My father was a drinker," he said.

Tony looked up with baleful eyes. "Mine, too."

"It hurts, doesn't it?"

"What does?"

"When you love them and they betray you. Fathers."

Tony nodded, sipping from his glass. "I guess."

"When you're a kid you can't rationalize things like hurt and pain. You can't just shrug it off and say, 'Yeah, my dad's an asshole. He's an alcoholic. That's why he does the things he does.' Instead, you start to think it's something that you did or didn't do that makes him that way. At that age you can't even say, 'Why doesn't he love me?' Though maybe you can articulate, 'Why does he hate me?' Because that's all you really know."

Tony kept nodding.

"Did he hit you?" Dan asked.

"Oh, yeah. Lots."

"The truth is, it's easier for them to raise a hand and strike out at whoever is nearest, even if deep down they love you. If you love them back, it hurts even more to think what a monster you must be to make them do that to you."

Tony wiped away a tear. "He said it was my fault. He found out I was gay."

"It's never your fault," Dan said. "It took me years to know that, but I won't forget it now."

The time crept past. Dan looked at his watch: nine eighteen. He was beginning to think he was mistaken. Maybe the text hadn't reached its destination. Maybe the Magus really was a myth made up to scare the fearful and gullible.

Nine thirty-five.

Nine forty-eight.

It was getting a bit late for a showdown. Nothing to do but keep waiting.

By eleven Tony had finished the bottle and lay passed out on the floor. He was gently snoring. Dan went to the window and looked out at the street. It was raining, a slight drizzle keeping everything wet. Everything felt like a disappointment. Dan eyed the slick pavement and wondered if CSIS was out there somewhere. If so, they were being as patient as he was.

It was nearly midnight when he heard the click. Someone had opened the downstairs door, which he'd purposely left unlocked. Dan looked over at Tony. Still sleeping. Dreaming of the father who never loved him. Furtive steps climbed the stairs, slow and secretive.

Dan clicked off the desk lamp and waited. The room was entirely dark.

He felt a buzzing in his pocket and looked at his cell. Donny's name showed onscreen. He couldn't have picked a more inconvenient moment. Clamping down on it, Dan stuffed the phone into his pocket. The buzzing stopped, then started up again almost immediately. *Not now, for fuck's sake!* Dan thought. And the buzzing died.

Footsteps stopped outside the door. There was a soft rap. Dan held still. After a moment the knob turned and the door opened, admitting a stab of light from the corridor. He couldn't make out the face of the person standing there. A hand reached in and fumbled for the switch.

Click.

Nothing.

Click.

Nothing.

The figure entered, closing the door behind him and stepping cautiously around in the dark. Then whoever it was stopped moving and seemed to be sniffing the air. Dan flicked on the desk lamp. In the gloom, he could just make out Peter Hansen's startled face. In his hand, a gun.

Hansen blinked, looked around and saw Tony.

"Tony!"

Tony sat up. His body seemed to shrink in horror.

"Tony, it's all right."

Tony stared at his husband standing across the room and holding a gun. Peter looked from Tony to Dan then back to Tony. Behind him, the door burst open and two men pounced. The gun went flying as they knocked Hansen to the floor and pinned him there.

For Dan, it was déjà vu. Steve Ross appeared behind them and came over to look at the man pinned to the floor. Only this time there was no slit throat, no victim lying dead due to CSIS incompetence, intentional or otherwise.

Tony was hyperventilating. He looked up. "Peter? What are you — ?"

Before Hansen could say anything, the two men bustled him out the door.

Once they'd gone, Steve looked quickly around the room, then came over to Dan. "How did you know it would be Hansen?"

"I didn't. I texted a number Simon Bradley had been hacking. Just like I texted you this afternoon to get you out of your office before I arrived. Bradley knew it was the Magus's number. I assumed whoever had it would respond, even if Bradley was dead."

"Was Hansen alone in all this?"

Dan shrugged. "That's for you to decide. All I know is that I texted the number with Tony's picture and Hansen turned up with a gun. Whether he killed John Wilkens and Simon Bradley isn't for me to say either. He could have had someone do it for him."

"I'll need a full statement from you. Tomorrow will do." Steve extended a hand. They shook. "At least you were right this time."

"It happens sometimes."

Dan walked him to the door. Steve looked back at Tony.

"And this one?"

"I used him. He had nothing to do with this. You can leave him with me. I want to talk to him."

THIRTY-TWO

The Magus

THE OTHERS HAD GONE. TONY sat on the couch, hunched forward like a small boy, holding his head in his hands and crying silently. Dan thought of all the things they had discussed, how Tony's father beat him when he drank, and how he'd married Peter because Hansen was nice to him and tried to help him clean up his life.

"Did you know?" Dan asked.

Tony shook his head. "No. I swear I didn't know."

"Would you have told anyone if you did?"

"I don't know," came the muffled reply. "I still love him. But why would …?" He trailed off, his body wracked with sobs. "I was supposed to disappear for good."

"After you met John Wilkens?"

"Yes. We met at a political function. He was a nice man, even if he was on the wrong team. All I knew was I was supposed to be friendly to him and tell him I had information for him. I was to try to get close to his wife."

"His wife?" Dan stared. "You met her, too?"

"Just once. That's who gave me John's private number. I passed it along to the Magus. To … Peter."

So he could tap his line, too, Dan thought. His mind was reeling. Anne Wilkens had said her husband had had no connection with Tony. He had believed her innocent of all this.

"Only I was surprised when we met," Tony went on. "She wasn't at all what I expected."

Dan was only half listening, recalling his conversation with Anne Wilkens and how strenuously she'd tried to convince him that she believed in her husband's innocence. Of course she had. She knew him to be innocent because she'd betrayed him. What had Nick said? That anyone who lied once would lie again. He turned back to Tony.

"Not what you expected. What do you mean?"

Tony looked at him in surprise. "Not really a trophy wife, was she? Must have been the money. Why he married her. I mean, her being so much older than him."

The penny dropped.

"She was older?"

"Oh, yeah. By a lot. Have you seen her? She could practically have been his mother."

Dan felt another buzzing in his pocket. Too late, he recalled Donny's insistent messages. He pulled his cell from his pocket: five missed calls. In the urgency of the moment, he hadn't felt a thing.

This time he responded.

"Everything's fine," he said.

"Well, good. So nice of you to let me know," came Donny's measured response over the soft exhale of a cigarette. "I mean, your office blew up and then you disappeared again for the second time this week. I was just, you know, wondering if you were okay."

"I'm okay."

"That's settled, then. At least now I can get some sleep. And I'm sure I shouldn't ask because it's probably classified information, but just where are you anyway?"

"In Corktown. A swank place across from the Body Blitz Spa. I should give them a call. I'll be needing them next, if they can fit me in."

"And Will?"

"Will Parker? No, he's not here. He wasn't involved."

Donny spluttered. "I thought you said you got my messages."

"I did. I haven't listened to them yet. What about Will?"

"Oh, shit, Dan! That's what I've been trying to tell you. Will has been lying to you from the very beginning. That family he bragged about? The wife and kids? They don't exist."

Dan felt a chill. "How do you know?"

"I know because I did a little asking around. I told you I'd heard differently about what he'd been up to the past few years. I talked to some friends of friends. Will Parker has been HIV-positive for nearly twenty years. There are at least two men who claim he infected them without telling them he was positive. He never married anyone, male or female. Definitely no kids in the picture anywhere."

Dan was alerted by a sound from the kitchen. "Just a second," he said, putting the phone on the side table. His brain was signalling an SOS as he headed to the kitchen. "Tony, get down on the floor!"

Tony gawped at him for a second then dove for the floor.

"Stay there!"

The kitchen was in darkness. Dan reached for the switch and felt something hard strike him across the face. He howled in pain and bent over, holding his arms up to ward off further blows.

"Back in the other room," Will ordered, motioning with the gun.

Behind him, the window was open onto the fire escape. Dan saw it clearly: Will sitting on the roof waiting for CSIS to leave before climbing silently down, balancing on the ledge as he lifted the latch and let himself in.

Dan's mind skipped backward over twenty years of sporadic connections, twenty years of struggling to piece together the mystery of Will Parker. Will the Radical. Will the Gifted Social Worker. Will the Solitary. And, of course, Will the Lawyer transformed into Will the Dutiful Government Employee. Bringing about the change from within he'd always said was necessary. Only Dan hadn't expected it in quite this way.

"Sit on the couch," Will said, backing Dan into the living room. He looked over at Tony. "You, too."

Tony got up off the floor and sat on the sofa beside Dan. "Who is this guy?" he asked.

"Don't you know him?"

Tony shook his head. "I don't know him."

"He's the Magus," Dan said. "The man who makes history."

"He's …? I thought Peter was …" Tony lapsed into a confused silence.

Will sneered. "You know what they say — history's a whore. She favours the man with the gold watch and the fat wallet. She lifts her skirt for the boys who run the show. The power-mad. The money-hungry. Someone has to change the balance."

"And this is your way of doing it?" Dan asked. "By breaking people's reputations so our side can win?"

Will shrugged off the comment. "We hardly live in an age of virtue and integrity, Dan. Take a look at the papers, the nightly news. Listen to our leaders. Do you think anyone is playing fair out there these days? Politics is war."

Dan shook his head. "Is it any different now than before?"

"A lot. It used to be you could win an election based on promises: a free chicken in every pot, lower taxes, legalized marijuana. Anesthetize the dull and stupid. And if your candidate stays out of trouble before the votes are tallied, all the better. But politics has become too sophisticated, the stakes too high. And most politicians are just not very good at staying out of trouble. You can't make people vote, but you can make sure the right people are set up to win." He gave a rueful smile. "Not that there are any moral giants these days. You get to see it all when you work for the government: bids tendered without real competition, years of waste and corruption, so much mindless incompetence. Governments get in and it's a free-for-all for their buddies. Payback time. It's how they think. Someone has to change that."

"In principle, I don't disagree with you. But not like this."

"Principles are the last things to go. People fight over them for decades until they can't remember why they're fighting. Vows? Promises? Forget about them. Our leaders do as soon as they're in power. The lunatics have taken over the government. Not exactly news, is it? I've always believed in being responsible to the people. This is just my way of doing it."

"Then you're insane."

"Is it insanity to fight hate and discrimination? Is it insanity to fight for fairness and equality?"

"Oh, I see. The Sermon of the Righteous," Dan said. "Rivers of fire and tongues of flame. What's the weather report? Big Wrath Coming. What you're saying is the end justifies the means. Might equals right."

"Why not?"

"Jesus Christ, Will. Two men are dead!"

Will shook his head. "Sometimes moral choices have to be made."

"Is that what you're doing? Making choices about who lives and who dies like some kind of angel of vengeance? Because I've got news for you — murder is immoral."

"John found out things we couldn't risk coming out before the next election."

"Because of Alec Henderson?"

Will sneered. "Alec Henderson is an ass. An egotistical, fatuous ass. I wasn't doing this for him. But his stupidity could have brought the entire government down."

"Then who were you doing it for? And why set up Hansen to look like he was behind all this?"

Will gave him a disappointed look. "I'm surprised at you, Dan. I'm not setting up Peter Hansen to lose. I'm setting him up to win. I believe in what Hansen stands for. I just didn't want this idiot" — he looked over at Tony — "ruining his chances. That's why I paid him to leave."

"Paid for with money from John Wilkens's account. Only Tony ruined your plan by gambling the money away and coming back into the picture."

"Sadly so."

"And in the meantime you were levelling the playing field, keeping a careful watch on our enemies."

"It's worked in the past. Very nicely, I might add. Pity you ended up with Simon Bradley on your doorstep. If he hadn't dropped his cellphone into your hands then none of this" — he swept the room with his gun — "would have happened. I'll take the phone, by the way."

Dan shook his head. "I don't have it."

"Don't fuck with me. You texted me with it earlier." He made a motion with his hand. "Please."

There was a sound of movement outside the door, muffled footsteps on the stairs. Will glanced quickly over his shoulder, then back at Dan. He pointed the gun.

"Stay there and don't make a sound."

He reached the door in three steps, slipping the bolt into place. Dan flew across the room, slamming his fists against Will's back. Will swung back and struck Dan with the gun again, knocking him to the floor.

He held the gun directly against Dan's head.

"I will fucking kill you!"

"Go ahead. You're going to anyway."

A floorboard creaked behind them. Will turned and aimed at the darkened kitchen.

"Drop it!"

Will fired, the flash illuminating the air around him. A return shot winged him, but he held onto his gun and fired wide, scattering plaster from the wall.

"Get down! Get down!"

Dan heard a shot and felt the reverberations as he dove for the floor. Two more shots followed. Will stepped backward, a look of surprise on his face. He dropped the gun and fell face-forward onto the floor.

The place came alive as figures swarmed into the room. Officers in uniform, plainclothesmen in dull grey suits. Dan wondered where they'd been hiding.

In plain sight, of course.

When he stood, he felt winded for a moment. *Getting old*, he told himself.

Nick's eyes locked with his. "I told you not to try this shit without me," he said before turning back to the room.

EPILOGUE

Grace

ONE OF THE MESSAGES DAN had missed during all the excitement was from Lester. He'd discovered a trove of hacked calls and evidence of interference in government operations on Simon Bradley's phone records. Among other things, it exonerated John Badger Wilkens III of any wrongdoing.

Anne Wilkens was the first person Dan called when he heard, explaining what had come to light and offering condolences for the revelation of her sister's involvement.

She was silent for a moment then said, "I blame myself for what happened to her. She resented me for taking her fiancé away from her. I don't think she ever recovered."

Dan wasn't about to say that not everyone who lost in love turned up years later looking for revenge. Even if Doris hadn't actively contributed to John Wilkens's death, she had helped bring it about.

Ked returned at the end of that week and took up residence in his old bedroom. The house suddenly felt a lot less lonely with his son around, Dan thought. Even Ralph regained some of his old liveliness. Yes, Dan thought, they would get through this together.

A few days later, Dan put in a bid on a small office conveniently located within walking distance from his house. The offer was accepted on the spot.

He invited Peter Hansen and Tony Moran over to settle his account for finding Tony. Not surprisingly, Peter had insisted he keep the money for his finder's fee.

"Won't you need it in your run for the legislature?" Dan asked.

Peter shrugged, glancing around at the empty walls. "Looks like you'll need it if you want to have a proper office. In any case, I can always sell some art to finance my campaign. But the gay community is backing me. I've got a fundraiser coming up next week. I expect you to be there."

"I will. I have high hopes for you."

Dan had already heard the details of how his text to the Magus had been forwarded to Hansen, alerting him as to Tony's whereabouts and resulting in his desperate, one-man rescue attempt. Will Parker had not been that far off from Baader-Meinhof tactics after all.

"And as for you ..." He looked at Tony, who still quaked like a rabbit. "I hear you've been cleared of everything."

Tony nodded. "Yes, once I explained everything to them they said I was free to go."

"That's good. You just got paid a lot of money to be someone's friend and pass along whatever he told you."

"They told me he was a spy." He hesitated. "Do you think I did anything wrong?"

"No," Dan said, truthfully. *Just really dumb.*

Dan took his time as he contemplated his next move. As far as he was concerned, the story was still unfinished so long as certain crucial questions remained unanswered. He thought long and hard about what he needed to do.

One morning at five, just two weeks after Will's shooting, he found himself seated in a large open kitchen in a ranch-style home. The skylight would soon flood the room with the morning's glow, revealing its opulent interior — fireplace, rugs, and an enviable collection of artwork — but he still had time to accomplish what he needed to do. It had been surprisingly easy to break into the house, but deactivating the alarm was another matter. He'd sweated over that for a considerable time before reassuring himself it had been properly decommissioned.

He'd been sitting there a while when the door opened and Steve Ross stared at him with bleary eyes. Steve's initial look of panic was instantly replaced with anger.

"How the hell did you get in here?"

"Your front door was open. I was passing by and I was afraid something very bad might have happened to you, so I let myself in."

"Bullshit!"

Steve looked around desperately, as though missing something.

"Your dog's okay. He's just drugged," Dan said.

"That's one more thing I'll have you charged with."

"Possibly. You know, I really have to hand it to you. You are smooth. I knew I was getting close enough to rattle someone's cage, but I couldn't figure it out. So I asked myself: what could John Wilkens have found that was so disturbing? Then, not long after I went stumbling around looking for who-knows-what, CSIS showed up. That should have tipped me off. It had to have been something extraordinary for Will Parker to call CSIS in."

Steve shook his head. "Will Parker is dead, thanks to you."

"Lucky for you. He can't testify against you. I'm sure that was convenient. Whose bacon were you really saving? What official secrets are you protecting? There's an election coming up. We all know how parties crumble at the first sign of a scandal. Did somebody from above order the kibosh?"

"Like I would discuss those things with you."

Dan shook his head. "All this crap about protecting the public good and here you are still abetting murders. How about that?"

"Where do you get the gall to ask these questions?"

"I have the gall because two men were murdered and you seem to want to overlook it because it's inconvenient to a member of the provincial legislature."

Steve waved a hand dismissively. "These things happen. That's life."

"Speaking of life, that was a cute little family photo on your desk at work. Did you miss it? I took it during our visit. Of course they're not really your family, are they?"

"No, they're not. But so what?"

"I showed it to Anne Wilkens. She identified you as the man who she was having an affair with. If you can call it an affair."

"Affairs are pretty commonplace these days. What does it prove?"

Dan saw him glance at the drawer next to the stove. "It's still there. But I took out the bullets, so unless you want to throw it at me it won't do much good."

"Are you wired?"

Dan shook his head. "I don't need to be wired."

"Then why did you come?"

"Just for a chat. John Wilkens came to you for a chat. Your name is in his calendar a week before his death. His wife showed it to me last week."

"That's feeble."

"John Wilkens —"

"Was a threat to national security."

"You set Wilkens up. We both know it. He discovered some emails linking Alec Henderson to the power plant cancellations. But he also found that someone had been tampering with the accounts, diverting money to the husband of a ministerial assistant, making it look as though he was stealing to pay for information. He tried to tell you what he knew and you had him killed."

"Did I? I don't remember. But you signed a non-disclosure agreement under the Security of Information Act."

"Yes, I did. Because you gave me no choice." Dan held out Simon Bradley's cellphone. "Unfortunately for you, this phone didn't sign anything. This is what you were looking for in my office, wasn't it? Why you decided to blow it up? Amazing the things you can find on YouTube. Did you know there's a whole section devoted to phone tapping? Simon Bradley was very, very good at it. You really need to brush up on it a little yourself."

"Pathetic. Don't think you can get away with it."

"No, Steve, *you* can't get away with it. And you won't. It's all here. All your private conversations with Will Parker. Bad luck when the spies are spied on."

"No matter what's on that phone, those are official conversations. Not admissible as evidence in any court. They'll be classified for decades."

"Right, classified information." Dan nodded. "I've also got a rapper who remembers you as the guy who offered him a gun to kill John Wilkens. Or how about the *Magna Carta*? No one is above the law. Next year marks its eight hundredth birthday. Happy birthday, Steve."

There was one final matter to be dealt with, this one of a personal bent. He'd been having chest pains off and on for the past few weeks, ever since Ked's graduation. At first, he put it down to stress. There'd certainly been enough of that lately. He ignored it for a few days until it returned forcefully late one night. *Indigestion*, he told himself, but resolved to call his doctor in the morning.

Whatever it was, it was telling him to be careful. He knew he couldn't go around swinging tire irons at cars forever. He envisioned himself chasing an assailant half his age and being felled right there on the sidewalk by his own internal attacker.

The next afternoon he was sitting in the doctor's office. His phone buzzed just as the receptionist called his name, beckoning him into a cubicle. He ignored the call, lying on the examining table and letting himself be poked and prodded while he answered the doctor's questions. *Any shortness of breath? Sometimes, especially going up and down the stairs at the warehouse. Any chest pains? Yes. How frequent? Often. What's often? Daily. Any panic attacks? All the time, doctor. All the time.* The doctor attached little cold disks to his bare chest, the wires trailing to a machine that looked like an over-blown coffee maker. Afterward he squeezed a ball and jogged on the spot while the doctor listened to his heart before telling him to go off and get dressed.

It was an hour before he checked the message. It was Nick, asking to meet at a local bar. But this time Dan's heart didn't leap at the sound of his voice. It was an exit meeting Nick wanted. Or maybe just an execution. In his current state of mind, one was no better than the other.

Dan showed up at the appointed hour and walked into a room full of jazz. A man who looked like Sam Smith leaned hard on the keys of a white baby grand. He was trying hard to sound like him, too.

Nick was seated at a table with his back to the room. Dan saw the scowl as he approached, the fingers tapping a nervous beat on the tabletop. A glass of something decorated with a lemon wedge sat in front of him.

He thought of his conversation with Donny earlier that afternoon. They had been talking about Dan's father, a man who was dead on his feet for most of his adult life. Grief had struck him down prematurely; he never got back up. As a result, he became a man who destroyed the things he couldn't live with, trying to find ways to leave them behind. Dan recalled the long silence of those black moods when his father stared off into the distance till the bottle was empty, or till he fell asleep, whichever came first.

"I resented him so much I couldn't even say 'I love you' to make him feel better when he lay dying."

Donny had him on that one. "Did you love him?"

"No."

"Then at least you didn't lie to a dying man."

"I could have said it to make it easier for him."

Donny had him there, too. "How many times in your life did your father tell you he loved you?"

Dan thought back. It was like looking over a long, unbroken panorama of grey. "Not once."

"So then? I don't think you owed him anything."

"I remember his dying words. He turned to me and asked, 'Did you ever feel like maybe you were an idiot your whole life?' At first I wondered: was he talking about himself or was he making a comment about me?"

"How did you answer?"

"I said, 'All the time, Dad. All the time.'"

Donny had put a hand on his friend's shoulder. "And in the short time you and Nick were together, how many times did you tell Nick you loved him?"

"Every day."

"And did you mean it?"

"Every time I said it."

Donny nodded, the sage concluding his talk. "You need time to think about what you're going to say to him tonight. But don't take too long. You have something good in your life. Don't fuck it up this time."

Dan shrugged. "He doesn't want me back. His message said he just wanted to finalize things between us."

"Whatever. Just don't be that stupid, emotionally distant schmuck you normally are. If you get a chance, take it."

Dan sat across from Nick now. The gash on Nick's forehead had healed. Thankfully there would be no scar for him to remember Dan by in years to come. Dan, on the other hand, still bore the welt where Will's gun had struck the side of his face.

"How are you?" Nick asked.

"Okay." Dan shrugged. "A bit sore. You warned me."

"I did. But you never listen to other people." Nick shook his head. "Sorry, that's not what I asked you here for. What I really want is to say that even though I'm a cop, I'm not ashamed to be gay. I just find it difficult to live with other people's attitudes at times. Maybe that's something I need to adjust to, as much as I would prefer that they adjust their attitudes instead. But I am a police officer, so I don't always get to act on my true feelings."

Dan nodded. In the background, Sam Smith's double tinkled "'Round Midnight," the theme song for lonely alcoholics.

"Okay, I'll keep talking, since you're doing the silent thing," Nick continued, fingering his glass. "I know you think life is perfectible, but to me it's hellishly disappointing more often than not. Still, it takes guts to accept and live with that. And in case you're wondering, this is soda I'm drinking. I haven't had another drink since the day I left. It was hard, but I held on. Mostly so I could tell you that and not lie."

A waiter came by. Dan nodded to Nick's glass. "I'll have the same, please." The man went away looking disappointed.

"Okay, that's good. Anything else you want to say?"

"Well, I could chew you out for those daredevil stunts you pulled recently, though I doubt it would stop you from doing it next time. But there's something that's bothering me, and it's hard for me to acknowledge, even though it's true. I think my real problem with most people is that no one takes the time to be noble anymore. They're all too afraid or self-absorbed or just plain stupid. There are no more heroes in real life. Except you."

"Except me?"

"Yeah, you. That's my problem. I still think of you that way. I wish I didn't. Your son thinks so, too. I talked to him yesterday. And we both agreed on that. So, yes, except you. But you're so damn worried you might turn into your father, you forget that."

Dan looked off for a moment. He sighed and said, "I'm not a hero. I threw you against a goddamn wall because you tried to walk away from me."

"Yeah, you did. Just like your father did to you. But you're not him. He's not you." He put his hands on the table, clasping them together. "What I want to say is, I forgive you."

"How can you?"

Nick sighed. "There you go again. Everything is impossible odds with you. How much do you want us both to suffer? You are just like your father in that way."

The memory came back, how he'd come home late from school after spending the afternoon with a friend. It had occurred to him to telephone and let his father know, but his father usually headed straight to the bar after work. Only this day his father had come home and seen Dan wasn't there.

By the time Dan returned, his father had worked himself into a rage. With one hand, Stuart Sharp backslapped his son, sending him sprawling against a doorframe. Dan fell to the floor and lay in stunned silence while his father left the room. Once his father's footsteps faded, he went upstairs to his Aunt Marge, who consoled him and bandaged his bleeding forehead.

When she finished, she told him to apologize. "Go in and tell your father you're sorry for what you done."

"What did I do?" Dan demanded.

Her look was stern. "You worried him, Danny. Tell him you're sorry and you won't do it again or there'll be no peace till you do."

Dan had gone hesitantly downstairs and stood in the doorway to the room where his father sat watching television.

"I'm sorry, Dad. I won't do it again," he said at last.

Without turning his head to look, his father said, "Do you know what I go through worrying, after what happened to your mother? Don't ever do anything so stupid again."

In that moment, whatever good Dan had felt for his father had died forever.

The waiter returned with Dan's drink and set it on the table. Nick was talking. Dan hadn't heard a word. "What?"

"I was saying that, with our work, either of us could die at any moment. I think of that every single day, but you don't. You don't let yourself."

Dan shook his head. "I don't choose to. What's the point?"

"That's what I mean. That's the difference between us. You're closed. You don't let things in. Life isn't straight lines, Dan. There are twists and curves all along the way. I try to be as open as I can. I'm easy that way. That's why you always know what I want and how to give it to me. With you, I'm always left guessing. There's this aloneness, this distance about you. I can't get through to you. It's like a power you have over me. It's not fair."

"I didn't ask for it."

Nick's fist hit the table, making the glasses jump. "No, you didn't, damn it. But it's still not fair. You get to call all the shots. Fuck you!"

Several patrons looked over at the two men arguing, and decided it was not worth their while to say anything.

Dan's thoughts crept back to the doctor's office, the electrodes attached to his skin monitoring his heart rate in spikes and dips on the screen beside him, searching for irregularities, the un-syncopated rhythm that would mark the impending end of his life.

After a few minutes, the doctor had unhooked him. Dan felt the disks pull at his chest hair, the pain pulling him back to the present.

"Get dressed and meet me in my office."

Dan had returned to the office and waited while the doctor looked over the results, his expression blank as unmarked paper.

"I want to remind you that at your age you shouldn't be running up and down stairs. You're not immortal, Dan."

Dan managed a smiled. "I thought I was."

"So do we all, at some point. But if you want to play god, eventually you're going to come face to face with the devil." He nodded. "Anyway, whatever it is, it isn't physical."

"But the pain —"

"Oh, I don't doubt what you're telling me, and from the sounds of it you've been under a lot of stress. But I think there's more to it than that."

For a second Dan thought he was about to be told he had something far worse than heart palpitations.

"But as I said, it's not physical," his doctor repeated. "How's your personal life?"

"I have trust issues," Dan said now to Nick.

Nick rolled his eyes. "So do I, Dan. I'm a cop. I don't really trust anybody. Kind of hard to work those issues out alone." He waited. "What do you do when you get thrown by a horse?"

"You get back on."

"Exactly. You get right back on. Otherwise, the fear gets to you and you never will. We all have trust issues. Forget your father. Isn't it enough that you and I both try to be good people?"

He waited, both of them sitting there not speaking. Somewhere in the background, Sam Smith's look-alike struck up a mellow tune. Customers drank and paid bills. Waiters drifted about with drink trays.

"I am what I am," Dan said. "And what I am is difficult and cantankerous and probably not worth the time you're taking to have this conversation."

"Fucking hell, Dan — you said it. You're all that and more. Don't you think I've learned that over the past year living with you?"

"Then what do you want?"

"You idiot. I want to come home." Nick extended a hand across the table top. "It's lonely without you and I'm tired of talking to you in my head. Please … I want to come home."

Dan looked away for a moment. He felt his shoulders quake as he looked down at Nick's hand and, for what felt like the first time in life, he grasped back.

ACKNOWLEDGEMENTS

MY GRATITUDE GOES OUT TO Don Oravec and Jim Harper, David Tronetti, Christian Baines, Liz Bugg, and Geordie Johnson for their support, as well as my solid-gold editor, Jess Shulman, who wasn't afraid to ask the hard questions that helped make this a better book. I'd also like to thank my parents, who raised me good and proper, and were nothing like Dan Sharp's parents. Further thanks are due to the Ontario Arts Council for a well-timed grant allowing me to complete the work. And, although his themes were different from mine, I acknowledge my debt to author John Fowles for the title of this book, similar to one he discarded years ago. As always, I was inspired by a variety of musical palettes along the way. The buzz on this one goes out to those English minstrels, William Byrd, Thomas Tallis, Orlando Gibbons, and Ralph Vaughan Williams. Cheers, lads!

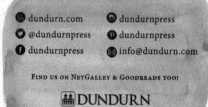

dundurn.com   dundurnpress
@dundurnpress   dundurnpress
dundurnpress   info@dundurn.com

FIND US ON NETGALLEY & GOODREADS TOO!

DUNDURN